SORROWFUL MYSTERY
(2nd Edition)

The 7th Bernie Fazakerley mystery

Judy Ford

SORROWFUL MYSTERY

Published by Bernie Fazakerley Publications

Copyright © 2017, 2018 Judy Ford

All rights reserved.

Cover design by Judy Ford

Madonna and Child image © 2018 Catherine Young

ISBN: 1-91-108347-3

ISBN-13: 978-1-911083-47-4

DEDICATION

Dedicated to members of the Mothers' Union worldwide and to families with young children everywhere.

O happy home, where Thou art loved the dearest,

Thou loving Friend and Saviour of our race,

And where among the guests there never cometh

One who can hold such high and honoured place!

O happy home, where two in heart united

In holy faith and blessèd hope are one,

Whom death a little while alone divideth,

And cannot end the union here begun!

O happy home, whose little ones are given

Early to Thee, in humble faith and prayer,

To Thee, their Friend, who from the heights of Heaven

Guides them, and guards with more than mother's care!

O happy home, where each one serves Thee, lowly,

Whatever his appointed work may be,

Till every common task seems great and holy,

When it is done, O Lord, as unto Thee!

O happy home, where Thou art not forgotten,

Where joy is overflowing, full and free,

O happy home, where every wounded spirit

Is brought, Physician, Comforter, to Thee—

Until at last, when earth's day's work is ended,

All meet Thee in the blessèd home above,

From whence Thou camest, where Thou hast ascended,

Thy everlasting home of peace and love!

Hymn by Karl J Spitta, translated by Sarah B Findlater

CONTENTS

ACKNOWLEDGEMENTS

I would like to thank the authors of a wide range of internet resources, which have been invaluable for researching the background to this book. These include (among others):

- Spinal Injuries Association http://www.spinal.co.uk/page/living-with-sci

- Wikipedia https://en.wikipedia.org/

- CatholiCity.com http://www.catholicity.com

- Google Maps https://www.google.co.uk/maps

- Disability and Jesus http://www.disabilityandjesus.org.uk/

- Singing the Faith Plus http://www.singingthefaithplus.org.uk/

Many of the hymns from which the chapter titles are derived, may be found in Singing the Faith, published on behalf of the Trustees for Methodist Church Purposes by Hymns Ancient & Modern Ltd, 2011.

I would like to thank Gillian Gilbert for reading the manuscript, giving helpful comments and pointing out typographical errors.

Members of the *UK Methodists* Facebook Group provided valuable insight into a variety of attitudes towards the practice of praying to saints.

I am grateful to Maryalice Hogg-O'Rourke, who gave me valuable advice and encouragement in preparing the Large Print edition.

GLOSSARY OF UK POLICE RANKS

Uniformed police

Chief Constable (CC) – Has overall charge of a regional police force, such as Thames Valley Police, which covers Oxford and a large surrounding area.

Deputy Chief Constable (DCC) – The senior discipline authority for each force. 2nd in command to the CC.

Assistant Chief Constable (ACC) – 4 in the Thames Valley Police Service, each responsible for a policy area.

Chief Superintendent ('Chief Super') – Head of a policing area or department.

Police Superintendent – Responsible for a local area within a police force.

Chief Inspector (CI) – Responsible for overseeing a team in a local area.

Police Inspector – Senior operational officer overseeing officers on duty 24/7.

Police Sergeant – Supervises a team of officers.

Police Constable (PC) – 'Bobby on the beat'. Likely to be the first to arrive in response to an emergency call.

Crime Investigation Unit (CID) – Plain clothes officers

Detective Superintendent (DS) – Responsible for crime investigation in a local area.

Detective Chief Inspector (DCI) – Responsible for overseeing a crime investigation team in a local area. May be the Senior Investigating Officer heading up a criminal investigation.

Detective Inspector (DI) – Oversees crime investigation 24/7. May be the

Senior Investigating Officer heading up a criminal investigation.

Detective Sergeant (DS) – Supervises a team of CID officers.

Detective Constable (DC) – One of a team of officers investigating crimes.

These descriptions are based on information from the following sources:

[1] Mental Health Cop blog, by Inspector Michael Brown, Mental Health co-ordinator, College of Policing. https://mentalhealthcop.wordpress.com/, accessed 31st March 2017.

[2] Thames Valley Police website, https://www.thamesvalley.police.uk , accessed 31st March 2017.

1 MOTHER DEAR, REMEMBER ME

Crystal manoeuvred the double buggy into the lift, placing her foot firmly against the door to ensure that it did not close before she and her two children were safely inside. She had perfected this technique over the five weeks since she had brought her newborn daughter home from the hospital to their two-bedroomed flat on the eighth floor of a tower block in the Headington district of Oxford. She pressed the button to select the ground floor and waited as the doors closed and the lift began its descent.

JUDY FORD

The flat was far from ideal for a young family, but with house prices the way they were in Oxford, it was the best that they could afford. The alternative would have been to continue living with her father-in-law in his large house on the other side of the ring road. He would have been delighted to have them, she knew; and in many ways, the attic rooms that he had offered them were superior to what they had here – not to mention the large garden with a swing, climbing frame and even a tree house. But it was *his* house, not theirs. It would have been bad enough if it had been Eddie's family home, but it was not even that. It was his stepmother's house, or rather, the house that she had inherited from her first husband on his untimely death. True, she had insisted that they were welcome to stay as long as they liked, but she had her own teenage daughter to consider. No, it was better this way, even if they were going to be a bit cramped for a few years until they could save up for something larger.

It was all very different from the home in Jamaica that she had left, less than six months previously. Their house there had been a single-story building with a veranda at the front and a small garden at the back. Her parents' house had been only a few streets away, next door to the church where her father was the minister and her mother ran the Sunday School. Except during storms, the doors and windows were left open, and the distinction between indoors and outdoors became blurred. Here, apart from their small balcony, going outside involved this tedious journey in the lift, negotiating tricky fire doors that were inclined to swing closed as she let go of them to push the buggy and its precious cargo through.

Crystal sighed. It had been a wrench to leave the land of her birth and all her blood relatives in order to come to this strange, cold, dark country. When she had married Eddie – the exotic stranger from across the sea – they had planned to settle permanently in Jamaica. However, when, the day after she realised that she was pregnant with their second child, the computer company for which he worked closed down, taking his job down with it, it was inevitable that he would look on both sides of the Atlantic for new employment. It was a bit of luck finding a job in Bicester, so close to where his father and stepmother lived. He could stay with them until he found somewhere for his small, but growing, family to live.

It had been another piece of luck that the hospitals in Oxford were short of nursing staff and willing to take her on to fill one of their vacancies, despite her imminent maternity leave. With their two salaries – and a generous gift of capital from Eddie's father, which provided a deposit – they had managed to buy a flat in a block that had once been owned by the council. That was a start. They had got their feet on the bottom rung of the 'housing ladder' that everyone here seemed to talk about so much.

The lift stopped at the fourth floor and an older woman with a walking stick got in. She looked down disapprovingly at the buggy and stood as far away from it as she could, within the confines of the lift.

'Good afternoon,' Crystal ventured

nervously. 'I don't think we've met before. My name is Crystal Johns. I live on the eighth floor. Are you one of our neighbours? We haven't been here long.'

She held out her hand and the woman took it, a little reluctantly, it seemed to Crystal.

'Myra Knight,' she replied. 'No. I don't live here. I've been visiting my son and daughter-in-law.'

'Would that be Morgan and Shona?' Crystal asked. 'I've met them. Their little girl is about the same age as my Ricky.'

'That's right,' Mrs Knight admitted, appearing to thaw slightly. 'They said there was a new couple with a little boy moved in a month or two back.'

'Well, it was February, so it's three months now.'

'And another little one, I see,' Mrs

Knight observed, nodding towards the buggy. 'How old is …?' she tailed off to avoid guessing the sex of the infant incorrectly or committing the monumental faux pas of referring to the baby as 'it'.

'She's five weeks now.'

The lift stopped and the mechanical voice informed them that they were on the ground floor and that the doors were opening. Mrs Knight stepped out first and then put her hand on the door to prevent it closing while Crystal pushed the buggy through.

'Thanks,' she said gratefully. 'It's so difficult, with the buggy being so wide.'

'Well, both children seem to be being very good for you,' Mrs Knight said generously. 'Kayleigh always shrieks her head off in the lift.'

'I expect it frightens her,' Crystal

suggested. 'It frightens me sometimes, seeing the doors closing all by themselves and feeling so shut in.'

They parted company at the entrance to the tower block and Crystal set off in the direction of the local recreation ground. She bent over the buggy and spoke cheerfully to her young son.

'We're going to the park, Ricky,' she told him. 'You'll like that, won't you? You can go on the swings and the slide and the see-saw.'

Ricky smiled and clapped his plump, brown-skinned hands in anticipation of the treat. He was a man of few words – 'bopple' and 'bikkit' to be precise – but, as his doting parents were keen to tell anyone who was willing to listen, he understood far more than he cared to let on of what was said around him. His mother smiled back into his eyes and then glanced towards her younger child.

Abigail, recently fed and changed, was sleeping peacefully with both arms lying above her head as if she were indicating surrender. Her surprising shock of red hair was standing up on end, contrasting vividly with the white sheet beneath it. The bright midday sunshine fell on her pale pink face, making her complexion look all the more pallid compared with the rich coffee colour of her brother's skin. They made an odd pair, Crystal reflected as she conscientiously adjusted the sunshade attached to the side of the buggy to protect her daughter from the effects of ultraviolet radiation. She shook her head in amusement at the thought that this was something that nobody in her family had ever needed to consider before.

It had all been a bit of a shock when

Abigail was born. She remembered, with a smile, the expression of amazement on the face of the midwife, who kept looking from her to the new baby and then to Eddie and back to the baby again. They had been the talk of the maternity unit – the black couple who had given birth to a white baby! Eddie had been so excited when he rang his father to give him the news. 'You'll never guess, Dad – she's white and she's got your red hair!'

Perhaps it was as well that they were living in England now. At least their daughter would not be the only white child in her class at school. And she had plenty of white relations here to prevent her feeling isolated in her own family. Eddie's family had all been tremendously kind when she arrived, shortly before Christmas the previous year. Peter and his wife had welcomed her into their home unreservedly. Eddie's sister, Hannah, visiting from her home somewhere in the north of the country, had given her an array of second hand baby equipment, including the useful double buggy, which combined a transportable cot for Abigail with a pushchair arrangement for Ricky. Her children (a few years older than Ricky) were white too, but then, she had married a white man, so it was less of a surprise. Genes were funny things. Presumably, Crystal must have a white, redheaded ancestor somewhere in her family tree, but neither she nor her parents had ever heard of any such person.

***

In a small house in St Albans, another

mother was also gazing down at her baby daughter. Georgia watched anxiously as Rachel grunted and twitched in her sleep. She had kept them awake with crying most of the night. Then she had vomited up her morning feed and it had taken hours of rocking in Georgia's arms to get her off afterwards. Now she was sleeping, but it seemed an unnatural sleep somehow. Georgia put out her hand and touched Rachel's cheek. It felt hot.

Could she be getting teeth? At just under three months that was not likely, but it was not unknown either. Perhaps the room was too hot. The weather had turned warmer recently. Georgia went to the window and opened it a crack to allow the air to circulate without causing a draught. Then she went back to the cot and peeled back the covers. In doing so, she touched Rachel's hand and was struck by how cold it felt. Burning hot cheeks and yet icy hands? That could not be the warmth of the room, could it?

Perhaps she should ring the doctor. They had talked about it before Nathan left for work that morning; but then Rachel had seemed more settled and they had concluded that they were being unduly anxious. They did not want to appear to be panicky parents overreacting at every minute change in their child's behaviour. But what if it were something serious, after all?

Georgia's breasts were swollen and uncomfortable, reminding her that it was time for Rachel's next feed. She would see how that went and then decide. It was strange that she had not woken for it already. Perhaps she too was exhausted after last night.

Georgia bent down and picked up her daughter. Her body felt strangely stiff and her limbs jerked in a way that they never had before. Then she started crying, making a high-pitched screaming noise that Georgia could not remember her ever having made before. She held her against her chest, supporting her head with one hand and walked round the room trying to calm her by rocking.

Eventually the screams died down and became a strange gasping sobbing. Georgia sat down and prepared to feed her. Bra and blouse were both sodden and sticky with the milk that her body had produced in response to the cries of her infant. She brought Rachel's mouth up to a nipple expecting her to latch on eagerly, as she usually did, but she showed no interest. Instead, she reverted to the high-pitched screams and jerky kicking of her legs.

Georgia was nearly in tears herself by now. She held Rachel to her and rocked rhythmically back and forth in the hope of calming her enough to take her feed. After what felt like hours, the screams subsided and the jerky movements of arms and legs died down into occasional twitching. Georgia ventured to offer the breast again and this time Rachel started to suck.

Not for long though. After only a few minutes, she released the nipple and she seemed to have fallen asleep. Desperate to relieve her own discomfort as well as concerned for her child's welfare, Georgia shook her in an attempt to wake her; but there was no response.

Georgia buttoned up her blouse and prepared to change Rachel's nappy.

Perhaps after that she would be ready for some more milk. The coldness of the plastic surface of the changing mat woke her and she started to cry again – not so loudly this time, but somehow all the more distressingly because of that. Georgia hurried to clean her and to fasten the fresh nappy, eager to return to the feed.

However, Rachel was still not interested. After a few half-hearted mouthfuls, she pulled her face away and refused to co-operate further. Georgia settled her back in her cot and stood looking down on her, an anxious frown on her face.

She made up her mind. She would ring the surgery and ask to speak to one of the GPs. Usually there was a doctor around for an hour or so after the morning surgery ended. She immediately felt better at the thought that she was doing something. She dialled the number and waited as it rang out. The receptionist took her details and then put her on hold while the doctor finished speaking to a patient on the other line. Georgia waited impatiently, walking round the room with her mobile phone to her ear. Then, at last, it was her turn.

'What can I do for you, Mrs Porter?' came a voice that betrayed a weariness beneath a tone of forced cheerfulness.

'It's my baby daughter, Rachel. I think she's running a temperature and she's not feeding very well.'

'Ah yes! Let me see … she's just coming up to three months now, isn't she?'

'Yes. That's right.'

'And how long has this been going

on?'

'Just today really. Well, she didn't sleep very well overnight and then today …'

'And this is your first baby, isn't it?'

'Yes. That's right.' Georgia paused and gave a nervous, self-deprecating laugh. Clearly, the doctor considered her to be a neurotic first-time mum. 'I don't suppose it's anything really – just me getting paranoid.'

'No, not at all. You're bound to worry. Now, you said she has a temperature …?'

The doctor went through what Georgia took to be a checklist of questions before bringing the conversation to a close with instructions to continue to monitor Rachel's symptoms, and to seek medical advice if any of a number of changes to her condition were to occur, but to endeavour not to worry unduly. Babies often had days when they were unsettled and reluctant to feed. It could well be a viral infection that she would throw off by herself within a matter of hours – a few days at most. If she did not want milk then try giving her water. So long as she was taking in sufficient fluids, there was probably nothing to worry about.

Georgia ended the call and put her phone away. She felt somewhat foolish. She should have realised that this sort of thing was just part of normal baby behaviour. Fancy bothering a busy, over-worked GP with her silly anxieties!

***

Felicity Mason – 'Flick' to her friends – settled her daughter, Mia, into her pram

19

and pulled up the hood to protect her from the bright sunshine. She turned to pull the front door closed behind her and set off down the short path to the stone wall that separated their modest house in Headington Quarry from the road. She chattered gaily to Mia as she guided the pram along the pavement.

'We're going to the shops to get something nice for Daddy's dinner. What do you think he'd like? I was thinking, maybe some of those sausages from the butcher that he said were so tasty, but they aren't very healthy, are they? Perhaps fish would be better for us. But he did like the sausages, and the butcher said they were low fat, so they're probably OK. What vegetables do you think he'd like with them? I know! I'll get some baking potatoes from the greengrocer's and do jacket potatoes. They're supposed to be good for you. And some tomatoes – he likes grilled tomatoes with sausages. Now what shall we have for dessert …?'

***

Not far away, in another road in Headington, another mother was preparing to take her baby out for a walk in the pleasant June sunshine. Little Esme was fractious and would not settle in her cot after her midday feed. Victoria Norris decided to take her out in the pram, in the hope that the motion would send her off to sleep. It sometimes worked – and then again, sometimes she would continue to cry as they walked and walked. Victoria hopefully placed an apple and a banana into the pram, next to Esme's feet. She had been too distracted to eat lunch; with luck there would be a few minutes of peace, while they were out, during which she could sit down and consume these.

The doctor in the hospital had warned Victoria that this sort of behaviour might be one of the consequences of the brain damage that had occurred during the difficult birth. The midwife and health visitor had both been solicitous in the first weeks after they came home – visiting frequently and offering advice – but it was more than a fortnight now since she had seen either of them. They must assume that she could cope on her own now – or else they were busy with other new mothers and did not have time for her anymore.

Victoria felt very alone as she pushed the pram along the pavement, choosing her route at random, concerned only to keep moving. She wished that she were back in her old home in Sunderland, where she had friends whom she had known since childhood and colleagues at the hospital where she worked, from whom she could have sought advice. Six months after the move, Oxford still seemed like an alien place where she knew nobody.

She sighed as she remembered John explaining why they needed to move. It had all seemed so reasonable at the time.

'You do understand,' he kept saying anxiously. 'I daren't let Debra know about the baby. She'd be so upset. Living here, you could bump into her at any time. And the house in Oxford is just the thing for raising a family.'

And so, she had allowed him to persuade her to resign from her job as a speech and language therapist on the stroke unit, and to move down to Oxford – 250 miles from her home and family and friends – to the house that John had inherited when his mother died, the house where he had grown up. All because he did not want his ex-wife to know that his new girlfriend was pregnant.

Poor Debra! She and John had been happily married – and happily child-free – for fifteen years before Debra developed symptoms of an early menopause. It was only then that they both realised how much they wanted to have a family of their own. Years of tests and treatments and hopes and despair followed, before finally they had tried to accept that they would never be parents. However, it had changed Debra forever and had created a barrier between them that John could not penetrate. Unsurprisingly, he had found intimacy elsewhere and, thirty years after their marriage, he had divorced Debra – generously handing over to her possession of the house that they had shared – and moved in with Victoria.

The prospect of becoming a father at last had been an unexpected bonus for John Middleton, but it had brought with it the prospect of further de-stabilising his first wife's mental condition. He remained very fond of Debra, even though living with her had become impossible. He could not bear the thought of 'rubbing her nose in it' as he described the situation were she to find out about Victoria's pregnancy. His business – something to do with engineering projects all over the world, as far as Victoria could make out –

could be run as easily from Oxford as anywhere else, and his mother's house had been lying empty since her death several months earlier. The move to Headington was an obvious solution to his problem; and he sought to sweeten the pill for Victoria by promising that, after one final three-month trip to China, to which he was already committed, he would pack in the globe-trotting and stay at home with his new family. His business partner could take charge of the international side of things from then on.

Esme's crying gradually subsided as she drifted into a restless sleep. Victoria risked pausing for a few moments to draw back the blanket, which her daughter had managed to pull up over her face in her agitation, and tuck it in safely beneath her chin. Then she started walking again, fearful that the pause in the motion of the pram would cause Esme to wake again.

Poor John! As his phone calls and emails made clear, he was so looking forward to returning home and seeing his daughter for the first time! What would he say when he discovered that she was not the perfect baby that he had been expecting? Victoria had not yet dared to tell him about the awful moment during labour, when the heart monitor had stopped, or her first sight of Esme, looking limp and lifeless and a strange blueish colour, or the soft-spoken doctor telling her gently that the brain damage due to oxygen starvation might be permanent. She had put it off time and again, and now he was due home tomorrow and he would see Esme and realise that something was wrong and Victoria would have to tell him – and would have to explain why she had kept it from him for so long.

And then what? Would he still want to give up the travelling and stay with her? Would he want to share the implacable crying and the difficulties over feeding, with the prospect that their daughter would never achieve the milestones that other people's children did?

***

A sharp yapping noise disturbed the silence of the office. It grew louder as Michelle Cohen fumbled in her handbag to find her phone. She must get round to changing the ringtone to something less annoying, she decided, as she deposited her diary, house keys, reading glasses and half a muesli bar on the desk and delved deeper into a sea of assorted till receipts and post-it notes. She found the phone and looked at the display. It was Georgia. What could she want? She never rang her mother at work.

'Hello Georgia, darling! Nothing wrong I hope?' Michelle tried to sound friendly and interested, but not overly concerned. Her own mother had been overbearing and unable to accept that her adult offspring were capable of making their own independent decisions. She was determined to allow Georgia the freedom to live her own life, unoppressed by constant un-asked-for maternal advice and ministrations.

'It's Rachel, Mum. I'm worried about her. She's very hot and won't settle and she keeps bringing up her feeds.'

'It could just be teeth coming,' Michelle suggested cautiously. 'I remember when you were that age, everyone said you were far too young for it, but you got your first teeth at twelve weeks.'

'Yes. Maybe you're right.' Georgia sounded dissatisfied. 'But would that make her keep being sick?'

'No. Probably not,' her mother admitted, her heart starting to beat faster with rising anxiety that she quickly suppressed. 'So perhaps it's a bug. Have you spoken to the doctor?' she added, trying to speak calmly.

'I rang the surgery and Dr Hodges said it was probably a virus and she'd throw it off in a day or so.'

'That's probably what it is then,' Michelle said reasonably.

'I know, but ... Mum ....'

'Yes?'

'I don't know ... she just doesn't seem

right. I'm scared … I mean, what if it's something more serious than that? What would you do, if you were me?'

'We-e-e-ell,' Michelle paused. Giving advice when you were specifically asked for it couldn't be considered interfering in her daughter's life, could it? But it was a big responsibility. What if she got it wrong? 'Why not give it a couple of hours and see how things go?'

'OK. I'll do that. Thanks Mum.'

'And if there's anything … I mean, if you'd like me to pop in on the way back from work?' Michelle ventured tentatively.

'Thanks. I'll let you know, Mum. I … I suppose I'd better let you get on now. Sorry for ringing you at work. I feel a lot better now.'

The call ended and Michelle put the phone back in her bag. As she stuffed the other items from her desk back in on top of it, she wondered whether she had got the balance right in dealing with her daughter. She did not want to be pushy, but was she perhaps just a bit *too* hands-off? *Should* Georgia have felt the need to apologise for having rung her? It was so difficult steering a path between appearing distant and uninterested and becoming an interfering old bag!

***

Debra looked up at the number carved into the stone gatepost and then down at the piece of paper in her hand. Yes! This was the house. She walked slowly up the path to the front door. She stood on the doorstep, hesitating to ring the bell. What would she do if Victoria answered it? What would she say to her? Why had she come? Was it idle curiosity to see what John's baby looked like? Or had she had some idea of confronting Victoria? But why would she do that? It wasn't Victoria's fault that she had been able to do for John the one thing at which she, Debra, had failed so miserably.

Ever since one of their mutual friends had let slip the fact that John's girlfriend was expecting a baby, Debra had been unable to think of anything else. It was so unfair that he could simply walk away and find a new partner to fulfil his desire for children, while she had no such easy option. She had got out all her old pregnancy and baby books, from the time before she and John had given up hope, and had followed through the weeks, imagining what Victoria must be experiencing at each stage. Nobody had told her when the baby was born, but it must be several weeks ago now – based on when the news had first reached her. She had to see it – the child that should, by rights, have been her own.

She rang the bell and waited. Nobody came. She peered in at the front window and saw a Moses basket in the corner of the room and an assortment of soft toys lying higgledy-piggledy on a long, green sofa. The friend who had told her that John had moved back to his mother's house, must have been right; but clearly, there was nobody in. Debra walked back down the garden path and looked both ways along the pavement. In the distance, she caught sight of a woman pushing a pram. That must be her! That must be Victoria, taking the baby out for a stroll in the June sunshine.

2 BROTHER, SISTER, PARENT, CHILD

Crystal crossed the road, looking round warily for traffic, and entered the small playground at the corner of Margaret Road Recreation Ground. She positioned the buggy under the row of trees that ran along the boundary between the park and the road, and applied the brake carefully. Abigail slept on peacefully while Ricky waved his arms and legs vigorously and broke into excited chatter in a language that only he could understand.

Crystal smiled down at him and hastened to undo the straps that confined him to the buggy.

'OK, OK! Don't be so impatient,' she admonished him gently. 'Mummy's getting you out as quickly as she can. There you are – see? Now, what would you like to go on first?'

She set Ricky down on his feet and took hold of the reins that were attached to a harness around his chest. He stood, wobbling dangerously for a moment or so before steadying himself by grasping hold of the side of the buggy. At fifteen months, he had been walking for some time, but he still found keeping his balance tricky, especially when taking to his feet after a period of sitting in the buggy. Frowning in deep concentration, he toddled off in the direction of the swings. Crystal followed, and soon she was lifting him up and fastening him into one of the baby swings.

'You'd better make the most of this,' she told Ricky, as she pushed him gently, to set the swing in motion. 'Mummy's going back to work next week, and Granddad Peter may not have time to bring you to play on the swings so often.'

Ricky ignored her remark. He was far too busy, swaying his body from side to side and singing a song of his own invention, to be concerned with making conversation. Crystal sighed to herself. She was very grateful for her father-in-law's willingness – eagerness, in fact – to look after the children for nothing, so that she could return to work and they could afford the mortgage on the flat. However, it was not the same as caring for her babies herself. Moreover, she doubted that any man – not even kind, dependable Peter – could provide her children with the love and security that their mother would have done.

Eddie had tried to reassure her.

'Don't you worry!' he had said. 'Dad's great with young children. I remember when Lucy was Ricky's age – she couldn't get enough of him. She liked him better even than her mum!'

Those remarks had not inspired confidence in Crystal. While she wanted Ricky and Abigail to be happy in the care of their grandfather, the idea that he might usurp her in their affections was not a welcome one. Moreover, the mention of Peter's stepdaughter, Lucy, only served to remind her that Peter already had his own family, and that Lucy might not take kindly to having her nose pushed out by two demanding newcomers. Jealousy could be a dangerous thing. Admittedly, Lucy had appeared to be delighted with her new nephew and niece, and had eagerly shared with Ricky some of her old toys; but seventeen was a difficult age and teenagers – especially girls – were notoriously changeable and unpredictable.

'Dee-daw! Dee-daw!' Ricky shouted out, interrupting her thoughts.

Crystal stopped the swing and bent down to speak to her son.

'See-saw?' she asked, pointing. This was a new word that he had never attempted before. 'Do you want to go on the see-saw?'

'Dee-daw!' Ricky repeated, nodding vigorously and attempting to stand up in the swing.

'OK. We'll go on the see-saw. Just sit still now, while I get you out.'

Crystal picked Ricky up and carried him across to the see-saw. She lifted him on to it and placed his hands on the handle, instructing him to 'hold on tight.' Then she proceeded to push the seat up and down with one hand, while holding her son, rather awkwardly, with the other. Really, the see-saw was not designed for a child as young as Ricky – or for one child alone. You needed someone else at the other end to balance it. However, a few days after they moved into the flat, they had met Shona Knight in the playground and she had suggested that her little girl, Kayleigh, and Ricky could share a ride. Ever since then, he demanded a go on the see-saw every time they visited the playground, failing to understand the difficulties that it presented to his mother in the absence of a suitably-sized playmate.

Working the see-saw became easier as Crystal settled into a steady rhythm. Her thoughts turned again to her imminent return to work. Perhaps it had been a mistake to turn down the offer of a more permanent home with her father-in-law. If they had not bought the flat, she could have taken her full entitlement to maternity leave, or worked part time, or … But then, it might have been years before they could afford somewhere of their own. Eddie was right – Peter was very good with the children, and she would still be able to spend time with them on her off-duty days. The main thing was to remember how lucky they were to have two healthy children after more than seven years of waiting and hoping and false alarms.

***

Flick stopped at the junction between Quarry Hollow and Quarry High Street. The corner of the Recreation Ground containing the children's playground was just opposite.

'Shall we take the short cut?' she asked Mia conversationally. 'Yes. That will be nice, won't it?'

She pushed the pram across the road and turned into the playground.

'Oh look, Mia! There's another baby here. Shall we go and have a look?'

She approached the buggy, which Crystal had left parked in the shade, and peeped into Abigail's carrycot.

'Look Mia! What a lovely baby girl! She's got a lot more hair than you've got – and such a gorgeous colour! I'll get you a nice ribbon like that one, when your hair grows. I wonder if she lives around here. Maybe you'll be friends with her when you're a bit older. I wonder who her mummy is.'

Flick looked round the playground, but the only adult there was a black woman giving her toddler a ride on the see-saw. She frowned. Had the beautiful red-haired baby girl been abandoned? Surely not? Oh, no – the mother was probably that fair-haired woman emerging from behind the slide holding the hand of a small child in pink dungarees.

'We'd better be going,' Flick murmured to Mia. 'Daddy won't be pleased if we forget to get his dinner, will he?'

She pushed the pram across the playground and out of the gate at the other side, and headed off across the grass.

***

Esme's crying became gradually quieter as the motion of the pram lulled her off to sleep. By the time Victoria reached the end of Ramsey Road, where it met the path along the edge of the recreation ground, the baby was sleeping peacefully. Victoria looked down on her. At last! She would cut across the grass and sit down on one of the seats by the playground to have her lunch before Esme woke up and started crying again.

She passed another mother and baby coming the other way. She seemed distracted and kept looking down into her pram. Perhaps she too had been up all night trying to calm a fractious child, and was now walking the streets in the hope of getting a few minutes of peace. They nodded perfunctorily, but did not speak.

The warm sunshine had attracted parents and grandparents from the surrounding neighbourhood to spend time with their offspring out in the open air. The playground was now busy with pre-school children running around and adults pushing them on the swings and the roundabout, helping them up the steps of the slide and holding their hands as they slid down again. Victoria steered the pram carefully round a black woman, who was bending down ready to catch her toddler when he reached the bottom of the slide, and headed for one of the benches in the shade of the line of trees that bordered the playground.

She parked Esme's pram next to a double buggy, glancing inside to see a pretty baby girl lying beneath an embroidered sheet depicting flowers and butterflies. She was sleeping contentedly with what looked like a smile on her lips. She must be about the same age as Esme, or perhaps a bit younger, judging by her size. Was she always as contented as this? Or did she too sometimes scream and scream and refuse to be pacified?

Victoria recollected herself and sat down abruptly on the bench. There was no time to waste speculating about other people's babies. Esme might wake at any moment. As she ate her meagre lunch, she watched the children playing. Would Esme ever be able to climb up the slide and launch herself down headfirst, like that little girl in the *My*

Little Pony tee-shirt? Would she ever swing from the climbing frame, like that blond-haired boy? Would she even manage to toddle around, unsteadily in her feet, like that black child in the Liverpool shirt? She finished her food as rapidly as she could and walked across the grass to deposit the apple core and banana peel in a bin. Sure enough, by the time she returned, Esme was already stirring again. Time to go – before she brought all the other mothers running over to see what Victoria could have done to her to cause her to scream so loudly and so inconsolably.

***

Debra hurried down the road, briefly breaking into a run when it seemed that she might be about to lose sight of her quarry. She slowed down again when she saw that Victoria – she hoped that it really *was* Victoria – had stopped. It looked like the end of the road. Where could she be going next? Now she was off again, striding out across what looked like a playing field. Debra quickened her pace again and soon came to the end of Ramsey Road, where a line of bollards marked the edge of the recreation ground. She stood aside to allow a woman with a pram to pass her. Then she set off over the grass in pursuit.

Victoria – she was convinced now that it must be Victoria – opened a yellow gate and went into a fenced-off area containing swings and slides. It was crowded with young children and their mothers and grandmothers, enjoying the summer sunshine. Debra skirted round the edge of the play area and took up a position behind one of the trees at the opposite side from where she had come in. She looked round and eventually spotted Victoria sitting on a bench. The pram – or rather, it turned out to be a buggy with a carrycot attachment, now that she was closer to it – was parked next to her. What now? Debra was torn between a desire to step up to Victoria and confront her, and a fear of making a scene and appearing ridiculous and pitiable.

She crept closer, still keeping behind the line of trees. Now she was only a few feet away and she could just see into the carrycot. So that was John's baby, was it? It looked very pale, hardly any different from the white sheet beneath it. She could not distinguish any facial features from this distance. Did she dare to come any closer?

Then Victoria got up and walked across the grass to put something into the litter bin. Debra stepped forward and peeped quickly in at the sleeping infant. Yes, there *was* something there that reminded her of John's face. She was not sure what, but a definite family resemblance. This baby ought to have been hers. She was John's wife, after all. She had only agreed to the divorce because he asked her and promised that she could keep the house in exchange for not making a fuss. She glanced across the playground and saw that Victoria had reached the bin and was about to turn round and come back. Debra beat a hasty retreat, back behind the nearest tree and then along by the railings to the entrance and out into the street.

She turned left, in order get out of

sight as quickly as possible. Good – there was a high wall here to shield her from view. What should she do now? She hurried along the road, which was called Quarry High Street, but which looked like no High Street that Debra had ever seen before. There were no shops, just houses, set back behind gardens bordered by stone walls. Where did it go? It hardly mattered now. She had done what she came for. Now it was just a matter of finding her way back to where she had left her car, and then … Well, she would think about that later.

***

Georgia looked down into the cot. Was she imagining it or was Rachel lying unusually still? She put her face down close to Rachel's mouth to check that she was still breathing. Immediately, she was struck by the warmth that was radiating from the child's cheeks. Alarmed, she picked her up and rested her on her shoulder so that Rachel's face was leaning against her neck. Surely, it should not be as hot as this? And why had the movement not woken her?

Georgia sat down and laid Rachel on her lap. She still did not stir. Her eyes were half-open, but she was clearly not conscious. Georgia spoke to her, softly at first, then louder. There was still no response. It was no good. Something was wrong. She must get medical help.

Georgia put Rachel back into her cot and considered what to do. The doctor's surgery would be closed for lunch now. In any case, she did not fancy trying to explain her concerns to the doctor who had so clearly thought she was fussing unnecessarily and who would, in all probability, continue to offer reassurance aimed at calming down an anxious new mother. A and E then? The nearest unit was in Watford, half an hour away. She had better get going then – or was she making a mountain out of a molehill?

As she strapped the still sleeping Rachel into her car seat, Georgia wondered if she was doing the right thing. Should she wait and go to the afternoon surgery at the doctor's? But she did not have an appointment. It might be a long wait, and if Rachel were to wake up and cry, the elderly patients in the waiting room would be impatient with her. She had, on a previous occasion, been asked to 'take that screaming child outside.' No. The hospital would be better, and it would probably be reasonably quiet in the middle of the day. Didn't most accidents happen in the late evenings when the pubs were closing?

3 WE HOLD OUR BREATH IN HORROR

'Just one more go,' Crystal told Ricky as he clambered laboriously back to his feet after his tenth (or more – Crystal had lost count) descent. 'Then we'd better check that your sister is still OK.'

Ricky grinned up at her and toddled off to make the climb up to the top of the slide again. Crystal followed him closely, ready to catch hold of him if he looked to be in danger of missing his footing. Another boy, impatient with Ricky's slow progress, pushed past him on the steps and Crystal steadied him as his hand slipped off the rail. The playground was becoming too busy now for children as young as Ricky; it was time they were going.

Ricky giggled happily, as he slid down and tumbled off the end of the chute, on to the rubberised surface of the playground. Crystal bent down and swept him up in her arms.

'Time to go now,' she told him.

Ricky squirmed and tried to get away, but Crystal held on firmly and started walking away from the slide towards the grassy border and the line of trees. Realising that his playtime was over, Ricky wriggled harder and started to cry.

'Don't make a fuss, Ricky darling,' his mother said soothingly. 'We'll come back another day. Be a good boy now.

You don't want your sister seeing her big brother crying now, do you?'

She carried him, still protesting, across to the waiting buggy.

'Quiet now,' she told him. 'Don't wake Abigail. She's still asleep, bless her. Now let's-'

Crystal broke off in alarm as she looked down into the carrycot and saw to her dismay that Abigail was not there. The pretty, embroidered sheet was turned down showing clearly the indentation in the mattress where she had been, but of the baby herself there was no sign. Crystal's heart beat faster and her mouth became suddenly dry. How could such a thing have happened? She held Ricky closer to her chest and looked around at all the other parents and children in the playground. Perhaps one of them had heard the baby crying and picked her up to comfort her.

Frantically she hurried round to each adult in turn, hoping against hope that one of them would be able to explain what had happened.

'Have you seen a five-week-old baby with red hair? ... My baby has been taken from her pram – have you seen her? ... I left my little girl in the buggy over there and now she's gone – have you seen ...?'

Nobody had seen anything. Nobody knew anything. Nobody could offer any sort of explanation. Crystal sat down on the bench next to the buggy and tried to gather her thoughts. A cluster of anxious onlookers gathered round her, many of them with young children, whom they gripped tightly by the hand or held in their arms. None of them had experienced anything like this before. It all seemed so unreal. A baby couldn't really disappear from a buggy in a busy playground without anyone seeing anything – could it?

'Better ring 999,' one of the other mothers said, holding tight to her own two youngsters as if she were afraid that they, too, might suddenly be snatched away. Crystal nodded silently and fumbled in her pocket for her phone. It seemed like a long time before it was answered. Her voice sounded strange and hoarse as she explained what had happened. The call handler was sympathetic and efficient. The police would attend immediately. Crystal should wait where she was for their arrival.

She ended the call and looked round again, as if she expected Abigail to have magically reappeared. What now? How long would it be before the police got there? What would happen then? What would Eddie say when he heard? She had better ring him right away – there might not be an opportunity once the police were there. She waited impatiently for him to answer. Perhaps he was busy or in a meeting? Perhaps she shouldn't have rung him at work. Too late now, he had answered.

Crystal told her husband what had happened, thinking all the time how unreal it sounded, as if it were happening to someone else. When she had finished, there was a long silence. He probably couldn't take it in either. Then, 'I'll be right over. Try not to worry. I expect there's a simple explanation.' Then there was a pause, before he added, 'Ring Dad. He'll know what to do.'

Then he ended the call and Crystal was left, gazing down at the phone in her hand, wondering what to do next. Eddie was right – his father would be able to help. He had been a police officer for years, before retiring to spend more time with his family. He was also the calmest, most reassuring person she knew – and calm reassurance was what she needed more than anything else right now.

***

As she drove into the hospital car park, Georgia wondered if she was doing the right thing. A large banner on the wall of the hospital informed her that A and E was only for 'people with serious and life-threatening emergencies' and that there were other, more suitable, facilities for most health problems. Did Rachel have a *serious and life-threatening* condition? Georgia certainly hoped not. But how could you tell in a baby as young as she was? Should she have called the 111 service? But they would probably have just said reassuring nothings the way the doctor had done. She was here now, so she might as well go in. They could always tell her to go back to her GP if they thought she was fussing about nothing.

Georgia need not have worried herself on that score. When she explained her concerns – apologising as she did so for troubling them when it was probably nothing much – the triage nurse immediately called a doctor who, after a few preliminary questions, took Abigail's temperature and listened to her chest, and then felt the soft spot on the top of her head.

'I think it may be meningitis,' she said to Georgia. 'We'll need to do some tests to be sure, but meanwhile we'll treat the symptoms. I want to admit her right away.'

'Meningitis? That's quite serious, isn't it?' Georgia asked, feeling as if her normal everyday world had suddenly vanished and been replaced by a strange, unfamiliar place that she did not understand.

'It can be. But there are several different kinds and some are more serious than others. If it's viral, then she'll probably throw it off naturally in a few days.'

'And if it's not?'

'Bacterial meningitis *is* sometimes dangerous, but it depends which organism is involved and how early on in the infection we've caught it. There's a very good chance that, even if that's what it is, she could make a full recovery.'

'But she might not?' Georgia asked fearfully. 'Do you mean she may die?'

'Try not to think about that,' the doctor said soothingly. 'Like I said, it may well be viral meningitis – or not even meningitis at all. We'll have her admitted and run the tests and then we'll know what we're dealing with. Now, take her back into the waiting area and someone will come and get you shortly.'

***

Flick put the last of her shopping on to the rack underneath the pram and set off for home, taking the route along the roads this time, instead of going across the recreation ground. As she turned the corner into Margaret Road, a police car came past with its siren blaring. She watched as the blue light raced along the street and then stopped at the corner by the children's playground. What was going on?

She quickened her pace. Up ahead she saw two police officers getting out of the car – a man and a woman. They crossed the pavement and went into the park. There were people there – standing in a huddle under the trees. Was someone hurt? An assault, perhaps? But then you would have thought there would be an ambulance.

Flick stared through the railings as she passed the playground. The police officers were talking to a black woman, who was sitting on a bench, hugging a small boy to her. About a dozen other adults – mostly women with young children in tow – were standing around, talking in small groups. The swings, slide, and roundabout were all unoccupied, and the shouts and laughter of children had been replaced by a murmur of conversation interspersed with occasional complaints from toddlers who did not understand why their playtime had been curtailed.

For a moment, Flick considered whether to join the crowd and ask what was going on. Then she looked down at Mia, lying peacefully in the pram, and decided against it. It was time that they were getting back. When you had a baby, life was regulated by feed times and nap times. Any delay now might mean that Mia's routine was disrupted and she would not settle in the evening and then dinner would be interrupted and Sam would get annoyed. He had said that he had a lot of marking to do. He would not be able to concentrate if Mia was crying.

Flick gave one last glance back at the huddle of anxious parents, and then crossed the road, bending over the pram and talking cheerfully to her daughter as they made their way up the final incline to their home.

***

Georgia opened the contacts list on her mobile phone and selected her husband's entry. It went straight through to voicemail. Bother! Nathan had said that he would be in court today, but she had hoped that it might still be adjourned for lunch. Judges seemed to take much shorter breaks than they used to. Her father, a solicitor specialising in criminal cases, said that they used often to have as much as two hours for lunch in his young day. Better not to leave a message. Whatever she said would either tell Nathan nothing or else alarm him.

Next, she rang her father's office. His secretary greeted her cheerfully and put her through at once.

'Hi Dad!' Georgia was suddenly at a loss as to what to say. 'It's probably nothing to worry about,' she began hesitantly, 'but I thought I ought to let you know.'

'Yes?' Her father sounded puzzled and concerned.

'It's Rachel. She's been admitted to hospital with suspected meningitis.'

'I see. Does your mum know?'

'I'm going to ring her now. I tried to get Nathan, but his phone's turned off.'

'I see. Is there anything we can do?'

'No. Like I said – I just thought you ought to know.'

Her mother was similarly downbeat. Sticking to her determination not to be an interfering, over-anxious mother, Michelle stuck to vaguely encouraging platitudes and an assurance that they would help in whatever way Georgia – and Nathan, of course – wanted them to.

'Do you think I ought to ring Nathan's dad?' Georgia asked her, as an afterthought as she was about to end the call.

'I would have thought that was Nathan's job.'

'Yes, I know, but … well, with me not having managed to get hold of Nathan?'

'I see what you mean,' Michelle hesitated. She was torn between the thought that, now that she and her husband knew about Rachel's illness, it was only fair that her other grandparent should be put in the picture too, and a wish to protect Georgia's father-in-law from news that would cause him unnecessary worry.

'I think it would be better to leave that for now,' she said at last. 'After all, there's nothing he can do, under the circumstances, is there?'

***

'Mrs Johns?' Crystal looked up at the sound of her name and saw a brown-eyed face surrounded by black hair looking down on her. It was a policewoman.

'Yes,' she answered. 'That's me.'

'You reported that your baby girl has been abducted. Is that right?'

'Yes – at least ... I left her here – in

70

the buggy – and now she's gone.'

'I see. Well, I'm Sergeant Tracy Burton and this is my colleague, Constable Malcolm Appleton, and we're going to do our very best to find your baby for you, but you're going to have to help us to do that. And first of all,' Tracy hesitated. However she put it, her next question was going to sound patronising. 'First of all, I have to ask – are you absolutely sure that you had the baby with you? I mean – could you have got distracted and thought you'd put her in the buggy when she was really safe at home in her cot? I know I sometimes do that sort of thing,' she added with a little nervous laugh.

'No. I'm quite sure. I remember seeing the sun on her face and having to move the shade to stop her getting burnt. She's got such pale skin, you see

– it's because of her red hair.'

Tracy fought down the impulse to wonder at the mismatch between Crystal's own appearance and her description of her daughter. There was no doubt a simple explanation. Perhaps the child was adopted or ... Before she could martial her thoughts and move on to her next question a woman from the back of the crowd pushed forward to have her say. She had firm hold of a boy of about four with blond hair and a very dirty face.

'I can confirm the baby was here,' she said. 'I had a peep in the pram just after we got here. There was a little girl with red hair tied up in a mauve ribbon. I noticed specially, because ....'

She hesitated before continuing, 'because there was no-one else here apart from this lady,' (she indicated

Crystal with an inclination of her head), 'and … but I asked her and she told me the baby was hers.'

'Thank you,' Tracy said, turning to the woman. 'We'll need to take a proper statement from you later, but tell me now – what time was it when you saw the baby?'

'I can't tell you to the minute,' the woman answered, pursing her lips in thought, 'but it can't have been long after one – it could even have been a minute or two before that. No, I tell a lie, it must have been about five past. I remember looking at my watch when we started down the footpath from Holley Crescent and it was one on the dot. So we must have got to the playground about five past and we left Josh's bike under the trees, next to this lady's buggy and that was when I looked in and saw the baby. I – I – I,' she looked towards Crystal and then back to Tracy, her face colouring with embarrassment. 'I couldn't see anyone – I mean I thought ….'

She took a deep breath and marshalled her thoughts. 'I saw this white baby with such pale skin and the only adult in the playground was this lady, and so I went up to her and asked her if she knew where the mother had got to, because it seemed odd leaving a baby on its own like that. And she told me it was hers. I'm sorry,' she added, turning to Crystal. 'I should've thought – that's to say, I shouldn't have assumed …'

Crystal waved her hand in a vague gesture, intended to indicate that no offence had been taken. She was starting to get used to the reactions of people seeing her with Abigail for the first time.

'Thank you. That's very helpful information.' Tracy thanked the witness and then turned to her colleague. 'Malcolm – call for backup. Tell them we need CID out here right away, and we'll need a team of officers to take statements. We need to get things moving – fast! It sounds as if the little girl can only have been gone a few minutes – an hour max – so if we get a move on we can probably track her down.'

'I know it's distressing for you,' she said, turning back to speak to Crystal, 'but try to stay calm. We need you to tell us as much as you can about what happened so that we can help you to find your baby.'

Crystal nodded and wiped her eyes

with the back of her hand. The presence of the police, and Tracy's sympathetic approach, had suddenly made the unbelievable situation horribly real. Ricky, on her lap, held close to her chest, felt a change in her breathing as she fought back sobs and, detecting his mother's distress, he began to cry. His world, too, had suddenly stopped obeying the normal rules and had become a terrifying place where anything might happen.

4 WHERE THERE'S DESPAIR IN LIFE

'I'm beginning to think that I might as well hang up my truncheon and retire,' DCI Jonah Porter remarked gloomily to his personal assistant as they reviewed his schedule for the rest of the week. 'Where have all the interesting cases gone? I'm wasted on all this minor assault and burglary. I want a nice juicy murder to get my teeth into!'

'That's a very unchristian attitude,' Bernie told him with a grin. 'You should be rejoicing at having made Oxford too hot for them to handle!'

'I suppose that must be it,' Jonah agreed, returning Bernie's grin with his own lopsided smile. 'I must have scared all the murderers and rapists away.'

A buzzing sound indicated that a call had come through on the mobile phone attachment on Jonah's wheelchair. With a swift movement of his left index finger, he accepted the call. They both listened intently to the news that a baby had been reported missing from a public open space in Headington. Jonah asked a few terse questions before ending the conversation by declaring, 'I'll get over there right away.'

'I told you, you should be careful what you wish for,' Bernie observed drily, torn between anxiety for the mother of the missing child, excitement at the prospect of new criminal investigation and pleasure at her friend's renewed vitality and improved mood as he prepared to launch himself into the task. 'I hope child abduction is sufficiently *juicy* for you.'

Jonah ignored her flippant remark. Now that he had a crime to investigate, he had no attention to spare for anything else. He manoeuvred his electric wheelchair out from behind the desk and Bernie leapt up to open the door to allow him out into the open-plan space where the more junior CID officers had their desks. Jonah called for silence and then explained the situation in a few words.

'Time is of the essence in a case like this,' he finished, looking round the room assessing each officer in turn to decide what role they should play. 'So this takes priority over anything else that isn't absolutely safety-critical. Andy!'

'Yes sir?' Detective Sergeant Andrew Lepage got to his feet, rather clumsily, knocking over a jar of paperclips on the desk in front of him as he did so.

'I want you to come with me. Where's Anna?'

'She isn't back from her antenatal appointment yet, sir,' came a voice from the back of the room. Jonah looked across and recognised Monica Philipson, an ambitious, but not always very reliable, detective sergeant.

Jonah made an effort not to show his annoyance at this news. He could do with a female officer to accompany him to speak to the mother of the missing infant, and DI Anna Davenport was one of his best, man or woman. He had been counting on her being available.

'Well, when she gets back, will

someone tell her to get straight over to the Margaret Road Recreation Ground and join us there. Now, Andrews, I want you to get together a team of officers and bring them over there to take statements. Apparently, there are quite a number of people who were in the vicinity when it happened, but it may be difficult to get them to stay around for long. I've told Uniform to take names and addresses and to keep them there as long as they can, but they're mostly parents of young children, so I can just see all our witnesses disappearing when it gets to time for the school run. And dogs – we need some tracker dogs to search the area in case the baby's been dumped somewhere nearby. Monica – you see about organising a call centre for people to ring in with information. We don't know if we'll need it, yet, but if it comes to that, I don't want there to be any delay. And put out a call for people to be on the lookout for anyone acting suspiciously with a young baby. Oh! And get on to all the hospitals and children's centres in case whoever it is decides to hand it in there. Right, Andy, let's get going!'

He led the way outside and into the car park. There, he had to wait for Bernie to put in place the ramp that would allow him to drive his wheelchair up into their specially adapted car. He sat in his chair, gazing around and going over in his mind all the things that he might need to do to take forward the enquiry. A car came past and pulled up a few spaces along.

'Hey, Anna!' Jonah called out to the tall woman with short blond hair, who got out. 'Come over here! I need you to come with us. Get in the car and I'll explain on the way.'

Bernie finished strapping Jonah, in his wheelchair, into the back of the car and then got out to transfer herself into the driving seat. Andy took the front passenger seat, allowing Anna to join Jonah in the back. She sat down opposite him and looked across enquiringly.

'I gather something is up?'

***

'So, what are we going to do about it?' Michelle demanded, sitting down on the corner of her husband's desk and looking him in the eye. 'Do you think we ought to go over to the hospital?'

Leslie Cohen took off his glasses and reached into his pocket for a handkerchief. Then he breathed on each lens in turn and polished them carefully before replacing them on his nose.

'What do *you* think?' he asked mildly.

'I don't know – that's why I'm asking you. I don't want her to think we don't care, but I don't want to make a big fuss about nothing. I mean ....' She trailed off, uncertain what she *did* mean.

'Well, do you think she wants us there? Would you have wanted *your* mother?'

'God, no! She'd have been demanding to see the consultant and cross-examining the nurses and threatening to put in a complaint about something-or-other that she didn't think was exactly as it ought to have been. You know what Mum was like. But I hope *I* wouldn't embarrass Georgia like that.'

'Well then, perhaps we should go over.'

'That's what I was thinking, but then I thought: Nathan doesn't even know about it yet and he's Rachel's father. I don't know if he'd like us to have been there before he even knew there was anything wrong.'

'Or he might be grateful that his wife wasn't left alone, even though she couldn't reach him,' Leslie suggested.

'But, if she really thought it was that serious, she'd have found a way of getting hold of him, wouldn't she? I mean – someone from his chambers would know how to get a message to him. And when she rang, she didn't say she'd like us to go over there, did she?'

Leslie sighed. He wished that his wife would admit that she was worried about her granddaughter and wanted to be there to hear the results of the tests, to give her daughter the benefit of her experience as a mother – only if she were to ask for it, of course – and generally to be the perfect grandmother. He decided to propose a compromise.

'Why don't we wait a few hours?' he suggested. 'I've got a client due in fifteen minutes, so I can't very well go over right away in any case. How about, we wait until after I get home and then give her a ring? Then if Rachel's still in hospital, we'll go over for evening visiting.'

'Yes. You're right. That makes more sense,' Michelle agreed, brightening up considerably, now that a decision had been made. 'I'll go home now and then I can have dinner ready for you when you get back, and we can go out straight away after that – if, as you say, Rachel hasn't been sent home by then.'

***

'How did the scan go, at the hospital?' Bernie asked Anna conversationally, after Jonah had finished briefing her on the child abduction case.

'It wasn't a scan – it was a follow-up appointment,' Anna answered in what struck both Bernie and Jonah as a rather strange voice. Jonah looked across at her sharply. The colour had drained from her face and she was twisting her hands together and making the knuckles crackle. 'The scan was last week, but they called us in to see the consultant.'

Nobody knew what to say. This was so unexpected. Moreover, neither Bernie nor Jonah liked to ask for more information. Anna was a colleague and a friend, but they had no right to know the details of her private life or medical history. Andy, at the age of 33 still single and living with his mother, felt out of his depth in such a conversation; he studiously kept his eyes to the front and his mouth shut. There was a long pause. Anna dropped her eyes and stared for a few seconds at her, as yet small, but unmistakeable, baby bump. She rested her hands on it as if cradling the unborn child. Then she took a deep breath and looked up at Jonah.

'They told us the baby has almost certainly got spina bifida,' she said, still in that strange, unnatural voice. Still no-one spoke. Jonah gazed back at Anna with a look of compassion. What could anyone say to that?

'I'm sorry,' he ventured, at last. Then, because this was something that he had his own strong feelings about, he added, 'but it's not really such a big deal, is it? I mean – it's just a spinal cord defect, isn't it? And, speaking from personal experience, that doesn't have to be–'

'I know!' Anna interrupted. 'That's what I said to Phil. I told him about you, and how you lead a full and active life, despite having a much more serious disability than what they're predicting for our baby. But he won't listen. He just keeps saying we don't have any right to have a baby that won't ever be able to live independently; and it wouldn't be fair on our kids because it would disrupt family life; and – and ...'

'You mean he wants you to have an abortion?' Bernie asked, trying hard to sound neutral on the subject. Her Catholic upbringing made it very difficult for her to understand how anyone could contemplate terminating a pregnancy, but she tried not to be judgemental and to accept that alternative views might be valid.

'That's right,' Anna answered miserably.

'And *you* don't,' Jonah said. It was a statement, not a question. He could see from Anna's face that she had made up her own mind and that a large part of her evident distress was not so much about the potential disabilities of her unborn child as the rift that had opened up between her and her husband.

'No.'

Jonah watched Anna's face. She seemed to be lost in thought. The colour was gradually coming back to her cheeks now. She looked at him and managed a small smile, in acknowledgement that he understood her predicament.

'He never wanted this baby in the first place,' she said suddenly. 'It wasn't planned. The doctors say it must have been the antibiotics that I took for that really bad chest infection I had over the winter. Apparently, some antibiotics can stop the pill working properly. Phil said ….' She gave a little gulp and then took another deep breath and started again. 'Phil wanted me to get rid of it from the start. He said he'd already put his career on hold for long enough, looking after the kids, and now they were just getting old enough for him to start making plans for expanding the business, I went and did this!'

Jonah remembered that Philip Davenport was a self-employed architect, who worked from home in order to care for their two children, while

Anna pursued her own career in the police service. Jessica and Marcus must be teenagers by now. It was no wonder that their father had been expecting to begin enjoying more freedom.

'He talked like he thought I'd done it deliberately!' Anna went on. 'He said if I wouldn't have a termination then I'd have to make my own arrangements for childcare. He wasn't going to sacrifice another dozen years of his life just because I wouldn't take a responsible attitude. He–'

'But we don't have abortion on demand here,' Andy blurted out, breaking his vow of silence. He was the product of a brief liaison between an undergraduate student and a much older postgraduate on a visit from Nigeria, who had turned out already to have two wives back home and who had disappeared back to Africa before his son was born. As such, Andy was painfully aware that he might never have seen the light of day if abortion had been more easily available to his mother.

'Phil said he could easily find a couple of doctors who would sign to say that it would be detrimental to my health to continue with the pregnancy. He reckoned it was pretty standard, what with me being older – and, in any case, I could always say that it would affect my mental health and nobody would argue.'

'You can't be any older than I was when I had Lucy,' Bernie commented. 'And she was my first.'

'Anyway,' Anna continued, sniffing and wiping her eyes with a tissue, 'I told him I wanted to have the baby and he said *on my head be it* and I said we'd manage somehow and he didn't need to have anything to do with it if he didn't want to. I assumed he'd come round to it in the end. But now ... The first thing he did when the doctor told us was ... he turned to me and said, "*now* will you agree to get rid of the wretched thing?" just like that!'

There was a shocked silence for several minutes. Nobody knew how to respond. Jonah tried to think of something comforting to say, but the only words that sprung to mind were angry ones castigating the insensitivity of Anna's husband. Bernie forced herself to concentrate on driving, as they approached the junction by the entrance to the recreation ground. Anna continued to dab her eyes and tried to compose herself.

They pulled up and Bernie got out so

that she could go round to release Jonah from the straps that secured him in the back of the car. He caught Anna's eye and gave her a gentle smile.

'Stay in here until you're ready,' he told her. 'Just take it slowly and don't be too hard on yourself.'

'No. It's OK. I'd rather be out there doing something – and that poor woman!'

***

'Nathan? Thank God! I thought you were never going to turn your phone back on.'

'What's up Georgie?' Nathan detected in his wife's voice a tone that he had never heard before.

'It's Rachel. I'm at Watford General. They've admitted her. They think it may be meningitis?'

'Meningitis? That's serious isn't it?'

'Not necessarily, apparently,' Georgia tried to sound calm and matter-of-fact. 'They've taken a blood sample and done a lumbar puncture and now I'm waiting for the results. They seem to be saying that if it's viral, it's no big deal, but if it's bacterial, it may be … well, then we do have to worry.'

'And do they *think* it's viral?' Nathan asked eagerly.

'I told you – we've got to wait for the tests to come back.'

'How long …?'

'Dunno. They didn't say. They just said they'd tell me when they do come. Nathan? Can you come over?'

'Yes. Of course. The court's adjourned now until tomorrow morning. I'll jump on the next train and be over there before you know it.'

'Thanks.' Georgia's voice sounded very small and frightened.

'And don't worry.'

***

'Crystal! I got here as soon as I could.' Peter Johns pushed his way through the crowd to speak to his daughter-in-law.

'Peter! I'm so glad you're here!' Crystal looked up and gave a watery smile. 'I just can't believe that this is happening!'

'DI Johns!' Tracy exclaimed as she recognised her former colleague. 'I don't believe it! Are you …? I mean is this …?'

'If you mean, is Crystal here my daughter-in-law and is it my granddaughter who's gone missing,' Peter answered, 'then, *yes* and *yes*.' He turned back to Crystal. 'Remember, most young babies that are snatched from their prams are taken by someone who wants a baby of their own – perhaps a mother who's lost hers and can't come to terms with it – so it's highly unlikely that they'll deliberately hurt Abigail.'

Crystal nodded and tried to smile.

'The main thing you can do to help,' Peter went on, 'is to try to remember everything that happened, from when you left the flat this afternoon to when you first found she had gone. Have a think about that, and then you'll be ready to answer the investigating officer when they get here.'

He turned to Tracy again.

'I assume that CID are on their way? Do you know who it is?'

'*Yes*, and *no*,' Tracy replied, copying Peter's laconic style. 'Malcolm made the call. He said they told him it would be top priority, but I don't know if they said who would be in charge.'

'Alright. Never mind that then.' Peter sat down next to his daughter-in-law. 'Whoever it is, I can guarantee that they'll be pulling out all the stops to find her,' he told her, putting his hand on her arm. She leaned towards him and he slid his arm round her shoulders. Recognising his grandfather's voice, Ricky cautiously lifted his head from where it had been buried in Crystal's neck and favoured him with a tentative smile. Peter returned the smile and put out his other hand to fondle the tight black curls on the top of Ricky's head.

'How about coming and sitting on Granddad's lap for a little while?' he suggested. 'To give Mummy a rest.'

5 I WILL WEEP WHEN YOU ARE WEEPING

'Sir?' Constable Appleton greeted Andy as he got out of the car and looked round, taking in the small crowd, standing around in huddles of two or three, chatting and pointing and, in some cases, looking at their watches and frowning. At the sound of Malcolm's voice, he turned and looked at him.

'DCI Porter is leading the investigation,' he told his colleague, taken aback at being addressed as 'sir'.

He was used to being the most junior member of any team, having only been promoted to the rank of sergeant a little over a year previously. 'And DI Davenport is assisting him.' He jerked his head in the direction of the car, from which Jonah was now emerging in his wheelchair. Anna followed him. Her eyes were red, but otherwise she appeared composed. Bernie was bending down to fold up the ramp and stow it away in the car.

'Constable Appleton!' Jonah called out, seeing the tall, fair-haired policeman and propelling his chair rapidly in his direction. 'Have you secured the scene?'

'We've rounded up everyone who was in the playground,' Malcolm answered. 'And I've been round them and got all their names and addresses and told them not to go anywhere. Hughes and Lightfoot are manning the two gates into the play area to keep out the public and monitor if any of the witnesses try to leave before you've had a chance to talk to them. The mother is over there on that bench – where Sergeant Burton's standing. Oh! And I think you ought to know that DI Johns is here.'

'Old Peter? Why on earth ...?'

'Apparently he's a relative or something. The mother rang him and–'

Without waiting to hear more, Jonah headed at full speed in the direction of the bench beneath the trees where Crystal was sitting, with Peter at her side holding Ricky on his lap. He was not quick enough, however, to get there before Bernie, who, at the mention of her husband's name had dropped the ramp and run at full pelt towards the playground. She did not wait to argue with Constable Gavin Hughes, who stepped forward to inform her that this was a crime scene and nobody was allowed in. Instead, she scrambled over the low railings, using a litterbin attached to the fence to give her a foothold. Then she elbowed her way through the crowd to stand in front of Peter, looking down anxiously at the little family group on the bench in front of her.

'Peter! And, oh Crystal! I'm so sorry! How did it happen?'

'That's what we're going to find out, isn't it?' Jonah answered, coming up behind her. 'Don't you worry, Crystal. Though I say it myself, I'm one of Thames Valley's finest and I don't often fail to solve a case.'

Peter looked up, smiling in spite of

himself, at Jonah's confident declaration. It was well known in the family that he considered his friend to be somewhat too big for his boots.

'Jonah! I'm glad they've put you on the case.' He turned to his daughter-in-law. 'It pains me considerably to admit it,' he told her, 'but Jonah's right – he *is* very good at his job. If anyone can get Abigail back safe and sound, he will. But,' he added, looking back at Jonah,' isn't there a conflict of interest here? I mean, you living with us and everything? I'm surprised they let you come.'

'We didn't know,' Bernie explained. 'They didn't give a name. The report we got just said that a woman had reported having her baby taken from its pram. We had no idea it was Abigail.'

'And if you think I'm going to waste

time checking with the powers that be whether or not I ought to be in charge of this investigation, you've got another think coming,' Jonah added. 'Let's get started. All being well, we'll be able to get the whole thing cleared up before anyone else twigs that there's anything to worry about.'

He turned to speak to Anna and Andy, who had come up behind him and were nodding and smiling at Peter, whom they both knew from his days as a Detective Inspector. Indeed, Peter had been Andy's mentor for several years after he joined the CID and he had great liking and respect for him.

'I want you two to start taking statements from the witnesses. The sooner we find out if any of them saw anything, the better. Constable Appleton has a list of names.'

'There's a woman here who says she saw the baby asleep in the pram at about five past one,' Tracy told them. 'Do you want to start with her? She says her name's Gail Carpenter.'

'Good work, Sergeant Burton. Yes. Anna – you interview Mrs Carpenter. Find out if she saw anything else. Andy – get the list from Malc and start going through it. With any luck, Andrews will be here any minute, with a team of officers to help you. Report to me if you hear anything interesting.' Jonah waited until he had seen Anna taking Gail Carpenter by the arm and guiding her to sit down on another of the benches that were arrayed along the grass border under the line of trees. Then he turned back to Crystal.

'I'd like you to take me through exactly what you did and saw this afternoon, starting from when you left the flat, and going right up to when you found that Abigail was gone. Can you do that for me?'

Crystal nodded.

'Good.'

Bernie took a small laptop computer out of a pocket at the back of Jonah's wheelchair and sat down on the bench next to Peter, ready to take notes.

'OK,' Jonah began gently. 'Now, can you remember what time it was when you went out?'

'I'm not sure,' Crystal looked at him anxiously. 'I didn't look at the clock. Ricky and I had lunch and then I fed Abby and changed her, and then we went out.'

'Don't let's worry about that then. Tell me about the journey. You walked here, I take it? Pushing the two kids in the buggy?'

'That's right.'

'And that takes – what? – fifteen or twenty minutes?'

'Something like that.'

'And we have a witness who says you were already here by five past one. So you can't have left the flat any later than, say, quarter to.'

'It must have been earlier than that. We'd been here five or ten minutes before she came.'

'You noticed her arrive?'

'Not exactly. There was no-one else here when we got here. She looked in the buggy when she arrived and then came over to me to ask if I knew where the baby's mother was.'

'Sorry?' Jonah looked puzzled. 'I don't get it.'

'I was the only adult in the playground

and she didn't think I looked like Abby's mother. You know – because she's white.'

'Oh! Yes. I see now.' A thought suddenly struck Jonah. 'Do you think she believed you, when you told her you were?'

'Oh yes! We had a little chat about my husband being mixed race and about red hair sometimes skipping a generation. And she said her little boy had blue eyes like his granddad, even though she and her husband both had brown ones.'

'I see. Now, going back to when you set off. It sounds as if it must have been not long after half past twelve. Do you think it could have been any earlier than that?'

'I don't think so. Like I said, we'd had lunch and I'd given Abby her feed.'

'OK. Now, did you speak to anyone on the way?'

'I don't think so.' Crystal tried to concentrate on remembering, but all she could picture in her mind was the empty buggy with its rumpled sheet and coverlet drawn back. 'At least ... there was the woman in the lift.'

'Go on,' Jonah said encouragingly. 'Was it someone you knew?'

'Not really. I mean, I'd never met her before, but she said she was visiting her son, and he's one of our neighbours. I know him a bit because they've got a little girl – Kayleigh – who's Ricky's age. They live on the fourth floor.'

'Did she tell you her name?'

'Yes.' Crystal closed her eyes and tried to remember. 'It began with a Y, I think.'

'Yvonne?' Bernie suggested, but

Crystal shook her head.

'Yasmin,' Peter offered. Crystal shook her head again.

'No. I'm sorry. I can't remember. But her surname must have been Knight, the same as her son's. He's Morgan Knight and his wife is Shona.'

'That's fine,' Jonah assured her. 'You're doing very well.'

'Now tell me – did Mrs Knight take an interest in Abigail at all?'

'What do you mean?'

'Well, did she ask any questions about her? Or pass any comments on her appearance or anything?'

'I don't know. She may have asked how old she was. People often do.'

'So you'd say she behaved just like any other stranger meeting you in the lift?'

'Yes.'

'When you got out of the lift, did you walk together at all or were you going different ways?'

'She had her car parked outside. So she got in that.'

'And you set off walking. Which way did you go?'

'I crossed over Wood Farm Road and went along Titup Hall Drive.'

Bernie obligingly produced a map on her computer screen and showed it to Crystal. Jonah looked down attentively at an identical map on the screen attached to his wheelchair.

'When I got to the end, I turned right,' Crystal continued, pointing out the route. 'And then left, along Quarry Road.'

'Good. Now think back. Imagine yourself walking along the road. Did you meet anyone?'

Crystal shook her head.

'Or did you see anyone watching you – or following you?'

'Not that I noticed. There wasn't anyone much around. I suppose people were mostly still having lunch. There was no-one here for a while after we got here. Then it started filling up later. It was when lots of bigger children arrived that I decided it was time to take Ricky home.'

'So you're not aware of anyone at all taking an interest in you or Abigail – apart from Mrs Knight and the woman who thought you couldn't be Abigail's Mum?'

'That's right. I'm sorry,' Crystal added, detecting a hint of disappointment in Jonah's voice.

'Not to worry! There are plenty of other people who were around while you were here. One of them may have seen something. So, back to when you arrived. You left Abigail asleep in the buggy while you played with Ricky on the swings and things – is that right?'

'Yes. I never thought ... I mean ... she was right there. I could see the buggy all the time.'

'Of course,' Peter said reassuringly. 'It was a perfectly reasonable thing to do. You mustn't blame yourself.'

'No. Of course not,' Jonah agreed. 'And I expect you looked across a few times, while you were playing, to check the buggy was still safe. Did you happen to notice anyone looking in on her or anything?'

'No. I saw a woman with a pram sitting on the bench next to it. I think she was eating something, but I didn't take much notice. She didn't stay long, I don't think. Other than that ... no, no-one.'

'Did you speak to any of the other parents – or did any of them speak to you?'

'Only the woman who was worried that Abby might have been abandoned.'

***

Michelle put the flapjacks into the oven and closed the door. In a reaction against her own mother's devotion to the kitchen, she had determinedly avoided acquiring any culinary skills and these were the only biscuits that she knew how to make. Consequently, they were what she resorted to whenever she wanted to provide a treat for her daughter. She filled the pan, in which she had mixed the ingredients, with cold water and left it soaking in the sink.

What time was it? Still too early to start making the dinner. It would be an hour or more before Leslie would be back. What could she do to fill in the time? Would it be too pushy to ring Georgia to ask for an update? After a few minutes thought, she decided that it would be perfectly reasonable to do so.

'Hi Mum!' Georgia answered. Michelle tried to analyse her voice to determine whether she sounded more or less optimistic than during her previous call.

'I'm home now,' she explained, 'so I just thought I'd ring and see if you have any more news on Rachel.'

'Still waiting for the test results, but one of the nurses said that her breathing seems to have improved, so I think she's moving in the right direction.'

'Her breathing? I didn't know she'd had trouble breathing.' Michelle's heart started beating faster at the thought that Georgia might have been shielding from her the seriousness of her granddaughter's condition.

'Not exactly trouble – just very noisy. Anyway, like I said, the nurse said it's improving.'

'Daddy and I thought we might come over for evening visiting – if she's not been discharged by then. What do you think?'

'Yes, of course. That would be fine. In fact, there's no need to bother about visiting times – just come whenever it suits you. They've told me she definitely will be staying in overnight. I managed to get through to Nathan and he's on his way now. So … see you later then.'

'Yes. We'll be over about seven then.'

***

'Let me through! It's my kid that's been stolen!'

Recognising his son's voice, Peter looked up and saw Eddie pushing open the gate and striding across the playground towards them. His face was a mixture of anxiety and anger. He paused momentarily as he caught sight of Peter. Then he hastened on, calling out as he came.

'Dad! How come-?'

'Your wife phoned me,' Peter answered.

'And Bernie? Aren't you at work?'

'Certainly I am,' his stepmother replied, pointing at the laptop.

'But ... Jonah! What are *you* doing here?' Eddie gasped, his eyes lighting on the man in the wheelchair for the first time.

'I'm the chief investigating officer,' Jonah told him, carefully concealing his annoyance at Eddie's failure to take that fact for granted.

With an effort, Eddie bit back the words that sprung to his lips: namely a demand to know why the police force had not seen fit to put a *proper* detective in charge of the search for his missing daughter. Six months on from their first meeting, he was still unable to believe that it was possible for a man who was paralysed from the neck down to be a functioning police office. Despite vehement protestations to the contrary, from Peter and Bernie, he was convinced that Jonah's employer must only have permitted him to return to his job after his disabling injury out of pity. Perhaps pity mixed with guilt, since it was likely that the unknown assailant who had shot him in the back had targeted him because he was a police officer. You couldn't help admiring his pluck, but nobody could possibly imagine that he played any more than a token role.

A lot had happened during the ten years since Eddie had last visited Oxford, on the occasion of his father's marriage to Bernie. Then, Peter had been a serving police inspector and Bernie was mathematics tutor at one of the Oxford colleges. Now, Peter was retired and Bernie had thrown up her career to become full-time carer for this friend of theirs, who had apparently once worked with Peter and with Bernie's first husband. To cap it all, Jonah was now living with them in their house, and caring for him seemed to dominate all of their lives. Bernie's daughter Lucy, for example, had been a lively six-year-old when Eddie saw her last. Now she was a young woman, working hard for her A' levels and, it seemed to him, devoting most of her spare time to looking after Jonah. It was all a very strange setup.

Coming back to the present, Eddie forced himself to give Jonah a brief smile and a nod in recognition of his statement. Presumably, some other officer bore the real responsibility for taking forward the investigation. That tall woman, for instance – the one whom the constable at the gate had called over to check that he should be allowed in to join his wife. She had introduced herself as a Detective Inspector. She looked competent. No doubt, she was really in charge and Jonah was being allowed to come along so that he felt that he was being useful. You had to feel sorry for him, having his whole world collapsing around him like that. It was no wonder that senior officers in the force had decided to humour him when he refused to accept his new limitations and be pensioned off; but it was surprising that Dad and Bernie had gone along with it. Bernie, especially, was not usually one to sympathise with people who were unable to face facts, however unpleasant they might be.

'I'm sorry.' Jonah interrupted Eddie's thoughts, speaking apologetically but firmly. 'I'm afraid I have to ask – just for the record – where were you between, say, noon today and one forty-five?'

'Why do you need to know that?' Eddie demanded, his anxiety for his daughter making him speak louder and more aggressively than he intended.

'Just routine,' Peter intervened. 'Statistically, most child abductions are done by family members. It's all just standard procedure.'

'I was at work,' Eddie said, trying to keep his rising irritation out of his voice. Why was it all taking so long? Why wasn't anyone out there, hunting down the person who had taken his daughter?

'Can anyone confirm that?' Jonah asked.

'My boss – will he do?'

'Of course. We'll need his name and telephone number and the address of your work.'

Bernie turned the laptop computer round and indicated to Eddie that he should type in those details. He knelt down on the ground in front of the bench and did so. Ricky, still sitting on his grandfather's knee, put out his hand and patted Eddie on the top of his head. He did not understand what was going on, but he could tell that his father was upset and it made him nervous.

Eddie finished typing and, looking up, found himself staring into his son's eyes. Ricky smiled broadly, hoping to dispel whatever it was that was making Daddy frown and speak so sharply. Suddenly tears were pricking the back of Eddie's eyes. He leaned forward and swept Ricky up in his arms, holding him tight against his chest. He staggered to his feet and went over to perch on the arm of the bench next to his wife. Peter got up to make room for him, and Crystal shuffled along the bench to allow Eddie to slide down next to her.

'Now what?' he asked.

'We need a photograph of Abigail that we can circulate to police forces across the country,' Jonah told him briskly. 'And we'll put copies out around the neighbourhood and on local and

124

national TV and in the papers.'

'I've got some on my phone,' Crystal volunteered, grateful at last to be able to contribute to the efforts to find her daughter.

'I've already downloaded the most recent one from your Facebook page,' Bernie told her, turning the laptop round so that Crystal and Eddie could see the screen. 'Are you happy for us to go with that one?'

Crystal nodded.

'Shall I ping it off to Sergeant Philipson?' Bernie asked Jonah.

'Yes. Tell her to get it sent out right away and to organise getting posters printed. Better put it on Social Media too. I'm going to get on to the Chief Super about a press conference. We need to be quick to get an appeal to the public on the six o'clock news.' He turned to Eddie and Crystal. 'Do you want to be there?'

'Yes, of course,' Eddie said at once, but Crystal hesitated.

'Will it help to find Abby?' she asked, after a short pause.

'Difficult to say,' Jonah told her. 'A direct appeal might make whoever's taken her realise the distress they've caused and consider giving her back, but to a certain extent that depends on why they took her in the first place. It might also generate public sympathy, but that can be a bit of a mixed blessing, and we want people to focus on looking out for Abigail, not on making a fuss of you. You don't need to make a decision right now – it's just something to think about. I'll set the wheels in motion and you can tell me what you've decided later.'

He pressed buttons on the keypad attached to the arm of his wheelchair to activate the mobile phone attachment.

'You need to remember,' Peter whispered to Eddie and Crystal, 'that footage of you at the press conference is likely to be replayed over and over again in the media – not just until we find Abigail, but when the case comes to court and when sentence is passed and, quite possibly when the perpetrator comes up for probation and even as an example of past history in all sorts of other contexts. It's up to you, but it might be worth considering only being there alongside Jonah and the Chief Super and leaving them to do the talking.'

'No,' Eddie objected. 'I want to have my say.'

'I'm sorry if this appears sexist,' Bernie said quietly, 'but if either of you makes an appeal for Abigail's return, I think Crystal might make more impact. People still tend to think that it's more natural for the mother to be distressed about a baby going missing. Fathers sometimes come across more as ...,' she searched for the right word, '... indignant that someone dared to violate their family.'

'Anyway,' Jonah broke in before Eddie could respond. 'I'll leave you two to think about that one. First I'd like you both to think back over the last few months – ever since you moved into the flat – and tell me if there's anyone who's been behaving as if they had a grudge against either of you.'

Eddie and Crystal both shook their heads.

'How about your neighbours? Do you get on OK with them? Are they friendly towards you?'

'Yes,' Eddie answered. 'Well – it's not like back in Jamaica, but they mostly say "Hi!" when we meet in the lift, and the people next door invited us in for a coffee the day we moved in.'

'And the lady on the other side said she'd be happy to baby-sit for us,' Crystal added.

'People don't really mix much,' Eddie went on. 'So we don't know many of them. There's a family on the fourth floor, who've been quite friendly. Morgan something-or-other.'

'Morgan and Shona Knight,' Crystal clarified. 'I told you about meeting his mother in the lift.'

'So there hasn't been anyone who seemed resentful of you being there,' Jonah pressed them gently.

'No. Why should they resent us?'

Eddie wanted to know.

'No reason,' Jonah answered equably. 'I just wondered. That's all. Now, I'd like you both to try to think if there has been *anyone* acting in a way that might suggest they could have a reason to want to take Abigail away from you. Crystal – you said that people are often surprised when you tell them that she's your daughter. Has anyone ever gone further than that?'

'How do you mean?' Crystal asked in a puzzled tone.

'Has anyone ever seemed not to believe that she really was your own baby?'

'I don't get it,' Eddie complained. 'Where's all this going?'

'I was just wondering if it was possible that someone might suspect your wife of having stolen a white baby. If they believed that, they might manage to rationalise to themselves that stealing her back was legitimate. So, Crystal, has anyone ever appeared to think it must be impossible for Abigail to be your baby?'

'No. I don't think so. Mostly they just seem interested.'

'OK. So, now let's widen it a bit further. Have either of you experienced any racial abuse since you moved to Headington?'

For a moment, there was a stunned silence. Then Peter spoke in a rather irritated tone.

'You're not trying to make out this is some sort of hate crime, are you?'

'I'm just exploring all the possibilities. Now – Eddie? – Crystal?'

'There was a woman on the bus,' Crystal said reluctantly.

'Go on,' Jonah prompted.

'It was a while back,' Crystal said, playing for time. 'Before Abby was born.'

'That's OK. Just tell me what happened,' Jonah said gently.

'The bus was crowded and I had Ricky on the seat next to me, so when I saw she couldn't find anywhere to sit, I picked him up and put him on my lap and she sat down next to me.'

Everyone waited expectantly for her to go on.

'Look – I'm sure this doesn't have anything to do with Abby's disappearance.'

'We won't know if you don't finish the story,' Jonah told her, speaking quietly and looking her in the eye.

'I said something about how full the bus was. And then … and then, she said it wouldn't be so full if there weren't so many people like me coming over here "taking our jobs and bleeding our NHS dry".' Crystal stopped again and looked round, first at Jonah and then at Peter and Bernie and finally at Eddie. They were all too shocked to speak. Crystal took another deep breath and went on.

'And then, she looked down at my belly and she said, "and then, when you're over here, you all start breeding like rabbits and filling up the schools with your brats so there's no room for our kids, and you all get straight to the top of the housing list so there's nowhere for us to live. Why can't you all go back where you came from?"'

'That's appalling,' Peter said angrily.

'Too right, it is,' agreed Eddie. 'Why didn't you tell me about it?'

'I didn't want you making a fuss.'

'Did you report it?' Jonah asked

seriously. 'We're trying to keep on top of hate crime, but we can't do anything if people don't tell us when it's going on.'

'No. Like I said – I didn't want to make a fuss. And besides,' Crystal looked round at them all again. 'It's all true isn't it? We *have* taken jobs that could have gone to local people; and we *have* used the NHS; and–'

'Nonsense!' Bernie interrupted. 'Eddie got that job fair and square because he was the best candidate. And you got your job because the NHS is crying out for more nurses. And–'

'And anyway, I was born here,' Eddie broke in, his voice rising in anger. 'I've got as much right to be here as that woman whoever she is – and you've got as much right because you're my wife.'

'And Ricky and Abigail are both British citizens,' Peter added. 'So you absolutely *must not* allow the likes of her to browbeat you into thinking you don't belong here.'

'I don't suppose you can remember the date and time and which bus it was?' Jonah asked, 'or a description of the woman?'

'No. Sorry.'

'Never mind. I doubt if it's relevant, anyway. Now, is that the *only* incident you can remember?'

'Yes, well ….' Crystal hesitated. 'Apart from a silly episode with some kids last week.'

'Tell me about it,' Jonah urged gently. 'Silly things are sometimes more important than they seem.'

'OK then, but I don't want to get anyone into trouble. They were only kids.'

Jonah nodded acquiescence.

'I was walking back from the shops and I saw this group of boys on the other side of the road. They must have been ten or eleven or so. Anyway, they were just hanging around, chatting together. And then, when I got closer, they started staring at me and pointing. And then they started nudging each other and laughing. And then a group of them pushed one of the boys to the edge of the kerb and he walked over the road and came and talked to me.'

'What did he say?' Jonah asked.

'He said, "Why don't you go back where you came from?"'

'So then I said, "I'm happy here."'

'And he said, "But you don't belong here."'

'He was only a young boy and I could see his mates on the other side of the road watching him to see what I did, so I

136

thought, "I'm not going to run away or look scared, because then they'll think they've won."

'So then I said, "Why do you think I don't belong?"

'And he said, "Because you're black."

'He looks so young and so ... earnest, and I think, maybe I can make him change his mind. So I says, "Come over here and have a look and I'll show you why I don't want to go back to Jamaica." And I points down at Abigail, lying there in the buggy. He hesitates, like he's not sure, but then, after a bit, he comes over and looks in and sees Abigail lying there asleep.

'And you should have seen his face – eyes wide like saucers they were – and his mouth drops open. So then, I says, "I'm so glad my little girl is going to grow up here in England, because, do you know? Back in Jamaica, there are people who would make fun of her because of the colour of her skin. Can you believe that?"

'And he don't say nothing, so I goes on, "but here in England people are mostly very accepting of people's differences, so I know my little girl is going to be just fine.

'And he stands there, just looking and thinking for quite a while. And then he asks if Abby really is mine, and I says, "Yes, my own flesh and blood".

'And then he says, "So her dad's white, yeah?" and I tells him, "No. he's black like me."

'He looks really confused then, so I says, "these things just happen sometimes. And do you know what it means?"

'Well he just shook his head, so I tells

him, "It goes to show that we're all just the same underneath!"

'Then his mates are hollering to him from across the street to come back, so he runs off. And I carries on home. And that's the end of that.'

'You were great,' Eddie said admiringly. 'I'd never have thought of all that – I'd just have belted him one.'

'I know. Why do you think I never told you about it?'

'Do you know the names of any of those boys,' Jonah asked seriously.

'No – and I don't want you poking around to find out. They were just young kids who didn't know any better.'

'I know, but they must have got their ideas from somewhere. And they may have told other people about you and Abigail – people who don't think it's right for a white baby to be brought up by a black woman.'

'Do you really think such people exist?' Peter asked sceptically. 'I mean – even if the woman is the baby's mother?'

'It's a possibility. We have to look at all the possible motives. And at the moment, we don't have a lot else to go on.'

'Sir!' Rupert Andrews called to Jonah from the other side of the railings that surrounded the playground. 'I've got a dozen officers here ready to go, but Inspector Davenport tells me they've finished interviewing the witnesses.'

'Excellent!' Jonah turned his wheelchair and headed towards the gate. 'Your team can start on house-to-house enquiries in the immediate neighbourhood. I want to know if anyone saw anything at all unusual, and in particular, anyone with a baby that they've not been seen with before. Have a look at this picture.' He rotated his computer screen so that Andrews could see the photograph of Abigail that Bernie had downloaded. 'She's quite distinctive. Not many five week old babies have that much hair.'

'Yes, sir.' Andrews turned to go. 'Oh! And the dog handlers are on their way,' he added over his shoulder.

6 WONDERFUL LOVE

Victoria looked down on her baby's sleeping form. Sleeping peacefully now – but for how long? She had settled surprisingly easily after her afternoon feed and now looked contented and tranquil. Victoria reached for her phone. This would make a good picture to send to John. He had been complaining recently that he didn't even know what his daughter looked like. It was difficult thinking about taking pictures when Esme was screaming the house down.

In any case, she did not want John to see her creased up as if in pain and purple in the face. This was just perfect.

'I don't know if you'll get this before you leave for the airport,' she wrote, a few minutes later. 'I can never work out the time difference. This is the latest photo of Esme. I took it just now – so it's bang up to date! I'm sorry I haven't sent you any since the one from the hospital, but the camera app on my phone hasn't been working. Missing you lots. Victoria. xxx.'

She pressed *send* and the email vanished into the ether. Not long now. This time tomorrow John would be back. How would he react when he saw Esme? They had so wanted that baby! But would he be able to cope with the reality, which was so different from what they had imagined it was going to be?

A ring at the doorbell interrupted her thoughts. With a final glance into the cot to check that all was well, Victoria went out of the bedroom, closing the door carefully behind her, and headed downstairs to see who was at the front door.

On the doorstep stood two uniformed policemen, one tall and skinny, the other older and more heavily built.

'Good afternoon, Madam,' the younger officer greeted her. 'I'm Sergeant Fox and this is PC Hughes. We're calling in connection with an incident that took place earlier this afternoon in the playground on the corner of Margaret Road.'

'What sort of incident?' Victoria asked, sharply. Something about their demeanour made her think that this was something serious. 'I was down there only a few hours ago and I didn't see anything.'

'A baby was taken from its pram,' Fox told her. 'We're calling at houses in the neighbourhood. Do you mind if we ask you a few questions?'

'No, of course not, you'd better come in.' Victoria stepped back, opening the door wide to admit them. Her heart was racing, bringing the colour to her cheeks, as she imagined the mother of the baby coming back and finding the empty pram.

'No need for that,' Fox assured her. 'This won't take long.'

'No. Please – come in. I've got my baby girl asleep upstairs and I'd rather be in the room with the baby monitor.'

She showed them into the front room, hastily gathering up the soft toys from the sofa so that they could sit down.

'I'm sorry it's such a tip,' she apologised. 'My daughter's only seven weeks and I'm still in a bit of a mess.'

'Don't you worry,' the older man assured her. 'This is tidy compared with what ours was like when our kids were babies. We had twins and we really didn't know what had hit us.'

They sat down on the sofa and Victoria perched on an easy chair opposite them, leaning forward and looking expectantly at them.

'You said that you were at the playground earlier?' Fox began, taking out his notebook and a pencil.

'Yes. That's right. Esme – that's my little girl – wouldn't settle after her midday feed, so I took her out for a ride in her pram. Sometimes that sends her off to sleep.'

'My youngest was just the same,'

Hughes agreed. 'I put in a good few miles pounding the streets at night, while the wife was minding the twins. It got to the stage where I used to look forward to being on nights for the sake of a bit of a rest!'

'So that would be, about what time?' Fox asked.

'One? One fifteen? I'm not sure.'

'Not to worry,' Fox reassured her. 'But I am interested that it looks as if you must have been there round about when the baby went missing. Did you happen to notice a double buggy parked at the side, under the trees? It was one of the ones with a sort of carrycot for a baby and a seat for an older child.'

Victoria paused as if thinking.

'Yes. Now you mention it, there was one there. Esme dropped off just as we got to the park. I hadn't had any lunch, what with her crying and everything, so I went in there and sat down on the bench to eat, while she was quiet. I remember now – there was a double buggy already there and I put Esme's pram next to it.'

'You didn't happen to glance in and see whether there was a baby in it?' Fox asked eagerly.

'Yes. I did, as a matter of fact. I know it was nosey, but it's difficult not to want to compare Esme with other babies.'

'Can you describe the baby to me?'

'I'm not sure,' Victoria hesitated. 'She was asleep. I remember thinking how peaceful she looked – not like my Esme! Even when she's asleep, she's usually restless.'

'You say *she*,' Fox pressed her. 'What made you think it was a girl?'

'I'm not sure,' Victoria said again. 'I

suppose it was probably the pictures on the sheet. It was unusual – embroidered with flowers and butterflies. It looked too pretty for a boy.'

Fox nodded, noting everything down.

'Did you see anyone else having a look at the baby?' he asked. 'Or anyone else showing any interest in the buggy?'

'I don't think so – but then, I wasn't there for very long. Esme woke up and I took her for another walk.'

'Can you remember what time that was?' Fox asked. 'When you left the playground, I mean?'

'No. Sorry.' Victoria looked round apologetically and bit her lip in thought. 'All I can tell you is that I can't have been there very long, because I was home well before half past two. I remember checking the clock in the kitchen to see how long it was before

Esme's next feed was due.'

'And did you go straight home from the playground?'

'No. Like I said, I was trying to get Esme back off to sleep; so we went on down Quarry Road, and then left, past the church. By then, she'd settled again; so I made my way back along the footpath that goes along the edge of the recreation ground.'

'You passed the recreation ground again?' Fox asked, with interest.

'Yes. That's right. But you can't see the playground from there − only the fields.'

'But someone could walk across the fields to get to the playground, couldn't they?'

'Yes, of course. That's how I got there in the first place.'

'Did you see anyone coming across

that way when you passed on your way home?'

'No.' Victoria shook her head. 'At least – not that I noticed particularly.'

'Thank you. You've been very helpful,' Fox drew the interview to an end. 'I think the officer in charge of this investigation may want to speak to you later, and he may ask you to make a formal statement about what you saw in the playground. So if you could just write down your full name and a number where we can contact you then we'll go and leave you in peace.'

He handed Victoria the pencil together with his notebook, open at a new page. She obediently wrote down the information and handed it back. They all got up and went out into the hall. Victoria went to open the front door, but Hughes intervened, speaking softly so as not to disturb the sleeping baby.

'Just one last thing. Could I just have a little peek at your baby girl?' he asked. 'I'll be careful not to wake her.'

Victoria gave him a puzzled look, but nodded and led the way upstairs. Hughes followed, his footsteps on the stairs surprisingly soft for a man of his bulk. Victoria opened a door and pointed silently towards the Moses basket, which lay on the double bed. Hughes tiptoed in and peered down on the sleeping infant. Her face was blotchy pink and red and she had just the smallest wisps of creamy white hair on her head. Her mother was right, he thought, she did not seem to be very peaceful. She reminded him of a cat, sleeping with eyes half open, ready to wake and spring into action at the slightest provocation. Seeming to sense his presence, her body went rigid and her face creased up as if she were about to cry. He backed out carefully, nodding his thanks to Victoria. Then they crept downstairs to join his colleague, who was waiting in the hall.

'What was all that about?' Fox demanded, as soon as they were safely outside with the door closed behind them. 'You surely weren't expecting to find the stolen baby up there?'

'Not really,' Hughes answered sheepishly. 'I just … It didn't quite ring true, going straight home like that after the baby woke up while she was in the playground.'

'She didn't,' Fox objected. 'She said she went round by the church.'

'Yes, I know.' Gavin Hughes was well

aware that his intellect was not his strong point. He was a good, solid, hardworking officer who shone in establishing a rapport with members of the public, but relied far more on instinct and experience than on brainpower in carrying out his duties. 'But this area used to be my beat, back in the day. It must be all of five minutes from Margaret Road to the church and another five minutes back again and, less than that along the footpath to Ramsey Road. Fifteen minutes isn't long to get a restless baby off to sleep so that it won't wake up again the moment you stop the pram.'

'Maybe she had things to do at home. Anyway, I assume the baby isn't the one we're looking for or you'd have said so?'

'No. She's about the right age, but the hair's all wrong. I'm sorry. It was just a hunch I had.'

'Never mind,' Fox grinned. 'At least we've found a new witness. The DCI should be pleased with us about that.'

***

Felicity Mason also received a visit from the police that afternoon. She looked in alarm at the sight of Sergeant Aaron King and Constable Malcolm Appleton on the step and immediately stepped outside and closed the door behind her. King made the introductions and explained why they had come, and Appleton took down her name and telephone number. Flick's eyes opened wide in alarm at the mention of a baby having been snatched from its pram.

'I don't see how I can help you,' she said nervously. 'I mean – I was only passing through the playground. I didn't stop there. My little girl's far too young for swings and that.'

'I'm sorry?' King said, holding up his hand to stop her flow. 'Are you telling me you actually went to the playground today?'

'Yes, of course. Isn't that why you're here?'

'No. These are just general house-to-house enquiries in the neighbourhood. However, if you *were* in the playground at all today, perhaps you could answer a few question about that. What time was it, for instance?'

'I really couldn't say exactly.'

'Approximately then?'

'After one – yes definitely after one.' She thought for a while then shook her head. 'No. I can't say closer than that.'

'Where were you going?' Appleton asked, hoping that this might prompt her memory.

'The London Road shops. We went through the recreation ground on the way and then we came back along ....' Her voice trailed off as she remembered the police car racing past, its siren blaring. 'I saw a police car. Was that what it was there for?'

'We attended the scene at 14.17,' Appleton informed her, 'in response to a call that was logged at 14.08.'

'Yes. That must have been about the time I was coming back from the shops. How awful! It must have happened just after I was there. Thank goodness I didn't leave *my* baby unattended. There was a buggy there, with a baby in it, left on its own. I thought at the time, perhaps I ought to do something about it, but then I thought I saw the mother coming back. Do you think it *wasn't* the real mother? She looked OK – and she had another little girl with her, so I never thought–'

'Can I stop you there?' King interrupted, holding up his hand again. 'Going back to the baby in the buggy – did you get a good look at it?'

'I did have a peep in,' Flick admitted. 'Just to see if she was alright – you know.'

'She? You're sure it was a girl then?'

'Oh yes! She had such beautiful long hair, tied up in a little top-knot with purple ribbon. And she had this really pretty sheet with flowers and butterflies all over it.'

'And her hair,' Appleton asked, 'do you remember what colour it was?'

'Auburn,' Flick answered without hesitation. 'Lovely long, auburn hair. Is that the baby that's been stolen? Did I really see her just before it happened?'

'It looks very much like it,' King admitted. 'Are you *sure* you can't be any more precise about what time that was?'

Flick thought again, but shook her head. 'No. I'm sorry.'

'Never mind. Now, you said you saw someone coming over to the buggy, and you thought it was probably the baby's mother – can you describe her to me?'

'She had fair hair. I didn't really notice anything else about her.'

'What made you think she was the mother?'

'I don't know really,' Flick shrugged her shoulders. 'I suppose it was just that there was nobody else around who *could* be. Apart from her, there was only a black woman with her little boy, playing on the see-saw.' She looked at her watch. 'Are we done now? *My* little girl will be waking up for her feed any moment and then her dad will be home and wanting his dinner.'

The two officers left, first having warned Flick that she could expect to be contacted again for a statement about what she had seen in the playground and leaving a telephone number for her to call if she were to see anything suspicious or remember anything that could be of help to the enquiry.

Flick watched them down the garden path and into the road, heading for the next house. Then she opened the door and went inside. She was greeted by the sound of crying and she hurried upstairs to Mia's bedroom.

'Don't cry,' she called out softly as she entered the room. 'Mummy's here now. Is Mia hungry then?'

She picked the baby up and carried

her downstairs to the kitchen where a bottle of milk was already warming in a bowl of hot water. She talked away all the time in the special voice that mothers reserve for their babies.

'Did those policemen ringing the bell wake you, then? Never mind – it's time for your milk anyhow. Can you wait while I change your nappy? No? Never mind – have your feed and then we'll see about that. They were telling me about a naughty mummy who left her baby all alone in the park and a nasty person came along and took her out of her pram. Can you imagine! Don't you worry – *your* mummy would never do anything so silly.'

**

'Georgie!' Nathan caught sight of his wife and hurried over to her. 'Is there any news?' he asked anxiously, sitting down next to her on the row of chairs in the waiting area outside the ward.

'They're still waiting for the test results.'

'And what then?'

'They say if it's viral meningitis then she'll probably make a full recovery in a few days. If it's bacterial, then, depending on which sort it is and how badly she's got it ...'

'Go on.'

'She could die.' Georgia hesitated and Nathan put his arm round her and held her tightly to him. 'Or she could have permanent disabilities.'

'Do you mean brain damage?'

'That's one of the things they said could happen – or deafness or epilepsy or ... all sorts of things. I didn't really take it all in.'

'But at the moment we don't know, do we?' Nathan reasoned, trying to look on the bright side. 'If it's viral meningitis then there's nothing to worry about.'

'Well, they only said she would *probably* recover. I've been looking on the internet and a proportion of people with viral meningitis go on to have after-effects too – especially children under one year old.'

'Well, don't let's think about that until we know for certain that it *is* meningitis. There's no point getting worked up about something that may never happen.'

'Yes,' Georgia sniffed and wiped her eyes with a tissue. 'You're right. I'm so glad you've come! It's been awful just waiting here on my own, with nothing else to think about except all the things that could go wrong.'

'I'm surprised your parents didn't come over. Thy must have known it'd take me time to get back from London.'

'Poor mum!' Georgia smiled and shook her head. 'She's so frightened of being an interfering mother-in-law that she hardly dares to speak to me about anything to do with you or Rachel. They rang to say they'd be over this evening after dinner. And that reminds me – have you told your dad?'

'No. I was waiting until I'd got here and seen how things were. I don't want to make him think he ought to come over here. It'd be such a trek for him and it's not as if he could do anything to help.'

'Yes. That was the sort of thing I was thinking too – although, on the other hand, it doesn't seem right, somehow, when my mum and dad know all about it.'

'But I know Dad. He wouldn't be prepared to just sit back and wait for news. He'd insist on being brought over here – and Peter or Bernie would go along with it for the sake of a quiet life – and then he'd be demanding to see the doctors and giving them the third degree over treatment options. And, ten to one, it'd turn out that one of them knew Mum and then they'd be off down memory lane and in the end–'

'OK. I get the picture. Let's wait until the test results come back and then decide.'

7 WITH HOPES AND FEARS WE COME

The crowd of onlookers had drifted away, and Constable Appleton had departed with the rest of the team to assist with the house-to-house enquiries. Sergeant Burton remained at the main gate of the playground, turning away anyone seeking to enter. Anna came over to Jonah, brandishing a sheaf of papers.

'I've collected together all the statements from the people who were in the playground,' she told him. 'And I've sorted them with the most interesting ones at the top. Would you like me to go through them with you?'

Jonah glanced down at the time on his computer screen. Then he looked up at her again.

'Is there anything there that gives us a lead that we could act on right away?' he asked.

'Not really. A few of them remember seeing the buggy, but nobody saw anyone approaching it or picking up a baby from it. And nobody saw anyone carrying a baby out of the playground. It's mainly just confirmation of the timings – and that's assuming that people really did know the time as accurately as they think they did.'

'In that case, give them to Andy to take back to the incident room and get them typed into the computer, so I can have a look at them myself in due course. Then I want you to take charge of searching the immediate vicinity, in case whoever took the baby got scared and dumped her before they'd got far. I need to organise a press conference and an appeal to the public. We need to get on with that to make sure we hit the six o'clock news.'

'Right you are,' Anna turned to go and nearly collided with the blue-uniformed figure of Chief Superintendent Alison Brown, who had arrived to see for herself how the case was progressing. She was followed by a plain-clothes officer of South Asian appearance. The two women nodded at one another as Anna hurried off to do Jonah's bidding.

'How's it going?' the Chief Superintendent asked Jonah. Then, without waiting for an answer, she turned to address Crystal and Eddie, who were sitting huddled together on the bench, with Ricky still on Eddie's knee, clinging to him tightly with his head turned away from all the unfamiliar faces and voices. 'Are you the parents?'

They nodded.

'Chief Superintendent Alison Brown. I'd just like to tell you how sorry we are that this has happened and to assure you that the police service is doing everything we can to find your daughter.'

'Thank you,' Eddie mumbled, looking up at her and then across at Peter, who was standing unobtrusively beyond the end of the bench, next to Bernie. Superintendent Brown followed his gaze and gave a start as she recognised her former colleague.

'Peter?' she said after a short pause. 'It *is* Peter Johns, isn't it?'

'That's right.' Peter stepped forward and shook her by the hand. He looked hard at her companion, but did not speak or offer his hand to him. Peter Johns did not often hold a grudge, but he found it hard to welcome the presence of DCI Arshad Khan. He hoped that the Chief Superintendent had not come to announce that he was to replace Jonah at the head of the investigation.

Then he turned and gestured towards Eddie and Crystal. 'And before you ask what I'm doing here, let me introduce my son, Eddie, and his wife Crystal – and their firstborn, Ricky.'

'Aa-aa-ah! I see!' Alison looked round at the Johns family, then at Bernie and finally towards Jonah.

'I only discovered who it was after I got here,' he explained. 'If you think there's a conflict of interest, I can hand over to someone else,' he added, the reluctance in his voice making it clear that this was not his preferred option. 'I just thought it was better to get things moving so as we don't lose any time.'

'Yes. Of course.' Alison considered the matter. 'And your conflict of interest would be because …?'

'Because I live with Old Peter, and his wife is my personal assistant – not to mention the fact that we used to work together.'

'If I'm going to exclude everyone who ever worked with Peter, I won't have a very large pool of officers to choose from,' Alison observed. 'What do you think, Peter? Are you happy to have Jonah leading the investigation?'

'That's not a fair question,' Jonah objected. 'He can hardly say to my face that he doesn't trust me to be up to the job.'

'It's nothing to do with being up to the job,' Alison said patiently. 'It's a question of whether your relationship with the people involved will make you biased. So Peter – what do you think?'

'I think it shouldn't be up to me to decide. Speaking personally, I can't think of anyone else I'd rather have on the case, because, whatever else you may say about Jonah, he's got an excellent track record of solving crimes; but that won't help you if anyone starts pointing the finger and saying you should have found someone who doesn't know me from Adam.'

'Please!' Crystal said suddenly getting up and taking hold of Alison's arm.

'Please just stop arguing about it. I don't care who's in charge, just so long as you find Abigail. She's overdue for a feed already and she needs me – us, I mean – to look after her. All I want is to get her back. If you switch who's in charge, that's going to delay things, isn't it? And Peter said that you haven't got anyone else who's as good as Jonah, so …?'

'You're right,' Alison said, briskly. 'We're wasting time. Jonah – you're in charge. Take all the officers you need – we've got to give this our best shot. That's why I've brought DCI Khan along. He's got lots of experience of dealing with crimes involving BME[1] families.'

---

[1] BME: *Black and Minority Ethnic* is a generic term used to describe people with African, Asian, Arab and Caribbean heritages.

'But not necessarily of knowing what to do with them,' Peter muttered under his breath, carefully avoiding meeting Khan's gaze.

Bernie, who knew a little of the history between the two men looked round anxiously, hoping that the addition of Khan to the team was not going to cause trouble. Things were already bad enough, without some sort of showdown between him and Peter.

'Now,' Alison went on, addressing Jonah, 'is there anything else you need from me?'

'I want to arrange a television appearance this evening,' Jonah said promptly. 'I want an appeal to go out on the national and local news asking the public to keep an eye out for the baby. She's quite distinctive, which is lucky; so people may well recognise her if they see her. We've got this picture.' He made the screen attached to his chair rotate to face Alison.

'I'll get on to that right away,' she agreed at once. Then she looked down at the photograph and her jaw dropped open.

'Thanks. I hoped you would. *Chief Superintendent* sounds so much more impressive than *DCI*. I'm sure they won't refuse.' Jonah grinned up at Alison, then his face changed as he saw her expression. 'What's up?'

'Nothing' she said hastily. 'I just – no, nothing.'

***

'I'm ho-ome!' Sam Mason called out as he struggled to open the front door without dropping the pile of exercise books that he was carrying. He taught

Geography at a comprehensive school in High Wycombe. Flick had taught there too, until a few weeks before their daughter was born. In theory, she was only on leave now, but it seemed increasingly unlikely that she would ever return.

'Let me help you with those,' she greeted him, emerging from the kitchen and taking hold of the pile of books. 'Where do you want them?'

'Is the kitchen table free?'

'Until dinner time.'

Sam looked at his watch.

'OK put them down there and I'll see if I can get them marked before dinner, so that we can have the evening together.'

He went into the kitchen, sat down at the table and picked up the first book, sighing as he opened it and saw the pages of illegible scrawl that this particular student had produced as his attempt at an essay on coastal erosion. Flick pottered round, making him a cup of tea and peeling potatoes for their evening meal. She had just put down the cup next to the pile of books on the table, when there came a sound from up above. Flick looked upwards.

'There's Mia crying,' she said. 'I'd better go to her.'

No!' Sam jumped up and stood between his wife and the door to the hall. 'It's time you stopped all that nonsense!'

Flick tried to push past him, but he stood firm and took hold of her by both elbows.

'Now listen to me,' he said, trying to speak calmly and rationally. 'Mia isn't crying. Mia isn't here at all. Mia's dead. You've got to accept that.'

Flick tried to pull away, but he held firm.

'That – that – that *thing* that you've got up there! That isn't Mia. It's just one of those crying dolls that you give to teenage girls to make them think twice about getting pregnant. It's not alive! It doesn't need you to go up there and stop it crying. Can't you understand that?'

'Yes! Of course I understand!' Flick shouted back, tears welling up in her eyes. 'I know she isn't real! But looking after her helps me.'

'No! It *isn't* helping you,' Sam insisted. 'It's just preventing you from coming to terms with what's happened. You've got to learn to let go of Mia. She's never coming back. You've got to face up to that. It's no good pretending.'

'You're wrong. You don't understand.

Looking after Mia *is* helping me. It's helping me to get back my confidence as a mother. It's helping me to believe that I could be trusted with another baby. It's helping me to stop thinking that it was all my fault!'

Sam let go of her arms and stepped back, defeated.

'Alright,' he said in a tone of resignation. 'Go up there and see to her, if you must.'

***

The recording of the television appeal went smoothly. In the end, Eddie and Crystal opted not to speak. They sat with Peter in dignified silence, next to Jonah, who did all the talking. On Jonah's other side, Chief Superintendent Brown added gravitas to the line-up. Finally, Peter made a personal appeal on behalf of the family, pleading with the kidnapper to return Abigail unharmed. When it was all over, Jonah turned to Eddie and Crystal.

'I know it's hard,' he said to them, 'but there really isn't anything more you can do now; so I suggest you go home. We'll let you know as soon as we hear anything at all.'

'And the same goes for you,' Bernie added, putting her hand firmly on Jonah's shoulder. 'It's time you were getting home for tea.'

'I'll send Andy out for a takeaway,' Jonah argued. 'I must just get back and have a look through those statements that he's been typing up for me. And then there was an interesting report from one of the house-to-house team that needs following up, and–'

'That will all have to wait,' Bernie

insisted. 'You won't get on any quicker if you make yourself ill by driving yourself too hard. Much better you come home with us now and have your physio – yes, your physio,' she repeated, seeing Jonah opening his mouth to protest, 'and a rest, and then eat your tea in a civilised manner. Then, if the TV appeal produces results, you'll be in a fit state to follow up on any new leads.'

'Oh all right,' Jonah grumbled. He knew that Bernie was right, but that did not make it any easier to accept. His disability did not often get him down, but at times like this he resented having to consider his own health ahead of pushing on to get the job done regardless. 'But, afterwards, I insist we go back in, so I'm on hand to deal with anything that comes up.'

'Alright,' Bernie reluctantly agreed,

realising that Jonah had made up his mind and would not be persuaded to do otherwise. In any case, she also wanted to get this case solved as soon as possible, for Eddie's and Crystal's sakes – not to mention the fact that, if Jonah was not on hand for the first flurry of responses to the television appeal, there was a danger that Arshad Khan might be the senior officer when the breakthrough occurred, and what would Peter's reaction be to that?

***

'Mum! Is that you?' Anna's daughter Jessica shouted down from upstairs as she entered the house on her arrival home from work. 'We've all had dinner,' she added, appearing at the top of the stairs. 'Yours is in the oven – not that it'll be any good by now. Why didn't you tell us you'd be late?'

'I'm sorry, love. I got tied up. A baby's gone missing and it's all hands on deck to try to find her.'

Anna hung up her jacket on a peg in the hall and went into the kitchen. She felt suddenly tired and very thirsty.

'You could've texted,' Jessica continued, following her in.

'Yes. I know. I said I'm sorry,' Anna replied wearily, pouring herself a glass of water from the tap and sitting down with it at the kitchen table. 'It was a bit hectic today. Where's your dad? I could do with talking to him.'

'He went out for a pint. He said he couldn't hang around all day waiting for you to roll in at whatever hour you saw fit.'

'Oh.' Anna recognised her husband's turn of phrase. This was clearly a verbatim report and it suggested that Philip was still angry with her. 'What about Marcus?'

'He's round at one of his mate's.'

Anna nodded. Then she braced herself to get up and investigate the food that Jessica had said was in the oven. It turned out to be the dried-up remains of a dish of home-made macaroni cheese. She put on a pair of oven gloves and lifted it out on to the table.

'This looks good,' she said without conviction. 'Did you make it?' she added, suddenly guessing the reason for Jessica's annoyance at her late return.

'I didn't have an exam this afternoon, so I thought, "I'll make something nice for Mum when she gets back". I should've known better.'

'I'm sorry. How was your exam? It was English this morning, wasn't it?'

'No. That was yesterday. It was Geography this morning.'

'Sorry. I lose track. How did it go, anyway?'

'OK. Not that you care!'

'I do, Jess. Honestly, I do! It's just I've got a lot on my mind at the moment.'

Anna hacked at the macaroni cheese with a knife, trying to separate it from the casserole dish in which it had been cooked. Eventually she managed to dislodge a reasonable portion, which she scooped on to a plate using a tablespoon. She sat down and began to eat, moistening each mouthful with water from her glass.

'*You*'ve got a lot on *your* mind!' Jessica said scornfully, sitting down opposite her mother. 'What about *me*?

I'm doing my GCSE[2]s, in case you hadn't noticed. I should've been revising this afternoon, but instead I thought I'd help out by making dinner for us all. I don't know why I bothered now!'

'Look, Jess,' Anna said through a mouthful of the unappetising food, 'I don't know how many times I have to say I'm sorry. Can you just give it a rest now?'

Jessica shrugged her shoulders. 'Whatever!' She tried to sound unconcerned, while in reality she felt tears pricking the backs of her eyes at the unfairness of it all. She got up and headed for the door. 'I'll be in my room – revising,' she added, once she was sure

---

[2] General Certificate of Secondary Education: examinations taken by school students in England at age 16.

that her mother could not see her face.

***

'Isn't Peter with you?' Lucy asked, as she helped her mother to set up the ramp to allow Jonah to exit the car on their return home.

'He's gone with Eddie and Crystal to collect some things from the flat,' Bernie told her. 'He's persuaded them to stay with us overnight.'

'How are they?' Lucy asked anxiously. Peter had rung her from the playground to let her know why he was not at home when she got back from school. 'It must be awful for them.'

'In shock, I think,' Bernie answered. 'It's the sort of thing that's hard to take in.'

They went inside and Bernie ran over in her mind the list of things that needed to be done. The attic bedrooms must be made ready for Eddie and Crystal, a meal had to be prepared for them all and, most importantly, Jonah must be got out of his chair for physio and skin-care and his urine bag must be emptied.

'I'd better see to you,' Lucy said to Jonah, secretly delighted to have an excuse to spend time with the man who had started out (when she was very small) as an honorary uncle and had now become a firm friend and confidant. 'Then Mam can start organising things for when the others get here.'

'Thanks love,' Bernie said gratefully. 'And before *you* start,' she added to Jonah, 'just remember that you've been in that chair and on the go without a break since lunchtime and if you don't do your physio like a good boy you'll be putting yourself out of action with pressure sores or something worse. We can't have tea until Peter and the others get here anyway.'

'Yes Miss,' Jonah replied in the meek tones of a small boy on being told off by his teacher. 'But you do promise I can go out again after tea, don't you?'

'Yes,' Bernie grinned and shook her head slowly, like a teacher humouring a trying but likeable pupil. 'But only so long as I get a good report from Lucy on your behaviour.'

***

'Any news from Georgia?' Leslie Cohen asked the moment he got home from the office. Michelle shook her head silently. 'I rang her to say we'd be over later, but she said they were still waiting for test results.'

'You've been baking.' Leslie looked

189

round at the flapjacks cooling on two wire racks. This unusual activity was a sure sign of his wife's anxiety.

'I thought I'd take some with us. I don't suppose Georgia has had much chance to think about eating.'

Leslie went over and put his arms around Michelle, drawing her close to him and speaking low in her ear.

'It'll be alright. Rachel's in good hands. The chances are she'll be fine – and if not … we'll come through somehow.'

***

Tea was a desultory meal. Nobody could think of anything to say. Neither Crystal not Eddie felt hungry, but they did their best to eat the fish fingers and chips that Peter had prepared. This was not his usual style of cooking, but it was the best he could manage in the time available, knowing that Jonah was keen to get back to the incident room with as little delay as possible.

Bernie collected the plates and put them in a pile next to the sink, before going to the large, walk-in larder in search of something for dessert.

'Is Anna OK?' Peter asked Jonah, as they waited while she served the last of the bottled pears from the previous season. 'She looked a bit washed out to me?'

Jonah hesitated and exchanged glances with Bernie.

'She's had some bad news,' he said at last. 'The scan showed up a problem with the baby.'

'What sort of problem?' Lucy wanted to know, sensing that they were not being told the whole story.

'They reckon it's got spina bifida.'

'That's like being born with a spinal cord injury – right?' Lucy asked

'I think so – roughly.' Jonah agreed.

For a few moments nobody spoke.

'How's Philip taking it?' Peter asked. He had worked closely with Anna at one time and knew her family. Philip always seemed to like to plan his life in meticulous detail, in much the same way as he might plan a new house that he was designing. Disruptions to the anticipated course of events always caused him disproportionate annoyance. Peter could not imagine him finding it easy to accommodate the prospect of a disabled child within his blueprint for family-life.

Jonah and Bernie exchanged looks again.

'I think,' Bernie said, after a long

pause, 'that's the thing that's really bothering Anna, more than the diagnosis itself.'

Peter raised his eyebrows questioningly, so she went on.

'Apparently he wasn't exactly chuffed at the idea of a new little Davenport coming on the scene in the first place,' she explained. 'According to Anna, he was all for her having a termination from the outset. This was just the icing on the cake, so to speak.'

'More like the last straw,' Jonah added. 'He was looking forward to getting his freedom back now the kids are growing up. I suppose he thinks, now, they'll be committed to a lifetime of caring.'

'But that's horrible!' Lucy exclaimed, looking round at each of the adults in turn. 'How can anyone even suggest killing a baby just because it's got something wrong with its spinal cord? It's not *its* fault!'

'I don't think that's quite fair,' Bernie intervened, glaring at Jonah. 'I'm sure what Phil Davenport is worried about is bringing a baby into the world that won't have a good quality of life.'

'What right has *he* got to decide?' Lucy demanded forthrightly, unwilling to be swayed by argument. 'How *can* he say that it would be better for their baby never to be born? How many disabled people are there out there who would rather not have been born? Take Jonah, for instance—'

'Lucy love,' Bernie cut in, 'I'm not saying he's right. I'm just saying that he has his point of view, and holding it doesn't make him some sort of monster.'

'*I* think it does though,' Lucy insisted. 'You'd have to be a monster to want to murder an innocent baby. And if he's really so bothered about its quality of life, it'd be more logical to wait until after it's born and you can see how badly affected it actually is. They could have made a mistake, or it could be a less serious type of spina bifida or–'

'Apart from anything else,' Peter intervened, speaking mildly in the hope of calming Lucy's indignation, 'to do that would be illegal.'

'Yes,' Lucy stormed on, 'it would be illegal because everyone agrees that it's wrong to murder babies; but I don't see why it's OK before they're born but a crime afterwards.'

'I agree,' Crystal added tentatively. 'I can't imagine how a mother could contemplate having an abortion;

especially not once you can feel it moving inside of you. I always felt my babies were people right from the first I knew I was expecting.'

'There you are!' Lucy cried exultantly. 'That's just what I was saying. The law's just trying to give people an easy way out when they don't want to face up to what they've done.'

'No, Lucy,' Bernie insisted. 'It's more complicated than that.'

'The Abortion Act wasn't just a whim,' Peter backed her up. 'A lot of people thought about it for a long time, and it took a lot of courage to get it through Parliament. It was all about trying to make things better for the mother while still recognising the rights of the unborn child.'

'I don't see–,' Lucy began.

'I know you don't,' Bernie cut her off

again, 'but give Peter a chance to have his say.'

'They set a limit based on the age at which the foetus would be able to survive outside the womb,' Peter continued. 'I always assumed that they were comparing the situation to turning off the life-support to a patient in a coma. The mother is like the life-support for the baby and if there's a conflict between her interests and that of the baby, you can see that there must be a case for allowing her to stop playing that role.'

'But we're not talking about when the mother's life is in danger,' Lucy objected.

'No,' Peter conceded. 'I'm just saying that, there is a rationale for distinguishing between before and after the baby would be able to survive independently.'

'Well I still think it's murder, however young it is,' Lucy said, stabbing viciously at a piece of pear with her spoon.

'I know you do, love,' Bernie sighed. 'And in many ways, I agree with you; but please try not to judge people for having different opinions – especially people like Phil Davenport who's going to have to live with the consequences of whatever decision they eventually go for.'

Lucy, unconvinced, continued to look sulky, but did not say any more. She could see that her mother did not want to continue the discussion and realised that infanticide was not a particularly suitable subject to be discussing in the presence of Eddie and Crystal at this moment.

Jonah looked round at everyone's

empty bowls and declared that it was time for him to get back to the incident room to find out whether there had been any response to the appeals on television, radio and in social media. Bernie, while regretting that he had not had as long to rest as she would have liked, concurred, on the grounds that the sooner they went, the sooner they could call it a day and turn in for the night.

Lucy helped Peter to wash up, while Eddie and Crystal put Ricky to bed and unpacked their overnight bags. Then they all congregated in the large living room, trying to make conversation, but with little success. Eventually Lucy got to her feet.

'I'm going to St Cyprian's to light a candle for Abigail's safe return,' she said, looking round at the others briefly before turning to go. Peter got up and followed her out into the hall.

'Do you mind if I come with you?' he asked, a little self-consciously.

'No. Of course not,' Lucy said, looking at him in surprise. 'But I thought you didn't believe in God and prayer and that.'

'I reckon it can't do any harm, can it,' Peter answered gruffly, feeling rather awkward, but determined to go through with the plan now that he had suggested it. 'I reckon Abigail needs all the help she can get right now.

8 THE PAIN THAT WILL NOT GO AWAY

'Police in Oxford are appealing to the public for information about the disappearance of a baby from a playground in the Headington area this afternoon.' Sam Mason looked up from his sausages and mashed potato to see a view of the familiar junction at the corner of Margaret Road. Blue and white police tape hung across the entrance to the playground and a uniformed police officer stood by the gate, looking rather bored.

'The incident happened between one and two,' the voice continued, as the camera moved along the outside of the railings to show the line of trees at the edge of the playground. 'Six week old Abigail Johns was in a buggy under the trees, where her mother had left her while she played with Abigail's older brother. A few minutes later, she came back to find her baby gone. DCI Jonah Porter, who is leading the enquiry, made this appeal for help to track down the missing child.'

The scene changed to what looked like the interior of a public building of some sort. The camera showed a crowd of journalists jostling for places near a large table raised on a dais. Then it homed in on the group of people seated behind the table. In the centre, a man with grey hair and clear blue eyes was speaking inaudibly. On his left, a woman in the uniform of a senior police officer sat listening attentively. Beyond her sat another woman, grey-haired and wearing glasses. On the other side of the speaker, Sam saw another middle-aged man and then a young black couple. They must be the parents of the missing baby. They looked very young and vulnerable. The woman kept dabbing her eyes with a tissue. Then the quality of the sound changed and the man's words could be heard clearly.

'We are appealing to anyone who was in the Margaret Road area of Headington this afternoon to come forward,' he was saying. 'They may have seen something that would help us. We are also asking people to let us know if they see anything that might indicate where Abigail is being held – perhaps something as simple as purchases of baby milk or nappies by someone whom you know doesn't have a baby. We think it's likely that whoever took her did so because they desperately want a baby of their own – perhaps a mother who lost hers through a miscarriage or a cot death – and so …'

Sam looked away from the TV screen towards his wife. Flick was sitting rigid in her chair, staring at the screen. For a few moments, Sam was unable to move. He sat looking back and forth from Flick to the television report and back again. Then he picked his plate up off his lap and set it down on top of a bookcase at the side of the room. He got to his feet and stumbled out of the room in a daze. Horrible pictures were forming in his head of Flick snatching a baby from its pram and leaving behind, in its place, that dreadful inanimate dummy that she had been caring for since Mia had died.

He somehow managed to reach the top of the stairs. He stood there, breathing rapidly, hardly daring to open the door of the little bedroom that had been Mia's nursery. He closed his eyes and forced himself to take a few long deep breaths. Then he opened his eyes again and went in.

It was very peaceful. The cot stood in the corner of the room, just as it had ever since they had put it there a few weeks before Mia was born. The gaily-coloured mobile, featuring characters from Disney's Winnie-the-Pooh, still hung above it. The pretty pink and white quilt lay in a hump. There was clearly something beneath it – but what?

Sam strode across the room, snatched up the quilt and hurled it aside. Then he looked down into the cot. The shape under the remaining clean white sheet did not move. He put both hands into the cot and picked it up. A feeling of intense relief flowed through his body as he confirmed that this was not, after all, a live infant. He collapsed on to the chair that Flick used to use when she gave Mia her night feeds, absent-mindedly hugging the doll to his chest and rocking it back and forth.

'Sam!' Flick's voice came from outside the door, sounding anxious and frightened. 'What's wrong?'

Sam looked up, his face tear-stained.

'Oh Flick, I'm so sorry! I thought ... I mean, when I heard them say that a baby had been taken, I was afraid ...'

'You thought *I'd* taken her?'

'Yes – no – yes! I thought you couldn't help yourself. I'm sorry! I should have known … I should never have …'

'No!' Flick flung herself down on the floor next to Sam's chair and put her arms around his waist. 'I'm the one who should be sorry. Ever since Mia died, I've been so wrapped up in myself. I never thought about you. I should have realised that you were grieving too.'

Sam let go of the doll and hugged Flick to him.

'No. It's not your fault. I should have been more understanding. I shouldn't have expected you to be able to just go back to how we were before.'

They were both crying now. They hugged each other tight and Sam kissed the top of Flick's head. The doll rolled gently to the floor and lay on its back, its lifeless eyes staring at the ceiling.

'Those poor parents!' Flick said at last, pulling a handkerchief out from her sleeve and wiping her face. 'At least we know where Mia is. They must be sick with worrying about what's happening to their baby.'

***

'OK, Bernie,' Jonah said briskly as they drove out through the gates of the house in Headington. 'Let's have it. What's with Old Peter and DCI Khan?'

'What do you mean?' Bernie asked, playing for time.

'That's what I'm asking you. I saw Peter's face when Khan showed up. He wasn't exactly over the moon at the prospect of him getting involved in the case, was he?'

'No,' Bernie admitted.

'So, go on then – spill the beans. What can Khan have done to upset Old Peter so much? It's not like him to carry a grudge.'

'Alright then,' Bernie sighed. 'It all goes back to when Angie was killed. Arshad Khan was part of the team that investigated it.'

'And?' Jonah prompted. 'Peter can't hold it against him that they never found out who did it. So what did Khan do that was so terrible?'

'It was his attitude. He was brought in because it looked like a racist attack. He was only a young detective sergeant then, but he was considered to be a bit of an expert on crime against ethnic minorities. Actually, I think that was mainly just because there were precious few non-white police officers in the force at the time. Anyway, he took it upon himself to give Peter a hard time over his attitude towards Angie's relationship with the West Indian community in Oxford. In Khan's opinion, Peter didn't understand what it was like for her to be a black woman in a white society. He thought Peter saw her as a white person with brown skin – which is probably sort of true, except that Peter would have said that *he* was equally a black person with white skin – and that he didn't do enough to encourage her to mix with other West Indians.'

Bernie sighed again.

'He was really obnoxious – especially when you consider that this was only a matter of days after Angie was killed. In the end, Peter snapped and shouted at Khan to stop piling on the accusations. Well, that frightened Lucy and she burst into tears, which only upset Peter all the more – you know how much he adores Lucy – and I had to ask Khan to leave.'

'So all that took place in your house?'

'Peter had to stay somewhere. His house was still cordoned off as a crime scene. I think that probably added credence to the theory that either Peter or I or both of us together could have killed Angie to smooth the way for us to get hitched.'

'D'you think that's what Khan thought?'

'Not really,' Bernie shrugged. 'I think he was more taken up with the idea that Peter hadn't been aware of the racism that his wife and kids were experiencing on a day-to-day basis and that his complacency had contributed somehow to her being targeted. He had a bit of a bee in his bonnet about white people wanting everyone to conform to their values and lifestyle.'

They pulled up in the police station car park and Bernie got out to set up the ramp for Jonah's wheelchair. To their surprise, Anna Davenport's car drew up alongside them. She locked it and came round to wait for Jonah to emerge.

'You didn't need to come back,' Jonah told her. 'You should be at home with your family.'

'My family don't seem particularly keen for my company,' Anna told him. 'Phil's gone out to the pub, Marcus is round at a mate's and I've just had a blazing row with Jess because I was late in and then forgot which exam it was she'd had today. I thought I'd just stay for an hour or so to see how the public appeal went and to give her time to calm down.'

They went inside and took the lift to

the first floor room where a team of officers was monitoring incoming phone calls and responses to the posting of Abigail's photograph on Facebook and Twitter. As they entered, Arshad Khan looked up from perusing a computer screen and came across to meet them.

'We're following up on a couple of possible sightings of the baby,' he told Jonah. 'One in Northampton looks plausible. The other is in Lanarkshire, which doesn't seem likely, seeing as it would require a private jet to get there in the time. However, I've asked the local police to look into it, just in case. Then there are two witnesses that cropped up via the house-to-house, who could be worth talking to again. Nothing definite, but they were there in the playground at the time the baby went missing. Shall I go round and interview them?'

'Let me read the reports and then I'll decide,' Jonah answered. If these witnesses really were significant then he would prefer to interview them himself. Moreover, Bernie's description of Khan's interview manner – albeit from a good few years ago, when he was significantly younger and less experienced – did not inspire confidence in his ability to obtain information from people who might well be nervous of police questioning.

'Very well.' There was something about the way Khan said these two words that conveyed dissatisfaction. 'Meanwhile, can I have a word – in private?' Khan glanced in a meaningful way towards Bernie.

'Certainly! Bernie will show you to my office and I'll be with you in five minutes.'

'Now, what was it you wanted to speak to me about?' Jonah said, entering his office less than three minutes later. He had waited just long enough for Khan to take a seat and for Bernie to switch on the kettle that stood on top of one of the filing cabinets in Jonah's office. He had correctly interpreted Khan's request for a private interview as being specifically aimed at excluding Bernie, and was determined that *he* would be the one who decided which conversations she was permitted to be privy to.

Arshad looked meaningfully in Bernie's direction and then back at Jonah, who continued to smile blandly.

'I'd rather speak to you alone,' he said.

'Yes,' agreed Jonah, pretending not

to understand. 'That's why we've come in here.'

'I mean that it would be better if *Mrs Johns* were not present,' Khan said at last, wondering whether Jonah could really be as obtuse as he appeared.

'*Dr Fazakerley* is my confidential personal assistant,' Jonah said, using Bernie's maiden name as a way of emphasising that she was here in a professional capacity and not as Peter's wife. 'She can be completely trusted not to repeat anything she hears outside of this room.'

'Very well.' Accepting that Jonah was not to be moved, Khan began, speaking rather tentatively and keeping watch on Bernie from the corner of his eye. 'I wanted to remind you that most child abductions are committed by members of the family.'

'Yes. I am aware of that.'

'And, in this case there's an added factor that we mustn't lose sight of,' Khan went on, continuing to watch both Jonah and Bernie closely. 'I'd like to draw your attention to the unusual circumstance of the child's physical appearance compared with that of her parents.' He paused.

'You mean: she's white and they're both black?' Jonah asked.

'Well … yes, in a nutshell. I'd like to suggest we have a psychological assessment done of both parents.'

'What for?' Jonah enquired, doing his best to sound interested in the idea rather than judgemental of it.

'To look for signs that they may have been finding it difficult to accept that the child was really theirs. I think, we ought to consider, as a hypothesis, the possibility that either or both of them could have rejected the child and wanted to get rid of it – her – I mean.'

'That's a very interesting idea,' Jonah said, speaking in a deliberately calm and measured tone. 'By all means follow it up if you think it's worth it. I would just like to point out a few things. Number one: the father has an alibi for the time of the baby's disappearance; his employer confirms that he was in their office on the other side of Bicester all afternoon. In any case, he is unlikely to feel any uncertainty about the child's parentage, in view of the fact that she looks the spitting image of her paternal grandfather. Secondly, the mother was in the playground with her other child for the whole time and so didn't have any opportunity to dispose of the baby anywhere, assuming that she wanted to.'

'If the baby was ever there in the first place,' Khan argued. 'Who's to say the buggy wasn't empty all along?'

'At least one witness, whom I spoke to at the playground,' Jonah answered. 'And potentially two more from the house-to-house. I've got those reports you were telling me about on the screen here. Two women confirm that they looked into the buggy and saw a baby girl.'

'It could have been a different buggy.' Khan was reluctant to abandon his pet theory.

'Yes, it could,' Jonah conceded, realising that this was a line of enquiry that Khan was determined to pursue. 'Tell you what – why don't you investigate the possibility that the mother disposed of the baby *before* going to the playground and then raised the alarm as a way of covering up what she'd done? You could start by talking to the neighbours at the flats where they live. We need to interview them anyway, so you can take charge of that aspect of the case, if you like. You can have Andrews,' he added generously. 'He's good at getting people to talk.'

'Very well,' Khan said again, sensing that he was being dismissed. He got up to go, turning to Bernie as he reached the door. 'I'm sorry you had to hear all that. I hope you understand that we have to explore all avenues and your family aren't being singled out for suspicion.' He paused, opening the door and stepping across the threshold before turning back and looking her firmly in the eye. 'And you do understand that you must not say anything about this to your husband or his son and daughter-in-law, don't you?'

'Of course,' Bernie answered coldly, getting up to close the door behind him. 'I am well aware of what *professional confidentiality* means, thank you.'

***

St Cyprian's Roman Catholic Church was an unimposing building of pale red bricks. It had been erected in the middle of the twentieth century to meet the needs of the growing numbers of people living in the rapidly expanding suburb of Headington. From the outside there was little to distinguish it from the surrounding houses, built in similar bricks and topped with the same red tiles. It had a small belfry at one end, housing a single bell. At the other end, a Celtic cross stood out against the sky.

The large rectangular widows along the side that faced the road looked dark, under their vandal-proof protective shields.

Peter was surprised by the contrast as he followed Lucy in through the light oak doors and found himself bathed in coloured light, which cascaded in through a large modern stained-glass window that filled the west wall. The uninspiring exterior had not prepared him for this. He looked up at the window in wonder. It depicted Noah's ark, resting on Mount Ararat, with the animals processing out and dispersing, watched by Noah and his family. Above the ark, and filling more than half of the space, a huge rainbow curved through the sky and disappeared behind distant mountains. Following the coloured arch with his eyes, Peter could see, behind those grey, rocky peaks, the suggestion of a yellow gleam. He smiled as he remembered Bernie's description of the window: 'You can't help thinking that the artist is trying to suggest that there's a crock of gold at the end of the rainbow!'

Peter had never been inside St Cyprian's before. Indeed, apart from a visit the previous year to the Metropolitan Cathedral in Liverpool, he had never been inside a Roman Catholic church at all. He was immediately struck by the difference between this and the interior of the Methodist church in east Oxford that he had attended with his first wife and to which he still technically belonged. His first impression was of being surrounded by pictures and statues – almost like entering an art gallery. The white-painted walls had a sequence of square paintings arranged along them at about head height – the Stations of the Cross, he supposed. Looking up, he saw that the white plaster gave way to blue as the walls curved inwards to form an arched ceiling. This was adorned with puffy white clouds, from behind which golden angels looked down with benevolently smiling faces.

At the far end of the ceiling, the blue became gradually lighter, changing to purple, pink, and then finally to yellow above the main altar. Peter supposed that this must be intended to symbolise sunrise. There was a hymn about that, wasn't there? Sun of Righteousness, arise – or something like that? Behind the altar was another large stained glass window. This depicted the Easter story, with the cross in the centre and, on either side, the empty tomb and Christ's ascension into heaven. A woman in a blue headscarf was engaged in cleaning the cobwebs from around the window with a long-handled duster. She looked round briefly at the sound of their footsteps on the tiled floor, before continuing with her work.

Lucy led the way, past a rather gory-looking representation of the sacred heart, to a wooden rail that ran along in front of a smaller side altar. A large wrought iron candelabrum stood just behind the rail. Three or four candles were lit, while a few more had burned down to stumps and gone out. A supply of fresh candles lay in an open-topped box attached to the wall. Also attached to the wall was a wooden box with a slit in the top and a notice explaining that this was for gifts of money in exchange for candles to light.

Lucy reached into her pocket and took out a coin, which she slipped into the box. Then she selected a candle, lit it from one of those already burning and set it in an empty socket in the candelabrum. Then she knelt down on the step in front of the rail and bowed her head in prayer.

Peter hesitated for a moment. Then he too dipped in his pocket and pulled out some change. He dropped two fifty pence pieces into the box and then picked up a candle, lit it and set it up next to Lucy's. Now what? He felt self-conscious standing there, but kneeling down would be even worse. He started wandering slowly round the church, looking at the statues and pictures. Was this what all the churches in England had been like, he wondered, before Oliver Cromwell purged them of popish idolatry?

Lucy got up and looked round for her stepfather. She spotted him a few feet away, standing, staring up at a tall statue – almost life-size – of a young woman in a blue gown and headdress holding a baby in her arms.

At least – it was the size of a baby, but it had the appearance of a much older child. Indeed, judging by their faces alone, the child could have been older than the mother. She was gazing into the distance with an anxious – almost frightened – expression on her face, clutching her precocious infant tightly to her, while he appeared to be struggling to get away, turning from her and raising his right arm aloft with two fingers outstretched.

Entwined about the woman's bare feet, which seemed to be standing on a, rather incongruous, small hillock of grass, was a long scroll bearing the words, 'And thy own soul a sword shall pierce.[3]'

Detecting Lucy's presence beside him, Peter glanced down at her and then back up at the statue.

'This is the Virgin Mary, right?' he asked.

'Yes.' Lucy wondered where this was leading. Peter had never seemed particularly interested in this sort of thing before. She looked up at the statue, noticing for the first time that, unusually in European art, both Virgin and Child were of Middle-Eastern appearance,

---

[3] A quotation from St Luke's Gospel, Chapter 2, verse 35, in the Challoner revision of the Douay-Rheims Bible. This is part of Simeon's speech to Mary when she took Jesus to the temple in Jerusalem at the age of eight days.

with olive brown skin and dark brown eyes beneath black brows. Mary's hair was hidden, but her son's tight black curls stood out like a halo around his head. The artist must have been conscious that this was a Jewish family from Palestine and not, as they were so often portrayed, blond, blue-eyed northern Europeans. The Madonna's expression was unusual too. Generally, she was depicted looking calm and serene, accepting her role in the incarnation with humble submissiveness. This Mary looked fearful, as if she were looking into the future and not liking what she saw.

'Do you pray to her?' Peter asked suddenly.

'Well, sort of,' Lucy said slowly. 'At least ... well, it's probably more correct to talk about asking her to pray to God on our behalf. Although, I don't know … Mam says that some Catholics treat the BVM like a fourth member of the Holy Trinity. So maybe … well, I suppose it doesn't make that much difference what you call it, does it?'

Lucy's mother had been the product of a mixed marriage between a Roman Catholic father and a mother who belonged to the Salvation Army. As an adult, she had joined the Methodist Church (through which she had formed a close friendship with Peter's first wife) as a compromise between those two extremes of Christian practice. She had brought up Lucy to appreciate her Catholic heritage, but with a healthy scepticism about things that her own mother had dismissed as *Holy Roman Hocus Pocus*. Prayers to the saints came into this category.

'No. I don't suppose it does,' Peter answered. 'I was just thinking,' he went on, sounding rather strange and dreamy, 'I was thinking that *she* would understand, wouldn't she?'

'You mean, she'd understand what it's like for Crystal?' Lucy asked, struggling to keep up with Peter's train of thought. 'Having her baby stolen?'

'Well, yes, I suppose so,' Peter said, sounding taken aback by this suggestion. 'But I was thinking more that she'd understand what it's like to see your son suffering and not be able to do anything to help.'

'Oh! Yes, I see what you mean.' It was Lucy's turn to be wrong-footed. Up until then, she had been seeing the current situation as primarily affecting Crystal and Eddie – and Abigail, of course, but she was too young to understand what was happening. Now she saw that Peter's trauma, while different, was as great as that of the baby's parents. She put out her arm and slipped her hand into his. 'I'm sure she does – understand I mean.'

Peter squeezed her hand gently.

'I suppose it's time we were getting back,' he said. 'I told Eddie we wouldn't be long.'

***

'Georgia!' Michelle quickened her pace as she caught sight of her daughter and son-in-law sitting on two plastic chairs next to a transparent plastic cot in the hospital ward. 'They told us you were here. Have you had anything to eat? I brought these in case you hadn't.'

Georgia looked up and saw her mother, standing in front of her, holding out a large tin, which, according to the words on the outside, had once contained Quality Street chocolates and toffees. She smiled weakly, recognising the tin and guessing its contents.

'Flapjacks?' she asked.

'That's right. I thought they might help ... you know ... give you something to do while you're waiting. And talking of waiting, is there any news about Rachel? Have the tests come back?'

'Yes – at least, they're still waiting for one of them, but they seem fairly confident that it's viral meningitis.'

'That's good isn't it?' Michelle asked, looking at each of their faces, trying to gauge their anxiety levels.

'Yes. Apparently it's nowhere near as serious as the bacterial forms,' Georgia told her.

'But?' her mother prompted, sensing

that there was more to be said.

'But, with her being so young, there could still be complications and even long-term problems.'

'They told us that the swelling around her brain isn't too bad,' Nathan added, 'which is a good sign. The main thing they're worried about is dehydration.'

'They've got her on a drip,' Georgia continued, pointing to the bag of saline solution hanging above the cot. 'She won't be able to go home until they're satisfied that she doesn't need any more intravenous fluids. She still won't feed, you see. They've tried feeding her through a tube, but she brings it back up again.'

Nathan got up and offered his seat to Michelle.

'Sit down here. I'll go and see if I can rustle up some more chairs.'

Michelle sat down next to her daughter, resting the tin of biscuits on her knees and clutching it with both hands. Leslie peered down into the cot. Rachel seemed peaceful enough – too peaceful, perhaps, as if she were unconscious rather than asleep. A slight movement of one hand reassured him that she was, at least, definitely still alive. He lifted his eyes and looked across at his daughter. Georgia appeared calm, but her eyes were frightened.

'Here we are!' Nathan was back with two more of the ubiquitous plastic chairs supplied on hospital wards for the use of visitors. He arranged them around the cot and both men sat down. Nathan turned to his mother-in-law. 'It was good of you to come over.'

'Not at all,' Michelle waved one hand

dismissively. 'We wanted to be here. I just wish there was more we could do to help.'

She opened the tin and handed round the flapjacks. Nathan took one, out of politeness, not expecting to be able to eat it. However, after biting into it, he was surprised to discover how hungry he was. He had eaten nothing since lunch.

'You *will* tell us if there's anything we can do,' Michelle said anxiously. 'We don't want to interfere, but if you think of anything ...'

'Of course we will, Mum,' Georgia assured her, wishing that her mother were not always so anxious about being accused of intruding. 'But right now, we just have to wait.'

'After all,' Michelle went on, determined to keep up the conversation and avoid any awkward silences, 'it's not as if Rachel's other granddad is in a position to do much. And it's no bother for us – really.'

'Yes,' Nathan agreed. 'That's why we decided not to tell Dad – not until we know for sure how Rachel really is. There's no point getting him worried, when there's nothing he can do about it.'

'Are you sure that's fair?' Leslie asked sharply, speaking for the first time since they arrived. 'Don't you think he has a right to know that his granddaughter is ill?'

'Well, yes, of course.' Nathan was taken aback. He had great respect for his father-in-law and felt uncomfortable at his evident disapproval. 'But – like Michelle said – he can't do anything. So we thought it was better to wait. Knowing Dad, he would probably be mad enough to insist on being brought over here to see her, which would be ridiculous!'

'Why ridiculous?' Leslie asked quietly. 'I would have thought it was only natural.' Neither Nathan nor Georgia replied, so he continued. 'You know your father best, but he strikes me as a very resilient character, quite capable of facing up to something like this; and, in his place, *I* would be considerably offended to think that you felt the need to protect me from knowing the truth.'

Nathan flushed red. For a few moments nobody spoke. Then Nathan stood up and took his phone out of his pocket.

'Yes. I suppose you're right. I'll ring him.'

***

The traffic was heavy on the M1. Debra wondered if it had been a mistake to try to get home that night, rather than finding a hotel and returning the following day. She switched on the radio, hoping for an explanation of the latest tailback and advice on the best choice of route beyond Sheffield. Should she leave the M1 and head for Doncaster or continue on it to Leeds?

'The baby's grandfather made this appeal for her safe return,' the news reporter said. Then a man's voice came over the airwaves, calm and clear, but sounding as if he were having difficulty getting the words out.

'I just want to say this to whoever has Abigail at this moment,' the voice said. 'I don't know why you took her, but I expect it's because you've had your own personal tragedy. Perhaps you've lost a baby yourself.' Debra's hands tightened on the wheel as she listened. 'I'm sure you don't intend Abigail any harm; but Abigail needs her own mum and dad – and they need her. We aren't interested in punishing you – we just want Abigail back home with us. So please, let us know where she is. If you don't want anyone to know who you are, leave her somewhere safe, and then tell someone where she is, so that we can go and find her and bring her home.'

Then the newsreader's voice went on to give details of a telephone number for members of the public to ring with any information they might have. Finally, the report closed with a reiteration of the facts. Debra's heart beat faster as she heard confirmation that the place and time agreed perfectly with her encounter with John's baby that afternoon. Could that have been Victoria's father speaking just now? He didn't have a Sunderland accent, but people moved about a lot these days, so that did not necessarily signify one way or the other. It didn't sound as if the police had any idea who might have taken the baby, if they were relying on appealing to her abductor to bring her back.

***

'Lucy? It's Nathan. I'm trying to get hold of Dad, but he's not answering his phone.' Nathan's voice sounded anxious, but that was not unusual. Jonah always said that his younger son was capable of doing all the worrying for the rest of the family as well as for himself.

'He's working late on a case,' Lucy told him. 'And I expect he's busy and not wanting to be distracted. Shall I ask him to give you a ring when he gets in?'

'Yes – well, no,' Nathan was taken aback. He had been so sure that his father must be at home – perhaps away from his chair, doing his functional electrical stimulation exercises and so not able to answer his mobile device – that he had not thought about what he would do if he could not speak to him immediately. 'Perhaps it would be better for you just to tell him I rang, and let him know that Rachel's poorly – nothing serious, just a virus.'

'What sort of virus?' Lucy asked suspiciously, convinced that Nathan would never have rung unless there were more to it than a simple cold.

'Nothing to worry about. I wouldn't have bothered telling Dad, only Georgia's parents are here with us so I thought it was only fair to let him know as well.'

'What do you mean? Georgia's parents are there with you?' Lucy became increasingly convinced that Nathan had not told her the whole story. 'They only live round the corner from you.'

'Sorry – didn't I say?' Nathan blustered. 'We're at the hospital. Rachel hasn't been feeding very well and she's lost some fluids, so they decided to keep her in overnight – just as a precaution. You will make sure Dad knows there's nothing to worry about, won't you,' he added anxiously.

'Yes, OK. I'll tell him that's what you said,' Lucy agreed, becoming increasingly annoyed at Nathan's patent refusal to admit to the seriousness of Rachel's condition. 'But it would be a lot easier if you could tell me exactly what's wrong with her. Jonah's sure to want to know.'

There was a confusion of noise and then Georgia's voice came on the line.

'Hi Lucy! I gather you're being asked to act as messenger. Tell Jonah that the doctors say Rachel's got viral meningitis. It sounds awful, but I've Googled it on my phone and usually people get better within a few days. They're only keeping Rachel in because she's so small and they want to be sure she doesn't dehydrate.'

There was more noise and then Lucy heard Nathan's voice again. Lucy deduced that he had snatched the phone back from his wife.

'Now, tell me about this working late business,' Nathan demanded. 'I thought Bernie had put her foot down and stopped him working out-of-hours.'

'It's a child abduction,' Lucy told him. 'So he doesn't want to waste any time.' She hesitated, wondering whether or not to reveal their own personal involvement in the case. Then, realising the hypocrisy of feeling annoyed with Nathan for not wanting to tell his father about Rachel's diagnosis, while she herself was not willing to be equally open with him, she went on. 'It's Abigail – Eddie's baby.'

'You mean Peter's granddaughter?' Nathan's voice sounded incredulous.

'That's right. Crystal took them to the park and left Abigail asleep in the buggy while she pushed Ricky on the swings and when she came back … no Abigail!'

'That's dreadful. I hope it works out OK in the end.' Nathan broke off and Lucy could hear a whispered conversation in the background as he conveyed the news to Georgia and her parents.

'Look – I'd better go now. Tell Dad not to worry about Rachel; and give our love to Peter and the others.'

***

On her way to bed, Victoria looked in on Esme. She had been unusually quiet all evening and Victoria wanted to check that nothing was wrong. She stood over the Moses basket and looked down. At first, she thought that Esme was staring back at her. The she realised that her gaze was glassy and unseeing. She hastily whipped off the coverings and picked the baby up. Her whole body felt rigid and her arms twitched in a strange rhythmic way.

The doctors had said that she might

have fits, but up until now, that had been one symptom of the brain damage that Esme had been spared. What should she do now? Victoria walked round the room holding Esme to her chest, with her face staring, with those unseeing eyes, over her shoulder. Should she go to A and E? On the other hand, maybe it would be better to ring the community midwife for advice.

Esme coughed and banged her head against Victoria's face. Then Victoria felt the little body in her arms relax and become soft and pliable again. Then the crying started. At least now they were back on familiar territory.

***

'And now,' Bernie said to Jonah as she followed him in through the front door on their arrival home, 'it's straight off to bed for you, and no arguments. I know you'll be wanting to be up and off first thing in the morning'

'OK Miss,' Jonah said meekly. 'I'll be a good boy.'

Although he would not admit it, he was feeling tired, as well as extremely frustrated at the lack of progress in finding the missing child. It had been as much as he could do to keep himself awake during the journey home in the car, and he was secretly looking forward to his bed.

'Any news?' Peter called out softly, clattering down the attic stairs. He had been sitting with Eddie and Crystal in their bedroom, because they had not liked to return to the living room leaving Ricky alone in his cot two floors distant.

''Fraid not,' Jonah answered laconically. 'A couple of lines to follow up in the morning, but nothing definite. I'm sorry,' he added, looking towards his friend as he reached the bottom step.

'Nathan rang,' Lucy said, appearing from the living room. 'He said to tell you that Rachel's been admitted to hospital with viral meningitis, but it isn't serious and you are not to worry about her. Oh! And he says to give their love to you, Peter, and to Eddie and Crystal. And they hope Abigail turns up soon.'

By now, Jonah, who had not been listening to the latter part of this short speech, had selected Nathan from the list of contacts on his mobile phone attachment and was waiting impatiently for him to answer the call.

'Dad!' Nathan's voice had a tinge of resignation in it. 'Good of you to ring, but there was really no need.'

'I'll go ahead and get the bed ready

for you,' Bernie said pointedly, speaking loudly enough that she was confident that Nathan would be able to hear.

'I suppose you heard that?' Jonah said, trying to sound light-hearted. 'So you don't need to worry I'm going to keep you talking. Just tell me this – Lucy said this viral meningitis isn't anything to worry about; is that what the doctors say? Or is that just your spin so as not to alarm poor old Dad?'

'Honestly Dad – they did say it will probably get better in a few days with no lasting effects. They're just keeping her in as a precaution, because she's so tiny.'

Lucy came up behind Jonah's chair and put her arms round his shoulders. As she kissed him affectionately on the cheek, she resolved to go back to St Cyprian's the following day and light

JUDY FORD
another candle.

9 WE OFTEN DREAD TOMORROW

'Ma-ma-ma-ma!'

Crystal slowly became aware of the rhythmic pounding of a small hand on her shoulders through the duvet and a small voice shouting in her ear. She opened her eyes, surprised to discover that she had been asleep. She had not expected to be able to drop off while she was still wondering and worrying about where Abigail was and whether she was safe and being cared for.

Ricky was standing at the side of the

bed with tears running down his face. He steadied himself by holding on to the bedclothes with one hand, while the other continued its pounding: bang, bang, bang, trying to attract her attention.

'How did you get here?' she asked, sitting up and reaching down to pull him up on to the bed beside her. 'It's naughty climbing out of your cot. You'll hurt yourself.'

Ricky buried his head in her nightdress and stretched his small arms as far round her chest as they would reach. Crystal hugged him to her and kissed the top of his head.

'Do you want to stay here with Mummy for a while?' She pulled the duvet up around them both and rested back on the pillow. 'Don't make a noise,' she whispered. 'We don't want to wake

Daddy, do we?'

***

On the floor below, Peter and Bernie had just switched off the light. Usually they were asleep by this time, but Jonah's late arrival home, and the further delay caused by his call to Nathan, had meant that the lengthy routine of putting him to bed had started late. Then, after they had come upstairs, Bernie realised that she had forgotten to put Jonah's chair on to charge overnight and she had to go back down to do that. Now they lay there side by side, each trying to formulate in their mind a plan for the following day.

'It's true what they say, isn't it?' Peter observed. 'It never rains but it pours. Just when I thought things couldn't get any worse, Nathan rings up with his news. Do you think Rachel's going to be alright?'

'I had a look on the internet while you were doing Jonah's skin care. As far as I can tell, Nathan's right in saying that it's bacterial meningitis that everyone's worried about. Provided it really is the viral sort, everyone seems to agree that it's not that serious.'

'Serious enough to keep her in hospital.'

'But probably it *is* just precautionary. Anyway, there's nothing *we* can do, so we'll just have to keep hoping everything turns out OK. At least Jonah had the sense not to insist on rushing off over there to see for himself.'

'Yes,' Peter agreed. 'I was half-expecting him – more than half, in fact – to insist on going. He must be becoming more reasonable in his old age.'

Bernie gave a little laugh. 'I'm not so sure *reasonable* is going to come into it tomorrow morning,' she said with a smile. 'I can foresee me having my work cut out getting him to take rest breaks and meal breaks and to trust other people to do things that he knows he could do better himself.'

'I know.' Peter put his arm around his wife's shoulders and pulled her closer to him. 'And I know he'd be like that whoever's baby it was, but I can't help wondering what's going to happen to us all if Abigail is never found – or if …'

'Would you rather someone else was in charge?'

'No.' Peter shook his head. 'I can't think of anyone I could trust more to do the job and not to give up until he finds her. I just … well, if anything happens to Abigail, I'm not sure that Eddie won't think that …'

'You mean he might blame Jonah?'

'Not exactly. It's more … I don't think he rates Jonah. I think he finds it hard to see beyond his disability.'

'You mean, he might think that the outcome would have been different if an able-bodied officer had been in charge?'

'Mmm.' Peter fell silent. Then, 'At least we've escaped having DCI Khan at the helm,' he murmured, turning on his side and drawing the bedclothes up over him as a way of indicating that he was settling down to sleep. 'I suppose we should be thankful for small mercies.'

***

Downstairs, in the bedroom that had been the breakfast room in the days before Jonah had moved in with Bernie and her family, Jonah was thinking

258

similar thoughts. He was not lacking in self-confidence, but he was well aware that criminal investigations often ended in failure, despite the best efforts of everyone involved. How easy would Peter and his family find it to forgive if any misjudgement on his part led to Abigail being killed or, what was perhaps worse, lost forever? Perhaps he should have insisted on handing the case over to someone else. But who would that have been? Arshad Khan, presumably. Peter would not have been happy with that – and Jonah, too, had little confidence that Khan was capable of leading an investigation of this nature to a successful conclusion. He had worked so long in the field of racially motivated crimes that he appeared incapable of keeping his mind open to alternative possibilities.

Could there be any truth in Khan's theory that either Crystal or Eddie was unable to accept a white baby as their own child? It seemed ridiculous. Jonah had seen them together, and nothing they had done or said suggested that Abigail was anything other than the adored daughter for whom they had longed for so many years. But the subconscious was a funny thing. Might they secretly harbour feelings that even they themselves did not acknowledge? Eddie had emigrated to Jamaica after his mother died. Peter had always worried that this might have been, at least in part, because he wanted to find somewhere where he was no longer the odd-one-out, a black man in a white world. If that were true, might he, subconsciously, be rejecting his white, red-haired daughter, who was a constant reminder of his own mixed heritage?

Then again, this was all pointless speculation, since Eddie was a dozen miles away when Abigail was taken. Admittedly, he could have paid someone else to steal her, but, while the subconscious might make a person behave oddly, it beggared belief to think that it might go to such lengths. No. if there was anything in Arshad's theory, it had to be more subtle than that. Perhaps something that Eddie or Crystal had said, which had prompted someone else to believe that they would welcome the removal from their lives of this problematic child? And that, almost certainly, brought them back to the hypothesis that the abductor was someone who wanted a child of their own and had taken Abigail in the belief that she would be happier with them than with her own parents.

***

'On the face of it,' Arshad told his wife, as he lay in bed waiting for her to finish removing her makeup and join him. 'The child's father has a copper-bottomed alibi.'

'So, what makes you think he could be involved?' Anita Khan asked, tossing a cotton pad in the bin and reaching for a pot of face cream.

'He may well not be,' her husband admitted, 'but, knowing his history, I can't help wondering. His mother was killed in a knife attack when he was only just turned twenty. That's the sort of thing that leaves a lasting mark on someone's personality.'

'And his father's an ex-copper, is that

what you said?'

'Yes. I didn't know Peter Johns very well, but, in the force, there were very few people who had a bad word to say about him. He's a real Mr Nice-Guy. The trouble was, he tended to assume everyone else was nice too. I'm sure he never had a clue about the racial abuse that his wife and kids were experiencing.'

'Until his wife was killed.'

'Not even then. I interviewed him. He would never accept that there had been anything more than playground taunting, and he wasn't even convinced that it *was* a racial attack. And that's another problem,' Arshad went on thoughtfully. 'We didn't exactly cover ourselves in glory over that investigation. It was seven years before the killers were brought to justice. Johns could be forgiven for being sceptical that I'll do any better this time.'

'Maybe it's as well you're not leading the enquiry,' Anita suggested, pulling back the duvet and climbing in beside him.

'Yes,' Arshad agreed. 'I can't say I was sorry about that – not when I saw how the land lay. I think I may be in for a bumpy ride, even so. Porter's basically given me all the bits that have the potential to upset Johns and his family. I can see why he's done it, but at the end of the day, I'm bound to turn out to have been the bad guy. Either the parents are completely innocent and I've been unnecessarily intruding into their private lives and undermining their relations with their neighbours, or one or both of them is involved in the kid's disappearance, in which case I'm responsible for breaking up the family.'

'Or you never get to the bottom of it and the parents are just left with everyone saying, "There's no smoke without fire",' Anita finished for him.

'That's just it,' Arshad agreed gloomily. 'I've got to ask the questions. But as soon as you ask, you sow the seeds in people's minds that you must have a reason for asking. And before you know where you are, it'll have got back to the family that a policeman has been noseying around, accusing them of stealing their own baby from its pram.'

'Not to mention the tabloids,' his wife observed. 'Some of them would love the idea of a black family rejecting a white baby.'

Arshad sighed.

'And, at the end of the day, the chances are all I'll be doing is making things more difficult for a young couple who are just the unfortunate victims of a particularly tragic crime. Oh well! Let's just hope whoever did it hears that appeal that Johns made and brings the child back.'

***

'I've made up my mind,' Philip Davenport said into the darkness as he and Anna lay in bed together. 'Brian Widecombe has asked me to go into partnership with him. I'm going to ring him tomorrow and tell him I'm in.'

'But he's based down in Exeter, isn't he?' Anna asked, feeling rather bemused. 'How can you …? Or do you mean, you'd run a branch of the business up here?'

'I mean,' Philip said, speaking slowly and clearly, as if addressing someone of limited intellect, 'that I'm going to move down there. The kids will love it – you know how much they always enjoy staying with Mum – and she'll be able to keep an eye on them when I need to be away from home on a job. It'll be absolutely perfect.'

'But, what about me? And my job?'

'That's up to you. Presumably, you could apply for a transfer to Devon and Cornwall Police. That is, if you give up on your crazy idea of having that deformed baby of yours.'

'Ours,' Anna corrected him. 'She's *our* baby. And they never said anything about her being deformed – just disabled.'

'Tell it your own way. All I'm saying is that it's up to you. If you want to go ahead with having it, you're on your own. You can keep the house here –

provided you pay the mortgage – but I'm taking Jess and Marcus down to live with Mum. I don't want their lives screwed up by having a cripple in the family and I'm not being lumbered with looking after the kid while you swan around doing your oh-so-important job.'

'I'm sorry, Phil. I never knew you felt like that. I thought you *enjoyed* being at home with the kids.'

'I did,' Philip conceded, 'when they were young. But now that they're older, I was looking forward to having the time to do the things *I* want for a change.'

'You could still do that,' Anna argued. 'I'll take the full year of maternity leave. And by then, we'll have a better idea what sort of childcare we need. We'll have enough to pay for it now that I'm a DI. Surely you don't really need to go off down to Devon?'

SORROWFUL MYSTERY

'You really don't get it, do you? One – going in with Brian is a great opportunity for me to do some really exciting things architecturally. Two – whatever wonderful childcare you organise (and I bet it won't be as easy as you're making out), I'll still have to put up with having the kid around the house, and what about when your job keeps you out after you're supposed to be back – like today, for instance? And, three – why should Marcus and Jess have to have their lives disrupted? Let me spell it out in words of one syllable: *I do – not – want – that – baby*. Either it goes or I go.'

'Not *it*,' Anna protested weakly. 'They told us she's a baby girl.'

'*It*,' Philip repeated emphatically. '*It* is not a baby anything – not yet. It's a foetus – a defective foetus. It's only chance that it's survived this long. We're just unlucky that it wasn't aborted spontaneously. The kindest thing for it, as well as for the rest of us, would be to get rid of it now, before it's developed enough to feel anything.'

'No! She's our baby. I can feel her. I've seen her heart beating on the scan – you'd feel different about it if you'd bothered to come. Why didn't you? You did with the other two. I remember when you saw Jess for the first time on the monitor in the sonography room. You were over the moon to see how perfect she was, even at twenty weeks. Why can't you feel excited like that about this baby?'

Philip sighed.

'How many times do I have to say it? I don't want another baby and this one certainly isn't perfect.'

'But she's ours. We can't just kill her.'

'Look Anna,' Philip said, more gently this time. 'Believe me; I *do* understand how you feel.'

'No you don't. I don't think you're even trying.' Anna rolled over on her side, as far away from Philip as she could get. Her instinct was to get out and go and sleep in the spare room, but she remembered that the bed was not made and the clean sheets were in the airing cupboard, which was in Jessica's room. This, probably pointless, gesture would entail disturbing the whole house and would inevitably lead to demands from their daughter for an explanation. 'Now, I need to get some sleep. It's going to be a busy day tomorrow.'

'Suits me.' Philip too turned over to face away from his wife. He wished she would try to look at things rationally. It was her hormones, he supposed, that made her unable to see that having another child – even one that did not come with all sorts of potential extra problems – was just infeasible in their modest three-bedroomed semi. It wasn't fair on Marcus and Jessica – and the child itself would be bound to suffer.

Anna closed her eyes, but sleep would not come. How could they have reached this situation? She wondered. How could you live with someone for twenty years and then suddenly discover that you didn't know them at all? Was Phil serious about moving to Devon? Or was he just using it as a threat to force her into agreeing to an abortion? What would Jess and Marcus say when he told them? They would be bound to go with him. They loved visiting his mother's house in Dawlish and, to be fair to Phil, he had always been there for them while they were growing up – unlike Anna, who had too often been too engrossed in her work to give them the attention they deserved. It looked as if she was going to be starting from scratch as a single mother of one child with potentially serious disabilities. How had this happened to her?

***

Debra turned over in bed, trying to get comfortable, but sleep continued to elude her. She felt restless and ill-at-ease. She wished John were there. She wished she could go back twenty years; back to before they had even thought of having children. They had been so happy together – so complete as a couple. She could not remember ever having had a sleepless night when John was lying there beside her. And even when he went away for those long trips abroad – that only made it all the better when he came home!

She could not stop thinking about John – and John's baby that should, by rights, have been hers too. They had been happy together. And he had said that it wasn't that he didn't love her any more. He *had* said that, hadn't he? It wasn't that he didn't love her – it was just that he needed more from a relationship. He felt that she had come to want him only as a potential father for her children and not for himself. She knew that she had made things difficult for him. Everything had seemed so pointless after it became clear that she could never conceive. She had found it impossible to find any enthusiasm for anything under the shadow of that crushing blow.

But could it be different now? Perhaps she could persuade John to come back to her now that he had proved himself with that younger woman. She could adopt the baby and it would be just as if it were their own. They would have to pay off Victoria, she supposed; but John had money. Thirty years of marriage must count for more than the two or three years that he had spent with Victoria – years when he had been abroad as often as he had been at home.

Yes. That was the solution. Victoria would be upset for a while, but she was young. She would find someone else. And at least *she* knew that she could have children.

***

Sam Mason woke to find that he was

alone in bed. Where was Flick? He reached out his hand and picked up the alarm clock from the bedside table. He peered at it in the dimness: 3 a.m. The space next to him, where she had been lying, felt cold. She must have been gone some time.

'Flick!' he called. 'Where are you?'

'Sorry. I didn't mean to wake you,' Flick apologised, coming into the room and climbing back into bed.

'I thought you said you were going to stop all this nonsense of getting up in the night to feed an imaginary baby.' Sam grumbled. 'I thought we'd agreed.'

'Yes. It wasn't that. I couldn't sleep, so I went downstairs for a glass of water, that's all.'

'Oh. Sorry.' Sam felt guilty. He should have been more trusting. After all, she had promised – after that tearful episode in the nursery, when he had as good as accused her of stealing someone else's baby. He rolled over and put his arm around Flick. 'I know it's hard for you. It's hard for me too. But we'll get through this – really we will.'

10 MORNING HAS BROKEN

'Would you like the last flapjack?' Michelle asked, holding out the tin to her daughter.

'Have we really eaten all those?' Georgia asked, taking the flapjack, breaking it in half and handing half to Nathan. 'When I saw the tin, I thought you'd made enough for a week!'

'That's what comes of being up all night with nothing else to do,' Nathan said, taking a bite. 'Mind you – I'm glad you brought them, Michelle. I can't believe how hungry I've been. It must be the waiting that does it.'

Leslie looked at his watch.

'Shall we go back to the ward? They said we could look in on Rachel again at seven and it's ten past now.'

***

'Oh Esme!' Victoria exclaimed in frustration, as she staggered bleary-eyed across the room for the tenth or eleventh time that night. 'Why can't you sleep like that baby we saw in the park yesterday? She didn't wake up screaming every five minutes, did she?'

The daylight was coming in through the thin curtains. There was no point trying to get back to sleep now. Victoria fed and changed Esme and then put her back in the Moses basket while she dressed herself. Esme continued to cry.

Victoria fumbled with the buttons of her blouse, getting them mixed up in the haste that was prompted by the sound of her baby's apparent distress. At last, she was ready. She picked Esme up and carried her downstairs, rocking her in her arms as she did so and murmuring to her soothingly.

When they reached the hall, Victoria put Esme in the pram and prepared to go out. Another day! Another day of walking, walking, walking – trying to lull Esme to sleep and to stop that constant crying!

***

'Can I help with the breakfast?' Crystal asked, coming into the kitchen and seeing Peter placidly cutting bread to make toast. He looked up and smiled.

'You can lay the table if you like,' he

answered, knowing that it was better for her to have something to do to distract her from constantly thinking about Abigail and what might be happening to her. 'And then, after that – does Ricky still have porridge for breakfast?'

'Yes – if you have it. If not, it doesn't matter.'

'Then maybe you could make that. You know best how he likes it.'

Crystal collected knives and spoons from the drawer. She was familiar with the kitchen from the time when they had lived here, before they found the flat. She started laying them out round the large wooden table in the centre of the room.

'I suppose there's no news?' she asked tentatively.

'No. I'm afraid not,' Peter told her. 'Jonah rang in first thing to check that nothing had turned up overnight, but nothing much has happened. They've confirmed that the potential sighting in Northampton was a false alarm and they've matched up the description of a woman seen approaching the buggy with one of the mothers who was still there when the police arrived. So just negative stuff really – eliminating lines of enquiry.'

Crystal took out a box of oats from a wall cupboard and measured a portion out into a pan. She added milk and water and took it over to the large gas cooker.

'Peter,' she said, still watching the porridge attentively to avoid looking at her father-in-law. 'Tell me honestly: do you think she's still alive? Do you think we'll ever get her back?'

Peter came over and put his hand

gently on her shoulder.

'I'm sorry, Crystal. I can't tell you what you want to know. I can only say that I really do believe what I said yesterday: that the most likely person to have taken Abigail is someone – probably a woman – who has lost a baby and is trying to replace it. And that means they probably know how to look after Abigail and want to keep her safe and well. If she was older, then I'd be much more worried, in case she'd been snatched by a paedophile. With a baby … well I reckon that probably the worst-case scenario is it could be someone who's stolen her to sell to a childless couple. In which case, they've got a vested interested in keeping her safe, haven't they? Either way, I think it's very unlikely that she's in the hands of someone who wants to harm her.'

'Thank you for making that appeal for them to give her back. Do you think it will work? I mean: will whoever's got her, give her back?'

'I'm afraid we can only wait and see. If it is a mother who's missing her own baby, then – yes, I think there's a good chance.'

'Would it have been better if *I'd* done it? If you think it's a mother, maybe she'd identify more with another woman?'

'I don't know,' Peter said slowly, taking the toast out of the toaster and putting in two more slices. 'It all depends …' He hesitated, unsure how to put what he wanted to say in a way that would not be hurtful to his son and daughter-in-law. He took a deep breath and tried to explain.

'I know DCI Khan thinks I'm too naïve

and head-in-the-clouds to realise, but there are some people out there who wouldn't be that interested in hearing what you had to say, simply because of the colour of your skin. They'd look at you and think that your baby being stolen didn't concern them. And then, when you add to that the fact that Abigail's white …. Well, there are even some quite respectable people out there who would be thinking what a hard time she's going to have growing up with both parents being so different from her. I can tell you for certain – there's no way you and Eddie would have been allowed to *adopt* Abigail.'

'Do you mean whoever took her may think they're saving her from being brought up in a black family?'

'I hope not, but … Like I said – whatever DCI Khan thinks, I do understand that race matters to a lot of people and it's possible that having a black woman appealing for the return of a white baby might not produce the response we're hoping for.'

'What's all that about DCI Khan?' Eddie asked, coming in, carrying Ricky in his arms. 'I saw the way you looked at him, Dad. Is there something wrong about him?'

'No – not at all,' Peter said hastily, wanting to avoid any suggestion that he lacked faith in the investigating team.

'Pop Ricky in his high chair,' Crystal said, sensing Peter's reluctance to expand on his opinion of Khan. 'His porridge is ready; it just needs to cool down a little.'

She turned to address her son, trying to speak normally, as if her world had not just been turned upside down and some of the pieces allowed to drop out.

'I'll give you some juice in your cup and then Daddy will help you with your porridge.'

Eddie lifted his son into the high chair and fastened the straps to prevent him climbing out. Then he turned to face Peter.

'Come on Dad,' he urged insistently. 'There's nothing wrong with him, but …?'

'OK, Ed,' Peter sighed. 'I can see you're not going to let this drop, are you? Look – it was a long time ago and I'm probably being totally unfair to the man.'

'But?' prompted Eddie again.

'He came round after your mum died. He was only young and he was so sure of himself …'

'He told your dad he was acting as if

he thought you and Hannah and your mum were white,' Bernie said forthrightly, coming in at that moment and sizing up the situation in an instant. 'He accused him of not believing that you'd ever experienced racial bullying at school and he told him he ought to have encouraged Angie to mix more with other West Indians.'

'But that's ridiculous!' Eddie exclaimed, looking towards his father for confirmation of this description of what had happened. 'He should've asked *me*, if he wanted to know about all that. It was completely the opposite way round. I never told Dad about the boys picking on me at school because I knew he'd go off the deep end about it and cause a scene. Who does this DCI Khan think he is, coming along and criticising-'

'Shut it, Eddie!' Peter's voice was

unusually sharp. 'I told you – it was a long time ago.'

'I'm sorry,' Bernie said, putting down the empty plastic cup that she had brought back from Jonah's room to be washed up. 'I shouldn't have said all that. As your Dad says, DCI Khan has probably changed his ideas a lot since then.'

'I've been looking up his record,' Jonah added, having followed her into the room while everyone's attention was directed towards Eddie's outburst. 'He's been very successful dealing with disaffected Asian youths; and he's got a growing reputation in more serious criminal cases.'

'There you are,' Peter said to Eddie, giving him a look that indicated that there was to be no further discussion. 'So just try to forget what Bernie and I said about him and give him the co-operation that he needs to help Jonah find Abigail.'

'Right! Now, let's cut the cackle and get a move on,' Jonah said briskly, positioning his chair at the end of the table and looking expectantly towards Peter. 'Toast and marmalade, please – and another cup of tea.'

***

'She looks a better colour this morning,' Michelle observed as she looked down into Rachel's cot.

'Oh yes – your little one's a lot better than she was,' agreed the nurse who had shown them into the ward. 'If she takes her next feed OK, I think we'll be taking out the drip.' She turned to Georgia. 'It says on the notes that you fed her during the night. How did that go?'

'Not bad. I mean, she didn't take as much as usual, but she didn't sick any of it up, the way she'd been doing yesterday.'

'There you are then! Just wait and see what the doctor says when she comes round later and I wouldn't be surprised if you're taking her home by lunchtime.'

'Do you really think so?' Georgia asked eagerly.

'Is it definite then?' Nathan added, before the nurse could reply. 'It's not bacterial meningitis?'

'That's what it says on the notes here – viral meningitis. And it looks as if she's fighting it – no problem!'

Rachel stirred, opened her eyes and then started to cry. Georgia reached into the cot and picked her up.

'Are you hungry then?' she asked, settling down on a chair at the side of the cot and cradling Rachel on her knee, taking care not to get tangled up in the trailing intravenous line. 'Let's see what Mummy can do about that, shall we?'

'I'd better be getting off to work,' Leslie said, seeing Georgia starting to unbutton her blouse. 'What about you, Mickie?'

'I'll give them a ring later and tell them I won't be in today.' Michelle had at last decided that staying with her daughter at such a time did not constitute being an overbearing mother – or perhaps she had decided that she did not care anymore if it did. 'There's nothing going on that someone else in the office can't handle.'

'Thanks Mum,' Georgia looked up briefly, before turning her full attention back to Rachel.

'Yes, thanks,' Nathan added. 'We really do appreciate you being here.' He looked at his watch. 'I'm sorry, Georgie, I'm going to have to go too. I'm due in court again this morning and you know what the trains are like.'

'That's fine. You go ahead. We'll be fine.'

'Right!' Nathan hesitated, feeling relieved, but at the same time slightly put out that his wife's attention seemed to be so much focussed on their daughter that his presence was of no consequence to her. 'I'll be off then.'

He leaned forward and gave Georgia a quick kiss on the top of her head, which was bent forward over her suckling baby. Then he backed away, keeping them both in sight as long as possible.

'Bye-bye, Rachel. Daddy will be back at tea-time.'

Leslie led the way out of the ward, holding the door for Nathan, who gave one final look back before finally turning to go.

'They'll be fine,' Leslie assured his son-in-law. 'And all the better for having us men keeping out of the way for a bit.'

***

In their house in Headington, Sam Mason was also getting ready to go to work. Flick was still in bed. She had declared her intention of having a lie-in after her restless night. Sam was not sure whether to be pleased or anxious about this development. On the positive side, she had not been up at six preparing a feed for the "Mia" doll that had been dominating her life for the last few weeks. Against that, her lassitude reminded him horribly of the days immediately following the real Mia's death – before she got hold of that doll, which had become so hateful to him. He hoped fervently that Flick was not reverting to the state that she had been in then.

As he chomped silently on his toast, he remembered those dark days. Flick appeared to have lost all interest in life. Sam would return from school in the evening to find her still in bed, or at best wandering aimlessly round the house in dressing gown and slippers. Friends would ring him to say that they had called round, but could get no answer when they rang the doorbell. Was Flick away? Did he need any help with the housework in her absence?

Some help with the housework would

certainly not have gone amiss, but Sam did not want anyone else coming in and seeing Flick's condition. This was something that they needed to deal with themselves. He valiantly strove to keep some sort of order, as well as keeping on top of his own work and, above all, trying to persuade Flick to start looking after herself again. He had seriously wondered if she would starve herself to death, and suggested tentatively to her that she should seek the help of a counsellor.

Then, overnight, things had changed, when some friend from school gave Flick that surrogate baby doll. Flick started to care for the doll in the same way that she had cared for the real Mia. At last, she had a purpose to her life again. Had he been wrong to persuade her to give it up? Was she right when she said that it was helping her to come to terms with her grief and start believing in herself again? Should he have allowed her to continue until she gradually lost the need to pretend that she still had a baby to care for, instead of snatching it away from her so suddenly?

Sam sighed. It was time to go. The M40 was always busy at this time in the morning. However, he was reluctant to leave Flick alone, now that her low mood had returned. He got out a tray and put it on the table. He added a bowl into which he poured cereal and then milk. There was enough coffee in the jug to pour a mug for Flick, so he did so and added it to the tray. He hesitated in the hall, on his way upstairs.

Then he put down the tray and went into the living room, where they had left the doll the previous evening, after Flick had promised that she would arrange for it to be given away. He picked it up and put it under his arm, so that he could carry the tray as well. Outside the bedroom, he put down the tray and the doll on the floor, so that he could open the door.

'I've brought you breakfast,' he said cheerfully as he entered with the tray.

'Oh Sam! That's very sweet of you, but there was no need,' Flick protested. 'I could easily have got it later when I came down. I'm not an invalid, you know.'

'Yes. I know, but the coffee was in the jug and it seemed a pity to waste it. And then I thought I might as well bring up some cereal as well.' Sam put the tray down on the low table beside the bed, where Flick could reach it without getting out. 'I'll have to go now.'

He hesitated, unsure of his next move. Flick looked calmer than she had been in those nightmare days following Mia's death, but she had made no move to try the food. She looked up at him and smiled.

'Bye then,' she said, almost as if she were pleased that he was going. She lay back on the pillow and pulled the bedclothes round her. She was clearly not planning to eat the cereal.

Sam stood there for a moment or two longer, still hesitating. Then he slipped out of the room and came back with the doll. He propped it up on the pillow next to Flick.

'I thought you might like to have some company, while I'm out.'

***

'Jess! Marcus! Come along! You'll be late!' Anna shouted up the stairs as she buttoned up her jacket, ready to set off for work.

'When can we expect you home?' Philip put his head round the kitchen door and called to her. 'I suppose you'll be out until all hours again.'

'I'm sorry, Phil. I just don't know. It's a missing child, remember? Think how *we*'d feel if it was our baby.'

'Which reminds me,' Phil added, coming out into the hall and speaking in a lower voice. 'Have you made your mind up about that yet? It'll only be worse the longer you leave it, you know.'

***

Debra peered bleary-eyed across her bowl of breakfast cereal at the television. It had been a long, tiring day yesterday and then she had not slept well. She felt exhausted and was very tempted to go back to bed for a few hours. This must be what it was like all the time for mothers with young children, she supposed. But perhaps, after a while, you got used to it.

She tried to concentrate on the news report in front of her. They seemed to be inside a church. The camera zoomed in on an array of small squat candles on a tiled floor.

'The church where the missing baby's parents worship each Sunday held a candle-lit vigil last night to pray for her safe return,' the commentator said. That was odd. John had never gone to church when he lived with her – and she had never been aware of Victoria doing so either.

The picture switched to show a woman in a clerical collar, who said a few sentences about how well-liked the child's family were and how many people from the local area had felt moved to attend the vigil.

Debra raised her mug of coffee to her lips, obscuring her view for a moment. When she looked again, the scene was of the railings outside the playground from which the baby had been taken. She recognised the row of trees and the swings and slide behind them. Tied to the railings, or propped up in front of them, was an array of bunches of flowers and soft toys. The camera panned along the line, allowing her to glimpse some of the words on the cards attached to the gifts: 'thinking of you', 'praying for your baby's safe return', 'from a mother to a mother', 'words can't express how we feel'.

Debra got up and switched off the television set. She carried the bowl and mug out into the kitchen and put them in the sink. Yes. She would go back upstairs and have a few more hours sleep. She needed it after yesterday.

11 WHAT CHILD IS THIS?

'When morning gilds the ski-ies,' the Reverend Alan Chambers sang softly to himself as he opened the gate to the churchyard on the way to say Morning Prayer in his small church in Headington. 'The heart awaking cries,' he continued, closing the gate carefully behind him.

It was a beautiful morning with clear blue sky and the sun slanting in through the trees and casting shadows amongst the graves. The dawn chorus was past its peak as the birds set about their business of searching for food for their growing broods.

'Alike at work and prayer,' Alan hummed, pausing to pull up a dandelion that had somehow escaped the eagle eye of the team of volunteer gardeners who had spent the previous Saturday weeding, in anticipation of a wedding scheduled for the following week. 'To Jesus I repair; May Jesus Christ be praised.'

He became aware of a new sound – discordant, shattering the peace of his little Eden. What was it? A cat? It sounded as if it were coming from inside the church. Had a cat got inside when his wife went in to arrange the flowers yesterday and been shut in all night? He listened again; it didn't sound quite like a cat.

JUDY FORD

The noise grew louder as he approached the porch that led to the south door. It was most definitely not a cat – it was a baby crying. Alan quickened his stride, hastening to find out what was going on. Two low steps up to the porch and now he was gazing in, waiting for his eyes to adjust to the relative darkness.

In the far corner, close to the heavy oak door that led into the church, there was a cardboard box lying on the floor. Its contents looked like a collection of old clothes, but they were moving and that was where the sound was coming from. He stepped quickly inside and knelt down by the box. Sure enough, it contained a baby – a baby with a red face, screwed up and howling.

Summoning the experience of forty years of administering infant baptism –

not to mention having played a role in the upbringing of four children and thirteen grandchildren – Alan reached into the box and picked up the child. He held it close to him and rocked it to and fro.

'What are you doing here then?' he asked rhetorically, peering into the box to see if there was a note to explain the baby's unexpected presence. He could not see one, but it was difficult to be sure without putting down the baby and making a thorough search of the blankets.

He got to his feet and started to walk about in the porch, rocking the baby and patting it gently on the back to try to calm it. It was probably hungry. Or cold: the sun had not yet got round to the porch and the thick stone walls made it cool in there, even on warm summer days like this one. At last, the crying diminished and finally the baby's head lolled against his neck and he knew that it was asleep – probably exhausted after all that crying.

'Morning vicar!'

Alan turned to see the cheerful face of Muriel Combes, one of his most faithful parishioners, who often joined him in the church for his daily devotions.

'Good morning, Mrs Combes.'

'And what have we here?' she asked, looking at the baby in his arms. 'A new little addition to the family?'

'Er … no. I found him – her – it – here when I got here this morning.'

'Abandoned, you mean?'

'So it would seem.'

'Is there a note?' Mrs Combes put out her walking stick and poked around in the box of blankets.

'I couldn't see one. I was thinking, perhaps I'd better take it back to the vicarage where it's warmer. And then we'd better contact the police. Yes,' Alan said decisively, bending down and wrapping the baby up in its blankets once more and then picking it up, box and all. 'Mrs Combes, will you stay here and let anyone else who comes for Morning Prayer know that it's cancelled today? I'm taking this little one back to the vicarage to warm it up and give it something to eat and let the police know about it.'

'And if the mother comes back for it?'

'Send her up to the vicarage. In fact – better come with her to see she finds us OK.'

'What are we all doing out here then? Forgotten your key, vicar?'

Turning to go, Alan nearly collided

with another member of his congregation. Graham Harris was a retired don, who often incorporated attendance at Morning Prayer into his regular after-breakfast constitutional.

'No. Morning Prayer's off, I'm afraid. Someone left this little stranger in the porch and I need to take it back to the vicarage to give it some TLC and inform the police.'

'There was a baby reported missing on the radio yesterday,' Graham said, looking down at the infant with interest. 'Do you think this could be the one?'

'Yes, of course!' Muriel agreed. 'I'd quite forgotten about that. I saw it on the TV – such a pretty little girl, with a little tuft of red hair all tied up in a ribbon on the top of her head.'

'This one doesn't have enough hair to tie up in a ribbon,' Alan said doubtfully.

310

'It could have been cut off,' Graham pointed out, 'to avoid discovery.'

'What colour *is* the hair?' Muriel asked, peering into the box. 'It's difficult to tell in this light.'

'It *could* be red,' Graham opined, 'or it might be blond. As you say, it's difficult to tell.'

'Yes. You're probably right,' Alan agreed, repositioning the box in his arms. It felt surprisingly heavy and he was keen to set off on the walk back to the vicarage without further delay. 'Now, I really must get her – if it is a *her* – into the warm.'

'You're back early,' Marion called to her husband, when she heard his key in the vicarage door. She looked over the bannisters, from where she had been cleaning the landing, to see him coming in, struggling to close the door behind him, while still carrying the heavy cardboard box. 'Did you forget something?'

'No. I found something. You'd better come down and have a look.'

Marion stuffed her duster into the pocket of her apron and hurried downstairs.

'It's a baby!' she said, looking into the box, which Alan had put down on the hall table. 'What a little sweetie! Do you think this is the little girl that was snatched from her pram in the park yesterday afternoon?'

'Well, that would make sense,' her husband agreed, 'but we don't even know that it's a girl yet.'

'We'd better find out then.' Marion picked the baby up out of the box and cradled it in her arms. The movement woke the child and it started to cry again. 'Poor little mite. I expect she needs changing anyway. I'll take her up and get her sorted out. Carla left some disposable nappies last time they came to stay. Can you get the carrycot out of the loft for me? We can't have a lovely little baby like you sleeping in a cardboard box, can we, darling?'

'She's a girl alright,' Marion told Alan a few minutes later, when he brought her the carrycot that his own children had all used nearly forty years previously. 'Now, while I try to settle her, could you get rid of this,' she handed him a disposable nappy wrapped in a plastic carrier bag, 'and then pop round to Laura's and ask if she can give us some formula milk –

just enough to give her a feed while we're waiting for the police. I'm sure she's hungry, poor little mite.'

'Hadn't we better ring the police first?' Alan asked. 'To get the ball rolling? And I'm not sure about feeding her. What about allergies?'

'Yes. You're right. Throw the nappy away, then ring the police, and *then* ask Laura for the milk. And if you're worried, you could ask the police if the baby that's gone missing had any allergies.'

'It could be a different baby.'

'If she is, then *nobody* knows what allergies she might have, but we can't starve her forever on the off-chance, can we?'

***

'This must be the place,' Sergeant Tracy Burton said as they slowed down outside the vicarage. 'Turn in there,' she added to Constable Appleton, who was driving. 'It looks like a car park for the church.'

They locked the car and skirted round the wall of the churchyard to the wrought iron gate that separated the car park from the grounds of the vicarage. To their surprise, their way was blocked by a sizeable cluster of onlookers who were standing around the gate or sitting perched atop the Cotswold-stone wall. At the sight of their uniforms, the crowd parted and they passed through, like Moses crossing the Red Sea.

'Are you here to see the baby that was found in the graveyard?' a young man called out as they passed.

'Is it the baby that was stolen from the park yesterday?' a woman asked eagerly.

'Have you told the parents yet?'

'Do you know who did it?'

'Has anyone been arrested?'

Tracy and Malcolm said nothing until they had passed through the gate and closed it behind them. Then they turned to face the crowd and Malcolm held up his hand for silence.

'We can't answer any of your questions at present,' Tracy told them. 'The vicar has reported an incident and we are here at his request. There is nothing for you to see here and it would be much better if you would all go home.'

'Can you confirm that they've found a baby?' someone called out from the back of the crowd.

'I can't confirm anything until we've had a chance to see what's going on.' Tracy replied coolly. 'If there's anything to tell, there will be a proper press conference in due course. Now, please – just go home.'

When they reached the front door, it was opened immediately by a grey-haired man wearing a clerical collar, who introduced himself as Alan Chambers, vicar of St Anselm's.

'Come in, come in,' he urged. 'I'm sorry about that lot out there. I've asked them to go away, but they won't take any notice. Word seems to have got out somehow and everyone's putting two and two together and coming to the conclusion that we've found the missing baby.'

He led the way down a rather dark passageway to a room at the back of the house.

'She's in here,' he said, opening the door and standing back to allow Tracy and Malcolm to enter. 'My wife's been trying to feed her, but with limited success I fear.'

'The poor little mite's probably missing her mother,' a woman greeted them, as they entered a large room that looked out over the extensive back garden. She looked up at them from the depths of a high-backed easy chair, one of several in the room, each a different size and shape, and each with its own unique floral print cover. Tracy idly wondered why, when they had gone to the trouble of buying loose covers for their furniture, they had not had a matching set made.

'I'm Marion,' the woman went on, looking down at the baby in her arms. 'Excuse me for not getting up, but I think she's just dropping off at last and I don't want to disturb her. She's taken about two ounces,' she added, looking towards her husband. 'So I'm hoping that will be enough to settle her down so she can sleep and then, when she isn't tired out with crying, poor little dear, maybe she'll be able to take some more.'

Tracy walked gingerly across the room and looked down at the baby. Her eyes were closed, but her face looked screwed up and tense. Then, as Tracy watched, the muscles seemed to relax; the baby's mouth dropped slightly open and her breathing slowed down. Marion smiled.

'There you are,' she whispered. 'She's off now. Just give her a minute or two and we can try putting her down in the carrycot.'

'Tell you what,' Alan said, speaking in a low voice so as not to disturb the baby. 'Why don't I take you both into the kitchen and get you a cup of tea? Then we can talk while Marion gets her settled.'

Tracy nodded acquiescence and they all slipped quietly out of the door and across the passageway into another large room. In the centre stood a heavy oak table, which Tracy thought had probably come with the house. Indeed, it was so bulky that it was difficult to see how it could have got there except by being built in-situ. It was surrounded by wooden chairs – of several different designs – painted in a range of pastel colours. The rest of the kitchen was more modern in appearance, although the fitted units and gas cooker both looked as if they had outlived their prime.

'Please take a seat,' Alan said,

waving in the direction of the table. 'I'll just put the kettle on, and then I expect you'll want me to tell you all about finding the child.'

He filled an electric kettle from the sink and set it back in its place on the working surface. Then he opened a wall cupboard and took out a teapot and four bone china mugs.

'I was on my way to say Morning Prayer,' he told them, as he spooned loose tea from a tea-caddy, the outside of which was decorated with a picture of a sandcastle and the message *a present from Margate*. 'So it must have been about quarter to nine or maybe a touch later.'

The kettle boiled and he poured water into the teapot.

'I saw her the moment I entered the porch, because she was crying –

screaming more like, in fact. Anyway,' he got a milk jug out of the fridge and poured some into each of the mugs, 'I picked her up and managed to quieten her down a bit and then a couple of my parishioners turned up for the service. So I left them to wait there and turn away anyone else who came, while I headed off back here. Then I rang the police and, well, here we all are.'

'And the reception committee, outside?' Tracy asked 'Where did they come from?'

'I don't know. They just turned up, wanting to know whether the baby was the same one that had gone missing yesterday. One of them said something about it being on Twitter. I can't think who was responsible for that. I'm sure Mrs Combes and Dr Harris wouldn't even know how to – but I suppose they may have told other people. Or maybe it was Laura. She's our next-door neighbour. She's got a little boy – about seven months. Marion borrowed some baby milk from her. Come to think of it, she did say something about how she'd seen a photo of the missing baby on Facebook. So, I wouldn't be surprised … Sorry. I'm rambling, aren't I?' He broke off, suddenly embarrassed at his long-winded explanation that did not really explain anything.

'Never mind,' Tracy smiled. 'Presumably you checked that there was no note with the baby? Or anything else to tell you who she was or who had left her there?'

'No – I mean yes, we did check, but there was nothing. I've got the box here that she was in.'

He got up and went back into the hall,

returning shortly with an empty cardboard box. Tracy looked it over, turning it round to view it from every side. There was nothing on it to indicate where it had come from.

'She seems to have settled now.' Marion came in and closed the door behind her. She sat down opposite Tracy and looked across at her eagerly. 'What now?'

'We'll contact Social Services to arrange for someone to look after the baby until her mother can be found. But, before that, please could you have a look at this picture of the baby that was snatched yesterday and tell me if you think this could be the same one?'

Tracy took out a copy of the photograph that Jonah had circulated, and put it down on the table in front of them. Alan and Marion bent forward to look at it.

'I don't know,' Marion said, after a long pause. 'The face is about the same shape, I suppose, but the thing that really jumps out at you in this photo is the hair. It's so unusual for a baby of that age to have any to speak of.'

'How old would you say the baby you found is?' Tracy asked.

'Quite young, but not newborn. At least a month, I'd say. Probably more like six or eight weeks.'

'Which would be about right,' Malcolm murmured.

'Yes,' Tracy agreed. 'And it also makes it less likely that it's a case of a young mother abandoning her baby. It's not that uncommon for teenage girls who have a baby by mistake to try to pretend it never happened, by leaving it somewhere, but that's usually soon after the birth. Do you think we could have a look at her?' she added, looking at Marion. 'To compare her with this photo? It's quite important that we know ... before we tell the mother of the missing baby.'

'Yes, of course.' Marion nodded, getting to her feet. 'Just try not to wake her. I'm sure she's tired out with crying and that's what made her so difficult to feed.'

They all trouped back into the living room, walking as quietly as they could. They stood in silence round the carrycot staring down intently at the sleeping infant. Tracy placed the photograph on a chair close by. They each looked at the child's face and then at the photograph and then back again.

'It could be her,' Tracy said softly. 'What do you think, constable?'

'All babies look the same to me, I'm afraid,' Malcolm confessed.

'And we haven't had a chance to see her properly,' Marion commented. 'She's either been screaming or asleep. So I don't know what colour her eyes are, for example.'

'I agree,' Alan concurred. 'I really can't say one way or the other.'

They returned to the kitchen and drank their tea while Tracy made phone calls.

'Social Services say they're a bit stretched but they'll try to get someone out before the end of the morning,' she told Alan and Marion.

'There's no rush,' Marion assured her quickly. 'We're happy to look after her for as long as it takes.'

'Thank you, but we need to get her checked over by a doctor and into proper temporary care while we look for her mother.'

'We've both been DBS-checked,' Marion assured her, 'and I used to be an Early Years teacher – not to mention bringing up four children.'

'It's not that we don't trust you to look after her. We just need to stick to the rules and, after all, we don't know if she has any medical conditions that might need treating. Sometimes parents abandon babies because they don't think they're going to be able to cope – if they have Down Syndrome, for example. Of course, in this case, we hope that we know who the parents are already and we'll be able to reunite them quickly, but we don't want to tell them that we may have found their baby until we're more certain. I've notified the officer in charge of the case and he will decide what to do about that.'

***

The officer in charge was in his office, scrolling through a summary of the evidence so far, on his computer screen, and pondering on how to prioritise the operation. He glanced sharply across at Bernie when Tracy told him that an abandoned baby had been found in a location close to where Abigail had gone missing. It was hard to imagine that this could be a coincidence.

'We need to move fast,' Tracy told him. 'There's already quite a crowd of people locally who are putting two and two together, so it can't be long before it's all over the media.'

'OK. Leave it with me.'

Jonah ended the call and looked at

Bernie again.

'Do you think it *is* Abigail?' she asked hopefully.

'Too early to tell. Tracy said she wasn't sure from the photo, so we need a better way of identifying her, before we tell Eddie and Crystal that we may have found her.'

'I could identify her,' Bernie suggested. 'Come to that, you probably could too. At least *we*'ve both seen her in the flesh, so to speak, and not just in a photo. Why not ring Tracy back and tell her we're coming over there?'

'There's been a change of plan,' Tracy told Jonah a few minutes later. 'We've decided to take the baby to the hospital for a check-up now, instead of waiting for Social Services. The crowd outside is getting restive and we've just had someone sneaking round the back and trying to take a picture through the window. This vicarage isn't designed to withhold a siege.'

'Right! We'll meet you there. I want to get a look at the baby before news leaks out to the parents. We don't want to get their hopes up if it's a different child altogether.'

He ended the call and then, with characteristic energy, headed for the door. Soon they were in the car park preparing to leave for the hospital. As Bernie was strapping him into the back of the car, Jonah's phone rang. It was Eddie.

'Why didn't you tell me?' he demanded angrily. 'It's all over everywhere that Abigail's been found in some graveyard or other, quite close to where she went missing. Why weren't we informed? Where is she? When-'

'I'm sorry, Eddie,' Jonah interrupted, trying to speak calmly despite rising irritation, partly with Eddie but more with the irresponsibility of those people who had broadcast their opinions on social media in advance of any statement from the police. 'I've only just heard about it myself. Bernie and I are on our way over to the hospital to-'

'What do you mean *the hospital*?' Eddie wanted to know. 'What's happened? What's wrong with her?'

'It's just a routine check-up. Something that has to be done whenever an abandoned baby is found. So, as I was saying-'

'But why didn't you tell us right away?' Eddie persisted. 'Are you keeping something from us? How come-'

'Eddie!' Bernie cut in. 'Please, just stop talking and give Jonah a chance to explain.'

There was a pause.

'Sorry,' Eddie said meekly. 'Go ahead.'

'The reason we didn't tell you – apart from having only just heard ourselves, as I said – is that we don't know yet that it really *is* Abigail. For all we know, it may be a completely different baby girl.'

'What are the chances of that?' Eddie asked, forgetting that he had promised not to interrupt.

'Non-zero,' Bernie said curtly. 'Which is why we wanted to make sure before telling you and Crystal.'

'We didn't want to raise your hopes, if it was only a false alarm,' Jonah elaborated. 'The officers who attended the scene weren't able to confirm identity from the photograph, so Bernie and I are on our way to see for ourselves. If it *is* Abigail then, of course, you and Crystal will be the first to know.'

'We want to come with you,' Eddie said. 'Now that we know about it, there's no point you seeing her first, is there?'

'No. I suppose not. Alright then – we'll call and pick you up on the way. Can you be ready to go in ten minutes? And in the meantime – don't speak about it to anyone, OK?'

'I don't think Eddie trusts me,' Jonah observed to Bernie as they drove round the ring road to collect Abigail's parents.

'Not so much *doesn't trust you* as *doesn't understand police procedure*,' Bernie replied. 'From his point of view, it's obvious that he should have been told the moment any possible lead comes up. He's frustrated that you can't keep him updated on every twist and turn of the investigation as it unfolds.'

'And it doesn't help when the world and his wife decide to chatter about every little thing on social media,' Jonah agreed. 'It's a disgrace that they found out about it sooner than we did.'

'Which I suppose is why he has a point when he says that we should have told him. In any case,' Bernie continued in a musing voice, 'you could say that we were being paternalistic in wanting to shield them from disappointment by not telling them anything until we were sure it was Abigail.'

Eddie and Crystal were waiting for them on the drive when they reached the house. Peter was on the front lawn, playing a chasing game with Ricky. They had agreed that he would stay at home with the toddler, who might become fractious if the identification process and any subsequent paperwork took a long time. Eddie went to the front passenger door, but Bernie signalled to them to get in the back.

'It's better if you're not visible when we arrive at the hospital,' Jonah explained. 'Any waiting journalists will start jumping to conclusions if they see the parents of the missing child apparently on their way to be reunited with their offspring. And I can't emphasise enough – *it may not be Abigail.*'

Eddie nodded and went round to the back of the car. Crystal followed him. As she took her seat opposite Jonah, he noticed that her eyes looked red, but her expression was more hopeful than it had been at breakfast that morning. He smiled at her, but could not think of anything to say that would not either raise possibly false hopes or sound patronising. Peter held Ricky up so that he could wave good-bye to his parents. Bernie put the engine into gear and they were off.

As Jonah had feared, a group of onlookers was clustered around the hospital entrance. However, also waiting for them were Tracy Burton and Malcolm Appleton. They ushered them in and soon they were entering a small room with one of the familiar transparent plastic hospital cots in the centre. Crystal and Eddie raced over to it and looked down in eager anticipation. Then their faces changed abruptly as they realised that this baby was not Abigail.

Crystal looked towards Jonah and shook her head, tears welling up in her eyes. Eddie gazed round the room with an expression of disbelief on his face. Bernie hurried over to see for herself. No, this was not Abigail. The sparse fuzz of pale auburn baby hair on her head was quite different from Abigail's thick red thatch. There was something different about her nose too, although Bernie could not quite put her finger on what it was. This baby answered Abigail's description, but she was not Abigail.

They all looked at one another. If not Abigail – who, then, was she?

12 SEEKING THE LOST

'Hi! Lucy! Wasn't that your stepdad on the news last night?' Lucy groaned inwardly, as she entered her form room and was immediately accosted by a cluster of girls, all eager for a part in the dramatic news story that they had seen unfolding the previous evening on their television screens.

'Yes,' she admitted.

'Go on!' urged Anthea Williams, a genial extrovert, who liked to share in any drama. 'Tell us all about it. Have they found the baby yet?'

'No,' Lucy replied shortly.

'It must be awful for her mum and dad,' said Leanne Mortlake earnestly. She was very serious-minded and prided herself on her ability to empathise with other people's problems.

'Yes. It is,' Lucy agreed. She walked to her locker and pretended to be very busy sorting out her books for her first lesson.

'What are the police doing? Have they got any leads?' Anthea persisted, following her across the room. 'Come on, Lucy! You must know.'

'What relation is the baby to you?' asked Paula Jones, one of Anthea's close friends and equally keen to share in any limelight that might be available. 'If your stepdad is her grandad, then you must be her …?' She broke off, unsure how to work out this strange family tree.

'I suppose Abigail must be my step-niece,' Lucy said. 'I'd never really thought about it before, but her father's my step-brother, so ....'

'What do *you* think's happened?' Anthea asked, still convinced that Lucy knew more than she was telling. 'You must have some idea.'

'I saw the police out combing the area with dogs,' volunteered Patsy Collingwood, whose house overlooked the recreation ground. 'And two police officers came round asking us if we'd seen anything.'

'And had you?' Anthea asked with interest. Lucy took the opportunity to walk away from the group. This was clearly going to be a difficult day. She settled down on a chair and pretended to be engrossed in studying her Biology textbook.

'No.' Patsy sounded regretful. 'It all happened before any of us got home. But one of Mum's friends from up the road said she saw a woman pushing a pram coming away from the park, round about when it must have happened,' she added, brightening up.

Lucy pricked up her ears at this revelation, but said nothing and kept her eyes down.

'Did she tell the police?' Paula asked. 'What did they say?'

'She told Mum that they wrote it all down and asked her if she could remember what the woman looked like.' Patsy was enjoying being the centre of attention. She racked her brains to think of anything more that she could add. 'Mum says, when babies are taken it's usually by some woman who's a bit unhinged because she's had a miscarriage or something.'

'My Dad said that a few years ago there was a case where a family made out that their baby had been stolen, when in actual fact they'd killed it and buried the body in the back garden,' Anthea told them. She was not at all pleased at the way Patsy had grabbed the interest of the group, and was intent on establishing that she too had expertise to contribute on the subject of missing children.

'Sshh!' Leanne hissed, looking across at Lucy, who was apparently still absorbed in her book. 'That's a horrible thing to say.'

'I heard about that one too,' Paula whispered. They all drew closer together so that they could speak without being overheard. 'From what I remember, it was an accident, but the parents were afraid Social Services would take their other kids away from them if they found out, and that's why they pretended the baby had been stolen.'

'Do you think-?' Patsy broke off as their form tutor entered the room and called for silence. Lucy put away her book and sat with her eyes front, carefully avoiding eye contact with any of her peers. Yes, this was going to be a long day.

***

'Right!' Jonah addressed his team. 'We now have a baby with missing parents as well as parents whose baby has been taken. It may be just a coincidence that both events happened within a mile of one another, but it's hard not to suspect that there may be some sort of link. However, that could be as tenuous as a mother who wanted to get rid of her baby – for whatever reason – hearing the news reports and being drawn to the scene of the crime. Maybe she thought, if she left her baby there, the parents of the missing one would take it in. The playground is still cordoned off, so the church may have been the nearest place she could find.'

He looked round the room, pondering on how to divide the work that needed to be done amongst the officers available.

'Alice,' he said at last, addressing a bright young Detective Constable who had only recently joined the team. 'I want you to do the rounds of the local GPs and community midwives and get the names and addresses of every woman who has had a baby between one and three months ago. We think that both babies are about six weeks old, but that may not be right. If this second one was born premature, for example, she may be older than she appears.'

'Yes, sir.' Alice got up to go. 'Are we looking for anything in particular?'

'The list is the main thing,' Jonah told her. 'But if anyone volunteers any information that would suggest that a mother may have had trouble bonding with her baby, make a note of it. As far as the GPs and midwives are concerned, we're trying to track down the mother of the abandoned baby. I hope they'll co-operate, but they may be reluctant to tell us about their patients' state of mind for fear of breaking confidentiality.'

'But *why* would a mother want to get rid of her baby?' Alice asked.

'I can see you've never had one,' Jonah smiled. 'If you'd been deprived of your sleep for a fortnight by a baby with colic, you'd understand why most parents have times when they wish they *could* get rid of their little darlings! It's just that most people manage to get through it without resorting to putting them in a cardboard box and leaving them in a church porch.'

'Or the baby could have something wrong with it,' Monica Philipson suggested from the back of the room. 'A friend of mine adopted a baby with cerebral palsy, who had been rejected by his mother because she couldn't cope with his disability.'

'Yes,' Jonah agreed, glancing across at Anna and noting with relief that she seemed calm. He had already decided to keep her focussed on the search for

Abigail, rather than allowing her to dwell on the subject of parents who did not want their babies. 'We don't have any reason at this stage to believe that the baby that the vicar found has anything wrong with her, but she's being given a thorough health check and I've asked the hospital to let us know if anything turns up. The other thing I want you to note down,' he went on, turning back to Alice, 'is if any of the babies have died. Remember – although you are ostensibly looking for the mother of an abandoned baby, this also gives us a chance to find out about potential child abductors.'

'Is the mother of the abandoned baby necessarily going to be local?' Andy asked tentatively. 'I mean, if you're right and she chose to leave it in Headington because she'd heard about the abduction, she could be from … well, anywhere!'

'Yes. You're right,' Jonah agreed, 'which is why we are also going to put out an appeal nationally for the mother to come forward. We need to get on with that, before people get it fixed in their minds that we've found the missing baby and they don't need to be looking for her anymore.' He sighed. 'This case just got a whole lot harder, as far as getting the public engaged is concerned. Now we're going to have *two* photographs circulating of *two* different babies, and we're asking people to tell us if they've seen one of them and to tell us if they know who the mother is of the other. Add to that the fact that lots of people can't tell one baby from another at the best of times and the chances of getting any useful information are practically nil!'

***

'According to my list,' Rupert Andrews said, as he and Khan emerged from the lift on the fourth floor of the block of flats, 'the first flat is occupied by Morgan and Shona Knight. He's a self-employed electrician and she works part time in a bar in the evenings. They've got two children, both below school age.'

'And his mother is supposed to have met Crystal Johns in the lift yesterday afternoon, when she was on her way out to the playground,' Khan commented. He had a good memory and, having meticulously studied the statements that Jonah and his colleagues had collected, he recognised the name. 'She talked as if she knew them quite well.'

'Let's hope so,' Andrews murmured.

'So far, most of the neighbours seem to hardly even have noticed they were there! There isn't exactly what you might call *community spirit*, is there?'

He rang the bell and they stood in the corridor waiting. There was a scuffling noise inside the flat and the sound of a child's voice. Then they heard the lock being turned and the door opened a crack to reveal a woman in her thirties, dressed in jeans and a tee-shirt, holding a toddler on her hip. A small boy peeped out from behind her legs. She looked at them with a questioning expression.

'Yes?' she asked in a puzzled tone. Arshad stepped forward, holding up his warrant card.

'I'm Detective Chief Inspector Khan,' he told her, 'and this is my colleague, DI Andrews. We're making enquiries in relation to the abduction of a baby from the children's playground at the Margaret Road recreation ground yesterday afternoon.'

'You'd better come in.' Shona Knight made way for them to enter the flat and then closed the door behind them. She led the way along a passageway, past several doors on either side and into a large, light living room. A Formica-topped drop-leaf table stood against one wall, folded down to make room for a small, gaily-coloured plastic slide. At the other end of the room, near to the glass door that led out on to a balcony, there was a three-piece suite, upholstered in a brown tartan fabric. Both the furniture and the floor were liberally strewn with an assortment of soft toys and other playthings.

'Sorry about the mess,' Shona apologised, putting down her daughter and gathering up toys to clear a space on the sofa for the police officers to sit down. 'I haven't liked to take the kids out today – with a baby-snatcher out there, I mean.'

They picked their way carefully across the carpet, trying not to step on any of the toy cars and wooden building blocks that lay about at random. Shona sat down on an easy chair and took her young daughter on her lap. The little boy stood watching for a moment or two and then got down on the floor next to her chair and started pushing round one of the toy cars. Shona looked expectantly towards Khan.

'As you are obviously aware,' he began, 'a baby was taken from a buggy yesterday afternoon. Did you also know that the family lived in this block of flats?'

'Oh yes! We know them. They haven't been here long, but their little boy is about the same age as Kayleigh.' She looked down at the toddler on her lap. 'I introduced her to the Mums & Tots group.'

'So you know Mrs Johns. Do you know her husband too?'

'I've met him a few times – especially round about when the baby was born. He used to take the little boy, Ricky, out to give Crystal a bit of peace and quiet.'

'I see. And would you say he had a good relationship with his son?'

'I suppose so,' Shona looked puzzled. 'What're you getting at? He was just a normal dad – as far as I could see.'

'Yes, of course,' Andrews spoke calmly, hoping to reassure Shona that the parents of the missing child were not under suspicion. 'We're just trying to get a picture of what the family was like – and what other people thought of them. You obviously got on well with them. What about their other neighbours? Did they fit in OK?'

'As far as I know. Like I said – they haven't been here long.'

'Mrs Johns was from Jamaica,' said Khan. 'She hadn't been over here long. Do you think there was any resentment of her, because she was an immigrant?'

'No – not that I knew of.'

'No racial abuse?' Khan prompted. 'Or name-calling?'

'Not that I ever saw – and Crystal never said anything. But maybe she wouldn't. I mean, with her being new here, she might not like to.'

'So she *did* feel that she was an alien in a foreign country?' Khan seized on this remark. 'She was uncomfortable about it?'

'No. I didn't mean that.' Shona looked at them both with a puzzled frown on her face. 'She did miss her mum and dad – she told me that. But she said she couldn't complain, because Eddie – that's her husband – had lived away from his family for twelve years, to be with her. Eddie's dad lives just round the corner. He's ever so good. He looked after Ricky – that's their little boy – while Crystal was at work. And when she goes back, he's going to look after ...,' she slowed down as she remembered that Abigail was missing and might never be found, '... both ... of ... the kids,' she concluded at last.

'Did it bother her that her son was being looked after by a white man?' Khan asked.

'No. Why should it?' Again, Shona

looked puzzled at the question.

'I thought she might be worried that he wouldn't understand their needs or their culture.'

'But … but it was Eddie's dad. He'd had two black kids of his own. He was great with kids. Crystal said Ricky took to him right away.'

'What about Abigail – the new baby?' Khan asked. 'It must have been a shock to her parents when she turned out to be white.'

'Everyone was surprised, yes,' Shona agreed, with a weak smile. 'But I think Eddie was pleased. He seemed very excited telling me about it the day she was born. And I expect his dad will have been pleased. At least …,' she hesitated. 'I'm not sure. I think maybe he was a bit embarrassed about the way everyone kept saying she takes after him. I think ... I think he doesn't like people noticing what colour people's skin is. Does that make sense?'

'Perfect sense,' Khan assured her. 'And what about people outside the family? Did you hear any comments about black parents having a white baby? Anyone suggesting that child would have a tough time growing up?'

'No.' Shona shook her head. 'Everyone just thought it was interesting that it could happen. That's all.'

***

A loud quacking sound from Georgia's pocket indicated that someone was trying to call her. She and Michelle were in the hospital restaurant having lunch. Georgia turned in her seat and took hold of her jacket, which was hanging on the back of her chair. Then she reached down and retrieved her phone.

'Hi Jonah!' she greeted her father-in-law, trying her best to sound cheerful.

'I just wanted to catch up on how Rachel's doing,' he told her.

'She's …,' Georgia hesitated. 'She's doing fine. We thought we were going to be bringing her home this morning, but when the doctor came round, she wasn't completely satisfied that she might not need more intravenous fluids. So they're keeping her in for a bit longer, just as a precaution.'

'You're sure about that?' Jonah asked sharply. 'And you're not talking things up to avoid worrying Poor Old Dad?'

'No, honestly!' Georgia protested, laughing in spite of herself. 'That's the unvarnished truth. The doctor said that getting a needle into a vein is so difficult in a baby Rachel's size that she'd rather leave it in longer than necessary than risk having to insert a new one if she takes a turn for the worse later. She wants to keep her in for one more night – *as a precaution*, that's all – and then she'll be discharged tomorrow. They've fixed me up with a bed here, so I can feed her in the night. Everything's going to be fine.'

'And what about you?' Jonah asked, detecting a hint of bravado in Georgia's voice. 'How're you bearing up?'

'I'm doing fine too. Mum's here with me,' Georgia told him, glancing across at Michelle, who was watching her intently. 'We've packed the men off to work and we're having a nice mother-and-daughter bonding session here at the hospital.'

'Good. Well, I'd better get off the line – things to do! Bernie and Peter send you their love.'

'Oh! I'm sorry!' Georgia suddenly remembered what case it was that Jonah was currently engaged in investigating. 'I forgot to ask – is there any news on Abigail's whereabouts?'

'No. We're following up on a few things, but nothing much so far. Oh! And don't believe everything you hear on the media. There was a baby found in St Anselm's church this morning and some of the papers are saying it's Abigail. It isn't, and we don't know yet where this one's come from. So, just be sceptical of anything you come across that isn't in an official police press release.'

'OK. I'm sorry there's no news. Tell them all we're thinking of them.'

***

'Hey Lucy!' Paula shouted across the

dining room as Lucy put her tray down on a table and started to decant her plate, bowl and cutlery. 'It looks as if your baby has been found – look!'

Lucy looked up to see Paula holding up a smartphone, with its screen turned towards her. Then, leaving her lunch on the table, she started across the room to see what it was that Paula was showing her.

'See!' Paula went on excitedly. 'They've found a baby girl in a churchyard in Headington, only yards from where she went missing – and here are the parents going to the hospital to collect her!'

Lucy gazed down at the photographs. She recognised the exterior of St Anselm's church and the entrance to the John Radcliffe hospital. Two figures entering there might well be Crystal and

Eddie, but seen from behind, she could not be sure. However, it was impossible to be mistaken about the next picture, which was of Jonah, also about to enter the hospital. She turned round and headed for the door, fumbling for her own phone as she did so.

Paula and Anthea watched her go.

'Ungrateful bitch!' was Anthea's opinion, as the door closed behind Lucy's retreating figure. 'She might at least have said *thanks*!'

'Shall we go after her?' Paula suggested, getting up. 'I bet she's ringing them to get the latest.'

'No.' Leanne put out a restraining hand. 'Give her some time. She's left her lunch behind – look! So she's bound to be back soon.'

Paula plumped back down in her seat, with a dissatisfied look on her face, and sat watching the door for Lucy's return.

'I still think she ought to have stayed around to give us the gen,' Anthea grumbled. 'What's the good of knowing someone who's got inside information, if they won't tell you anything?'

'Mam!' Lucy said, a few moments later, when Bernie answered her call. 'Is it true? Have they found Abigail?'

'No love. I'm sorry. It was just a false alarm.'

'But it says on-'

'I know, love; but it's just irresponsible reporting. We've seen the baby they found at St Anselm's and she's nothing like Abigail – well,' she corrected herself, 'I suppose she *is* quite like Abigail – same age, same colouring, but her face is quite different.'

'Oh!' Lucy said, feeling suddenly very let down. She wandered out of the building and walked aimlessly across the yard towards the playing fields. 'So – there's no news? You still don't know where she is?'

'No, love. That's why we didn't bother to tell you. We weren't expecting you to hear about that other baby turning up.'

'So you *will* ring me if there's any news?' Lucy asked anxiously.

'Yes – but only once we know it's real news and not just silly speculation.'

'Yeah. OK.' Lucy ended the call and stood motionless for a few moments looking down at the phone in her hand. Then she thrust it into her pocket and strode off across the field.

The playing fields had been created by levelling an area of hillside. This meant that the lower and upper fields were separated by a steep grassy slope, which was a favourite place for students to sit during breaks and at lunchtime. Lucy threw herself down on it and lay staring up at the puffy white clouds moving slowly across the blue summer sky. What business had Paula got, showing her that news report without checking her facts first? And what sort of stupid journalist wrote things like that without taking the trouble to make sure it was true?

Then her anger subsided and was replaced by misery, as she thought about how much worse it must have been for Eddie and Crystal – and Peter, too – having their hopes raised and then dashed in such a cruel way. Was the investigation really not going anywhere? Mam hadn't sounded very hopeful, but maybe she was just being cautious so as not to raise her hopes too far. What if-?'

'Hello, Lucy!' Mrs Pettigrew, Lucy's Chemistry teacher loomed over her, casting a shadow and blocking her view of the sky. 'Is anything wrong?'

'No. I'm alright – thank you,' Lucy added, as an afterthought.

'So there wasn't any particular reason why you left your lunch behind and came out her?' Mrs Pettigrew settled herself on the grass and sat staring out across the lower field.

'I – I – well,' Lucy hesitated. Then she took a deep breath and began to explain. 'You've probably heard on the news about a baby being abducted in Headington yesterday?'

'Yes,' Mrs Pettigrew said, encouragingly.

'Well, her granddad is my stepfather.

'Oh. I see. I didn't know.'

'No. Well, Paula and Anthea found this report that she'd been found, and they showed it to me – back there in the dining hall – but it wasn't true! It was just some stupid journalist putting two and two together and making a hundred and three. And I rang my Mum and she says they aren't any further forward with finding Abigail. And it's going to be just so awful for poor Peter if they *don't* find her. Eddie probably wouldn't have come back from Jamaica if it wasn't for Peter being here. And …' she trailed off, lying back and putting her arms across her face to hide her tears.

'Perhaps you ought to take the day off,' Mrs Pettigrew suggested kindly. 'Why don't you go home? I'll let your form tutor know.'

'No.' Lucy wiped her eyes and sat up. 'It would only make things even worse for Peter, if he thought it was interfering with my education. I'm OK. I just want to be on my own for a bit.'

'OK.' Mrs Pettigrew thought for a moment. 'Would you like me to have a word with the other girls and tell them to cut you some slack?'

Lucy hesitated. She did not like to think that she could not cope with anything that life threw at her – and what was a bit of banter from Anthea and her cronies compared with losing a baby? Then she nodded.

'OK. Thanks.'

***

Victoria gazed down into Esme's cot. She looked peaceful with her eyelids closed lightly – not scrunched fiercely together as if she were afraid of opening them and seeing something hideous or terrifying. There was none of the red blotchiness on her skin caused by her frequent bouts of crying. Since returning from their morning walk, she had been amazingly contented. She had consumed her lunchtime feed eagerly and without the usual fuss, and then, afterwards, she had drifted off into this tranquil sleep such as Victoria did not remember having seen before.

'Daddy will be back soon,' she whispered softly. 'He's so looking forward to seeing you. You will be good for him, won't you? He'll be tired after coming all the way from China.'

She tiptoed out, leaving the door open a crack so that she would hear if the baby woke and started crying. Perhaps everything was going to be alright when John got back after all.

***

Flick reached out a languid arm and switched on the radio that stood on the bedside cabinet. The pips announced that it was one o'clock and time for the World at One. She lay back on the pillow and closed her eyes. She supposed that she ought to get up – but what was the point? What was the point of anything now that Mia was gone? The newsreader announced the headlines, but she was only half listening. Then came something that made her open her eyes in surprise and listen intently.

'Oxford Police have issued a statement saying that the baby that was discovered this morning in a church in Headington is *not* the missing infant, Abigail Johns, who was snatched from her pram in a nearby playground yesterday.'

Flick sat up, alert now. If not the missing baby – then who was it?

'The identity of the baby has not yet been established. Police are appealing for the mother to come forward, but so far no-one has claimed the baby girl, who is believed to be between four and eight weeks old. We will give the number to ring if you have any information at the end of this report, but first over to our Oxford correspondent.'

Flick leapt out of bed and crossed the room to the desk where their computer stood. She pulled out one of the drawers, looking for a pen. At last! Here was a blue ballpoint. Now what about something to write on? She found a discarded tissue box in the waste bin under the desk. That would do! She flattened it down on the desk and sat with her pen poised. Only just in time! She wrote down the number carefully.

Should she ring right away? Yes, of course! Otherwise, someone else might get there before her and claim the baby for their own. But she must get her story straight first. She would tell them that she had suffered from post-natal depression – lots of mothers got that. And it wasn't a lie – everyone agreed that she had been depressed. And so, in a fit of despondency, she had taken her baby to St Anselm's and left her there. She hadn't known what she was doing, but now she regrets it and wants Mia back. Yes – that ought to do the trick!

She took out her phone and keyed in the numbers.

13 SWEET SPIRIT COMFORT ME

The doorbell rang.

'I'll get it!' Eddie called from the living room, heading out into the hall.

Crystal, who had been helping Peter with the washing up while Eddie played with Ricky, put down the tea towel that she was holding and made for the door, hopeful that this might be news about Abigail. Peter struggled to take off his rubber gloves and then followed her.

'Good afternoon,' Arshad greeted them, holding up his warrant card. 'I don't know if you'll remember me from yesterday. I'm DCI Khan and this is my colleague DI Andrews.' He glanced over his shoulder towards Rupert Andrews who was standing behind him, a little lower down the ramp that led up to the front door from the drive.

'Have you found Abigail?' Crystal asked breathlessly, pushing past Eddie in her eagerness.

'No. I'm afraid not,' Arshad said apologetically. He felt awkward about this visit, and even more so when he saw Peter waiting patiently in the background. 'We just need to ask you some more questions, I'm afraid. May we come in?'

'Yes, yes, of course,' Eddie made way for them to enter and then closed the door behind them. Everyone stood awkwardly in the hall wondering what to do next.

'Come into the living room,' Peter said at last, leading the way. As they entered the room, Ricky looked up from the floor, where he was sitting, busily engaged in building a tower from brightly coloured wooden bricks. At the sight of two strange men invading his territory, his face crumpled and he burst into tears. Crystal ran forward and swept him up in her arms, murmuring comfortingly in his ear.

'Sit down,' Peter said, indicating the large sofa and a range of easy chairs.

Eddie and Crystal sat together on the sofa while the two police officers each took a chair. Peter hesitated and then sat down next to Crystal. All three looked across at Arshad expectantly.

'I'm sorry to have to ask these questions,' he began. Then he stopped.

It was tremendously awkward having to question the parents of a missing child with the intention of gauging whether they could have been responsible for her abduction – or worse. In this case, it was doubly difficult because of the presence of his ex-colleague who was clearly already resentful of his involvement and suspicious of his methods and motives.

'I'm afraid that we have to explore every possibility,' he began again. 'And that includes asking you some rather personal questions about your family life and your children.'

'What sort of questions?' Eddie demanded, aggressively. 'What are you implying?'

The anger in his father's voice frightened Ricky and he started to cry again. Arshad looked towards Peter, suddenly thinking of a ruse to get him out of the way.

'Inspector Johns,' he said. 'I think perhaps it would be best if you take the little boy away somewhere else while we talk to his parents.'

Peter nodded silently and leaned across to pick up his grandson.

'Come along Ricky,' he said. 'These men need to talk to Mummy and Daddy, so let's go out in the garden. Would you like to play in the sandpit?'

Ricky nodded and smiled up at Peter, as Crystal released her hold of him. They went out through the open French window, on to the wide paved area behind the house. Arshad got up and closed the door behind them. Then he turned back to address Eddie and Crystal.

'I realise that this is going to appear

very intrusive,' he resumed apologetically, 'but it could have a real bearing on what happened to your daughter. You see, we have to try to imagine how people around you see your family. In particular, what sort of reaction do you tend to get when people see that your daughter is white? What did your neighbours say, for example, when you brought her home from the hospital?'

'They were surprised,' Crystal answered, 'but mostly they'd seen Eddie's dad, so they were more just interested than anything else, and some of them talked about it being fascinating the way things sometimes skip a generation. Why does it matter?'

'So nobody suggested that it might be difficult for her at all, in the future, growing up as a white girl with black parents?' Arshad persisted gently.

'No.' Crystal looked round wide-eyed, still unable to see the point of this questioning.

'And you didn't have any concerns on that score yourselves?'

'No. Of course not!' Eddie retorted angrily. 'What're you trying to say? Are you accusing us of something?'

'DCI Khan is just wondering if you were perhaps a bit … apprehensive, let's say, on behalf of your daughter – with her looking so different from the rest of the family,' Andrews said, speaking for the first time. 'I mean – you were probably expecting that she would look more like your other child, weren't you?'

'I suppose so,' Eddie conceded grudgingly. 'But, just because we weren't expecting it, doesn't mean we wish she'd been different.'

'Abigail is our precious baby,' Crystal protested. 'We love her just the way she is. We don't want to change her colour.'

'No. Of course not,' Arshad said hastily. 'But, as DI Andrews said, it must have given you pause for thought, didn't it?'

'Well, Eddie did have a bit of a joke about it with his dad,' Crystal said, smiling as she remembered the conversation that Eddie had had with Peter, when he rang him from the hospital to tell him that he now had another granddaughter. 'He said that Peter might need to vouch for him that he really was Abby's father.'

'Oh?' Arshad turned to Eddie. 'Why was that?'

'It's just an old family joke. Something that happened to me years ago.'

'Go on.'

Eddie sighed.

'Look – this is all just wasting time. It's got nothing to do with Abigail.'

'I'll be the judge of that. Tell me about this incident in your past.'

'It was nothing – just some stupid woman jumping to conclusions. Oh alright! Here goes. It was years ago, like I said, when I was still at uni – only it was the holidays so I was at home. I was looking after Lucy-'

'Lucy?' Arshad asked.

'Bernie's daughter. She was two at the time, and Bernie had to go to London for the day so-'

'Bernie, as in DCI Porter's PA?' This time it was Andrews' turn to interrupt.

'Yes – only she was still working for the university then. My mum and dad were Lucy's godparents, but they were both on duty that day, so I volunteered to babysit, while Bernie went off to London, like I just said.'

'Go on,' Arshad said, as Eddie paused to consider how best to tell the story.

'I took Lucy to the park. She threw a tantrum and some interfering old bat told a passing policeman that a big black man was trying to run off with a little white girl. Then he tried to arrest me; so I got him to call my dad and he came over and got everything sorted out[4],' Eddie finished in a rush, keen to get it over with. 'It was all a storm in a teacup. We laugh about it now.'

'But it *was* something that you

---

[4] You can read about this in *Two Little Dickie Birds* © 2015 ISBN 978-1-911083-13-9

immediately thought of when you saw your daughter's colour,' Arshad commented.

'No! Well – yes, I thought of it, but only as a joke. I told you – it's part of our family folklore. Stop trying to pin your own stupid hang-ups and inferiority complexes on us. If there's one thing I learnt from my dad when I was growing up, it's not to judge anyone by how they look on the outside. Abby could have had two heads and a forked tail and she'd still have been our daughter. Can't you get that through your thick head?'

'I'm sorry, sir,' Arshad retreated into formality. 'I didn't intend to cause offence.'

'Look, what is it with you lot?' Eddie stormed on, getting to his feet and pacing round the room. 'Do you *always* go round trying to blame the victims when you investigate a crime? It was the same when Mum died, wasn't it? Bernie told me all about it. She said you seemed determined to make out it was Dad's fault Mum was killed. *You* thought my dad had killed my mum because he wanted to marry Bernie, didn't you? Well you were wrong about that, and you're wrong now!'

'I really am very sorry,' Arshad began, but Andrews cut in, speaking quietly and calmly, but forcefully.

'I think we'd better go now.' He got up and held out his hand towards Eddie. 'I know it's hard to believe, but we really are doing our best to find your daughter. I've worked with your dad and he was the best boss I ever had.'

Eddie stared for a moment before taking the proffered hand and shaking it. Andrews turned towards Crystal.

'Mrs Johns?'

She got up and shook hands. Eddie went over to the door and held it open for the two police officers to go out. Then he followed them into the hall, ushered them through the front door and stood watching as they walked down the slope to their car. Arshad turned to face him.

'I really am very sorry,' he repeated. He waited for a few moments, but Eddie continued to stare at him in stony silence, so he turned and got into the car. Eddie stood watching until it disappeared behind the high copper beech hedge that bordered the property. Then he turned and went back inside.

There was nobody in the living room, but the French window was fastened open again, so he went through it and found his wife playing with Ricky and

Peter in the sandpit at the edge of the patio.

'They've gone,' he said, in answer to his father's questioning look.

He sat down on the edge of the sand pit and started picking up handfuls of sand and letting them run through his fingers. For several minutes nobody spoke. Then Eddie could hold back his anger no more.

'Who does he think he is?' he demanded, speaking low to avoid frightening Ricky. 'Coming round here and insinuating that we would have preferred Abigail to be black!'

'What do you mean?' Peter asked sharply.

'What I said. He kept on and on, asking if we were worried she'd feel out of place in a black family, and if the neighbours thought it was strange, and

... I can see now, Dad, why you used to get so het up when people commented on me and Hannah. I always thought you were making a fuss about nothing.'

'I suppose he thought ...,' Peter began, trying to be fair and to put the best construction possible on Arshad's words; but he trailed off, unable to finish the sentence.

'He *thought* that we did away with her because we didn't want a white baby in the family,' Eddie growled, just loud enough for Peter to hear. 'That's what he *thought*! He's a racist bastard; that's what he is!'

'Did he say that?' Peter asked in a shocked voice. 'Did he actually accuse you?'

'Not in so many words, but I could see that was what he was thinking.'

They sat for several more minutes

without speaking. Then Peter got to his feet and brushed the sand from his trousers.

'I'm going out for a walk,' he said, stepping out of the sandpit and starting across the patio. 'I won't be long. I just want to get some exercise and clear my head.'

Eddie watched him go, and then got hastily to his feet and ran after him.

'You're not going to put in a complaint about DCI Khan, are you?' he asked anxiously. 'I shouldn't have said that about him being a racist. I was just angry with him, that's all. He's probably just doing his job. I mean – I suppose some parents *do* reject their kids, don't they? You won't do anything …?'

'Don't worry,' Peter assured him, with a grim smile. 'I told you – I'm just going for a walk to clear my mind. And you're right – if I was in charge of this case, *I'd* have to be asking whether the parents could have had a hand in the baby's disappearance. I'm just grateful that you have an alibi – and that the Chief Super allowed Jonah to stay on the case.'

***

Walking aimlessly through the streets, Peter discovered himself outside St Cyprian's Church. He stopped and stood for a few moments looking towards the open outer door, through which he could see sunbeams slanting in and picking out the carving on the inner doors. Then, without knowing why, he walked up the path and slipped silently inside.

The sun was shining from a different direction today and the room was no longer bathed in the colours of the rainbow. The stained glass on the western wall looked duller than before, as light poured in through a row of windows along the southern side, each of which depicted a different saint against a clear glass background.

Peter looked round. The place seemed deserted. Didn't they worry about thieves getting in and stealing the brass candlesticks or the ornate crucifix from the altar? That leather-bound Bible must be worth something too – not to mention the cash in the collecting box where he and Lucy had lit their candles the previous evening. Less than twenty-four hours ago! It felt like a lifetime.

He walked slowly down the aisle, strangely drawn towards the statue of the Madonna and Child, which stood by a pillar separating the small chapel with the candelabrum from the sanctuary where the main altar stood. 'And thy own soul a sword shall pierce,' he read again, looking down at the improbable mound of painted stone grass, which, he now noticed had white lilies growing amongst it.

He stood motionless, staring up at the pale brown face and the sad brown eyes of the Virgin. Then he lowered his own eyes to take in the curly black hair and bright, eager face of the child. He appeared to be struggling to get away from his mother, who was holding him tight, seeking to protect him from whatever unknown danger she feared for him. It was uncanny! The figure looked so much like Eddie as a child – the same curly black hair and dark brown eyes – the same look of determination and dislike of being constrained (especially when it was done for his own good) – the same-

'Can I help you?' a voice asked gently.

Surprised, Peter turned his head and saw a man standing next to him. It was a priest – presumably, this was his church. He looked young, for a priest – perhaps in his mid or late thirties, Peter thought – with straight black hair and brown eyes.

'No – thanks – I was just …'

'Are you new to the area? I don't think I've seen you here before.'

'No. It's not … I don't … I'm not a Catholic,' Peter said incoherently.

'That's fine,' the priest assured him. 'We welcome everyone here. Was there a particular reason …?'

'No, no … well … yes!' Peter turned to face the priest and their eyes met. The priest looked back for a second and then an expression of understanding crossed his face.

'I *do* recognise you now,' the priest said, in tones of compassion. 'You're the grandfather of that little girl that's gone missing, aren't you? You were on the box last night appealing for her return.'

'Yes,' Peter admitted. 'I was just ...,' he looked sheepishly towards the statue, feeling rather foolish.

'I am so sorry!' the priest was saying to the back of his head. 'I've been offering prayers to St Anthony for her safe return.'

'St Anthony?' Peter asked absently, with his eyes still fixed on the Virgin and Child.

'The patron saint of lost things,' the priest explained. 'That's him over there.' He pointed towards one of the windows on the south wall. Peter looked across and saw a stained-glass picture of a man in a monk's habit, holding a child in one hand and a book in the other.

'My stepdaughter told me that Catholics don't really pray to the saints – only ask them to pray to God on their behalf.'

'I suppose that depends on what distinction you make between *praying* to someone and *talking* to them. She's probably trying to make it clear that the saints can only answer our prayers through *God*'s grace – that they aren't like little gods themselves. Your stepdaughter's a Catholic, I presume?'

'Well ... not exactly. She took her First Communion here, but mostly she and her mum go to the Methodist church.'

'You wouldn't be talking about Lucy Paige, by any chance?'

'Yes. I suppose you probably know her – and my wife, Bernie.'

'Lucy was in the first class of kids that I prepared for communion. She certainly kept me on my toes! A very forthright young lady – quite a challenge for a young priest in his first parish.' The priest smiled and held out his hand. 'I ought to introduce myself. I'm Father Damien Rowland – and you must be Peter Johns.'

Peter acknowledged the truth of this statement and shook Father Damien's hand, smiling at his description of Lucy aged nine years.

'Lucy thinks a lot of you,' Father Damien went on. 'She was extremely definite that, if God is going to consign you to hell for all eternity just because you don't believe in Him, then she doesn't think much of God and she'd rather go to hell with you!'

'That sounds like Lucy,' Peter agreed, smiling in spite of his dismal mood. 'She's not one to keep quiet when she has an opinion on something.'

They stood for a few moments without speaking. Peter felt rather awkward, standing there in a strange church, surrounded by statues and images that he did not understand; but he did not like to walk out, now that the priest had engaged him in conversation. Father Damien felt a pastoral responsibility towards someone who, while not exactly a member of his flock, was certainly deserving of sympathy and had, by whatever means, been drawn to enter his church; but how to offer support without appearing to be attempting to proselytise?

'I usually make myself a mug of tea

round about this time in the afternoon,' he said eventually. 'Why don't you join me? It'll be more comfortable in the Presbytery, and we can chat more easily without being surrounded by this cloud of witnesses,' he added, glancing round at the statues and stained-glass saints.

Peter hesitated and then nodded. Father Damien started back down the aisle towards the door. Peter gave one final look at the olive-skinned Virgin before following him. This was turning out to be a very strange afternoon!

***

'Right, Anna,' Jonah said, swivelling his chair round to face his colleague, who was sitting at her desk, apparently engrossed in something on her smartphone. 'I want you to take the list that Alice Ray has compiled, and prioritise interviews with the women on it. Any who suffered miscarriages or stillbirths or whose babies have died, are potential suspects for our child-abduction – especially if they live near the Margaret Road recreation ground or have any reason to go there.'

Anna did not reply, so he glided over to her and looked to see what she was studying so intently. She sensed his presence and switched off the display, but not before Jonah had seen that she had been reading an email on her private account.

'I'm sorry, sir. You were saying?'

'Constable Ray has made a list of all the women in the Headington area who gave birth within the last three months. Get her to print you out a copy and then come and join me in my office.'

Anna nodded. She was vaguely aware that this was not what Jonah had said before, but she had been too distracted by Philip's email to pay proper attention. His plans for the move down to Devon were clearly much more advanced than she had realised.

***

'I was impressed by that appeal you made,' Father Damien said, pouring tea into mugs from a large, green teapot. 'There was no hint of malice in it – no demand for vengeance.'

'I don't know about that,' Peter shrugged, taking hold of the mug that Father Damien had placed in front of him. 'Whatever I may have felt about whoever took Abigail, I said the only thing we *could* say. The only hope of getting her back is to make them think they can return her without any repercussions for them. It's just plain common sense and pragmatism.'

'I'd say it was more than that. It was as if you really cared for the perpetrator. I don't think it would have come across like that if you hadn't been sincere – if you didn't understand what might have made them feel compelled to take her.'

'Yes, well,' Peter felt awkward at receiving what seemed to him to be undeserved praise. 'That's what I have to keep telling myself – that they only took her to try to fill a big gap in their own life – that they've suffered their own tragedy and therefore can't think about anyone else's feelings. I don't suppose I'll be feeling so forgiving if it turns out that she's been taken by some sadist pervert who goes round hurting children for the fun of it – like the Moors Murders or something.'

'Surely that's not likely? The scenario you described in your appeal – of the woman who's lost a baby – must be much more probable, isn't it?'

'That's what I keep telling myself – and I hope that Eddie and Crystal haven't even thought of the alternative – but such people *do* exist.'

They sat in silence for a few moments, each lost in his own thoughts. Then Peter looked up and addressed the priest.

'You've got me all wrong, anyway,' he said. 'I've got all sorts of angry, unforgiving thoughts in my heart. That's how I came to be in your church. I had to get out of the house for a bit, to cool off. It's just that ... well ... they're not directed at the person who's taken Abigail.'

Father Damien looked at him and raised his eyebrows, but did not speak.

'It's one of the police officers who's conducting the case,' Peter explained. 'I know he's only doing his job, but …'

Father Damien continued to look at Peter with an expression of interest, but without speaking.

'The thing is: a significant proportion of child abductions are done by members of the child's own family – estranged fathers upset at being denied access, or foreign parents or grandparents wanting to take a child to live abroad, or ex-partners wanting to punish the child's parent and so on. And you also get some parents who, for one reason or another, reject their own kids and want to get rid of them. There have also been cases of parents accidentally killing a child and then staging an abduction to cover it up, because they're afraid of being blamed. Anyway, that means that the police *have* to consider those possibilities – and *that* means questioning the parents about their relationship with their kids and so on.'

'But?' Father Damien prompted gently.

'It's the *way* he's been questioning them. He came round this afternoon, trying to make out Eddie and Crystal must have found it hard to bond with Abigail because she's got a different colour of skin from them. He's ...,' Peter trailed off, turning red with embarrassment at giving way to his feelings.

'Go on – he's what?'

'No. It's just me. You see, it's not the first time ... There's some history between us. I shouldn't let it get to me like this. I'm being unfair.'

'Oh?'

Peter picked up his mug in both hands and took a slow draft of tea. Then he put it back down on the table and looked across at the priest, who returned his stare with a look of compassion. Peter took a deep breath and began his confession.

'You see, the thing is – I've never really forgiven him for the way he spoke to me after my wife was killed. I suppose you know that Eddie's mother was attacked by a group of youths and stabbed to death?'

Father Damien nodded.

'Well, Sergeant Khan, as he was then, was an up-and-coming young officer with a special interest in inter-racial tensions. He was convinced – or at least that's how it seemed to me –

that Angie's death was something to do with us living as if we were just the same as all the white families around us. He thought – and he actually said as much – that I didn't understand what it was like for Angie and the kids being black in a white society. He as good as told me that I ought to have taken more interest in her roots and encouraged her to mix more with the local West Indian community. I've always taken the line that we're all the same underneath and you shouldn't treat people differently because of how they look, but these days we're told to celebrate diversity and that treating people fairly isn't the same as treating them equally.'

Peter took another long draught of tea, and sat thinking for a few moments. Father Damien watched him, but said nothing.

'I suppose that's what really gets me,' Peter resumed. 'The fact that he may have been right. He knew about a whole load of incidents of racial bullying at school that Eddie had never told *me* about. Was that because he thought I wouldn't understand? Could there be something in this idea of Khan's about parents subconsciously rejecting kids that are too different in appearance from themselves? I mean ....' He paused and sighed quietly. 'I've found being a dad to Lucy a whole lot easier than it was with my own kids. Is that because, deep down, I don't really relate to them as mine?'

'Has it ever occurred to you that it could be quite the opposite?' Father Damien asked quietly. 'Isn't it at least as likely that your relationship with your stepdaughter is easier because there's less at stake – because she *isn't* your own flesh and blood? If you get it wrong, you haven't failed as a dad, because you're not her real dad in the first place. Everyone knows being a step-parent is really difficult, so nobody is going to judge you. You can afford to take risks in your relationship with Lucy, because, at the end of the day, you could just walk away from one another.'

'I couldn't walk away from Lucy,' Peter protested. 'That's just it – I feel as much for her as for my own kids.'

'Yes, of course,' Father Damien agreed. 'But for different reasons. There isn't the same instinctive need to protect her, just because she's yours. In a sense, she – and her mother – have had to earn your love. And there's another thing – aren't some of the things about your own kids that annoy you most, the faults that you recognise in yourself? There's none of that with a step-child. You may feel obliged to correct her for behaving badly, but at least you don't have to imagine that she's inherited the tendency from you!'

Peter looked up and smiled.

'You know, I think you may have something there. Going back to Khan and the racial bullying – the thing that upset me most was the way Eddie had been afraid to tell me about it, because he thought I'd go off the deep end and cause a scene (which I probably would). That's just exactly the way I used to behave when I was a teenager and people ragged me about my ginger hair – or about being in a children's home. The last thing I wanted was adults getting involved and blowing it out of all proportion.'

'And I'd also say,' Father Damien said earnestly, 'that you wouldn't be agonising about all this – and you wouldn't have been able to make that appeal last night – if you didn't care about your son very much.'

Peter coloured again and lowered his eyes. He sat silently, staring down into his mug.

'Lots of people have been saying that they're praying for Abigail,' he said, after a long pause. 'Do you think it'll do any good?'

'Prayer always does good.' Father Damien hesitated and then went on, 'but that's not the same as saying that prayers will bring your Abigail back safely. Praying isn't a sort of magic that makes things happen automatically.'

'You mean God might not want Abigail to be found?'

'No. I mean he might not be able to-'

'But I thought he was supposed to be able to do anything?' Peter interrupted.

'Not even God can do things that are a logical impossibility – such as drawing a round triangle or making that mug of tea both full and empty at the same time or giving whoever it is who has taken Abigail the freedom to decide what to do about it, and at the same time forcing them to give her back.'

'So what's the point of praying about it then? What good *can* it do?'

'All sorts of good. It can give Abigail's parents – and the rest of the family: you and Lucy and Bernie and everyone else – comfort and strength during the waiting. Maybe it was God's guidance, prompted by prayer, that led you to come into my church this afternoon – and maybe it was God leading me to go in at the same time.'

'But can it do anything to help find Abigail?'

'Like I said – God can't *force* the person who's holding Abigail to hand her back, without violating their freewill; but He can work through their conscience to encourage them to make that choice for themselves. And He can work through other people too – maybe people that they meet saying things that make them realise the enormity of what they've done, or maybe the news broadcasters saying just the right words to make them stop and think. God may have been helping you to find the right words for that appeal that you made yesterday.'

Peter still looked dissatisfied, so Father Damien tried to think of another way of explaining.

'I know this is hard to believe,' he said, leaning forward across the table, 'but, whatever happens in the end, God cares just as much about Abigail as you and your son and daughter-in-law do. It's just … well … he has to care for the perpetrator too. It's like … You've got two children, haven't you?'

Peter nodded. 'Yes. Hannah's up in Leeds. She's been talking about coming down to be with Eddie and Crystal, but I told her not to, because there was nothing she could do to help.'

'Think back to when they were both small, and imagine that you found your daughter hurting your son – quite deliberately. You'd be upset for your son, wouldn't you? But you'd also be upset that your daughter would do such a thing. And you wouldn't stop loving her, even though what she was doing was hurting your son, whom you love too. And suppose you could only protect your son by constraining your daughter in a way that injured her? How would you choose between them? That's how God feels in a situation like this.'

Peter sat thinking for a minute or so. Then he finished his tea and glanced down at his watch.

'I'd better be going. Lucy will be out of school soon and she'll worry if I'm not there when she gets home. Come to that,' he added, with a grin, 'I bet Eddie's on tenterhooks, expecting me to have rushed off to report Khan for harassment. I'd better get back and put him out of his misery.'

They walked together to the door of the presbytery.

'Thanks,' Peter said, as he stepped through. 'Everything seems a lot clearer now. But … how come? I mean – you've never married; you don't have any kids of your own. How is it that you know so much about …?'

'People tell me things. It's my job. When you were a detective, you used to go round asking people questions and they told you all sorts of things about their private lives. I don't even have to ask the questions – people just come along week by week and tell me about all their family rows, and about how angry they feel with their kids or their parents or their spouse or their in-laws. I spend all my time looking in on other people's families and trying to help them to patch up the squabbles and re-direct the anger and – quite often – to forgive themselves for not being perfect.' He reached out and laid his hand on Peter's shoulder. 'There's a reason why Roman

Catholic priests are called *Father*. And *we* often worry that we're not doing it as well as we ought to be doing it, too.'

He stood on the step, watching Peter as he walked down the path and turned into the road. As soon as he had disappeared round the corner, Father Damien turned and pulled the door closed behind him. Then he made his way back to the church, murmuring to himself the words of the prayer of Our Lady of Fatima: *O my Jesus, forgive us our sins, save us from the fires of hell, and lead all souls to heaven, especially those most in need of your mercy.*

14 AMAZING GIFT OF LOVE

'Mrs Felicity Mason?'

Flick looked at the plump young woman in a brown trouser suit who was standing on her doorstep. She had a small briefcase in one hand while the other was extended towards Flick, holding up an identification card.

'I'm from Social Services,' the woman continued, looking at Flick through the thick lenses of a pair of black-framed glasses. 'My name's Ruth Hammond. I've come about your call regarding the baby that was left in St Anselm's church.'

'Yes – yes, come in!'

Flick opened the door wider and stepped back to allow the woman to enter. She stepped carefully over the threshold, pausing in the hall to glance down into the pram that Flick had positioned there, where she could not fail to notice it. Flick followed her gaze, noting that she appeared to be studying the way that the blanket was pulled back, revealing an indentation in the mattress below. Flick hoped that she could not tell that this had been made by a lifelike doll and not by a real baby.

'Sit down,' Flick told her. 'I'm sorry about the mess.' She hastily gathered up a dummy and two plastic squeaky toys from the small coffee table. 'Would you like something to drink?'

'No thanks.' Ruth looked round the room, taking in the cluster of soft toys lying on the sofa, the bouncy baby seat in the corner of the room and the large photograph on the mantle-piece of a young baby in an embroidered dress. Flick noticed her gaze resting on the photograph and she went across and picked it up.

'This is Mia,' she told Ruth, holding it out towards her. 'We had this taken when she was two weeks.'

Ruth looked closely at the child in the picture and tried to compare it in her mind with the baby that she had seen in the hospital cot that morning. It was difficult to know whether they could be the same child – babies change so quickly at that age.

'She's beautiful,' she said, hoping to win Flick's confidence by using the same bland compliment that she employed when speaking to any of the young mothers whom she encountered in the course of her work. 'And how old is she now?'

'Seven weeks and three days,' Flick answered promptly.

That sounded about right – perhaps close to the upper end of the estimate that the doctor had given, but well within the margins of error. Ruth bent down and opened her briefcase to get out her notes.

'I feel such a fool now,' Flick said, becoming impatient with Ruth's measured approach. 'I don't know what came over me this morning. I suppose it was the lack of sleep that stopped me being able to think straight. She just wouldn't stop crying, you see. So I put her in the pram and took her out for a walk to try to get her off to sleep, but she just kept on and on, and I started to think I was never going to get any rest ever again. And then, when we got to the churchyard, I suddenly couldn't take it any longer and I left her there. I knew the vicar would be along soon – he comes every morning. I've seen him there before.'

'I see,' Ruth noted all this down in a spiral-bound notebook.

'So – when can I have her back?' Flick demanded suddenly, unable to bear the suspense any longer. 'Where is she now?'

'The baby that was left in St Anselm's is still in the hospital at the moment,' Ruth told her, speaking calmly and trying unsuccessfully to make eye contact with Flick who, unable to control her growing agitation, was looking wildly round the room. 'We haven't identified a foster home for her yet and the doctors are a bit worried about her.'

'Why? What's wrong with her?' Flick asked sharply, her eyes widening in alarm. 'It can't have been because she was left out – it's so mild today and the reports said she was found before nine.'

'They think she may have an underlying medical condition.'

'What sort of condition? Was that why she wouldn't stop crying? Why didn't I think? I must go to her! She needs me.' Flick got out of her chair and turned to head out.

'I'm sorry, we can't allow that,' Ruth said, getting up and placing herself between Flick and the door. 'I know you're worried and I can understand that you want to be there; but we don't even know – not officially – that she *is* your baby.'

'Of course she's mine!' Flick protested. 'I've got her birth certificate. Look! Here!' She opened the drawer of a small bureau that stood next to the window and snatched up a piece of paper, which she thrust into Ruth's hand.

Ruth unfolded the paper and looked down. Sure enough, it was a birth certificate for a child born a few weeks earlier. She sat down again and noted down the details: *Mia Sophie Mason, female*. Then she looked up at Flick and held out the certificate to her.

'Thank you. Now, I'll need the name and address of your GP, please.'

Flick grabbed the notebook and pen from Ruth's hands and scribbled down the details.

'Here you are! *Now* can I see Mia?

When can she come home?'

'I'm afraid not,' Ruth said apologetically. 'We have a range of checks that we need to do. You have to understand that we do need to be sure that you really are the mother. And then …,' she hesitated. It was always difficult to explain to parents, when their suitability as parents was called into question. 'Well … you *do* see that we have to put the baby's safety ahead of every other consideration, don't you? And, a mother who leaves her baby in a churchyard … well, we need to be sure that you have all the support that you need to be able to cope with a baby, before we can allow her to come and live with you again.'

'Yes. I suppose so,' Flick's face fell. 'How long will all that take? What will happen to Mia in the meantime?'

'We'll see that she's well looked after,' Ruth assured her. 'And as soon as we've established that you really *are* her mother, we'll arrange for you to visit her. Now, I'd better get off and set the wheels in motion.'

Flick watched from the window as Ruth walked down the path and got into the car that she had left parked on the road outside. How long would all that checking take? Why couldn't they just hand the baby over to her? She wanted her – nobody else did. That social worker had said that they couldn't find a foster home for her. There must be something that she could do to persuade them to change their minds.

***

'Sir?' Monica Philipson crossed the room and stood in front of Jonah, who had been engaged in a discussion with Anna Davenport and Rupert Andrews about priorities for the next stage in their hunt for Abigail. 'I thought you'd want to know – we've had a call from Social Services about the baby that was abandoned in the church.'

'Go on.'

'A woman's come forward claiming to be the mother. A Mrs Felicity Mason, from Quarry Hollow.'

'Quarry Hollow?' Jonah mused. 'That's the road that leads down from the ring road to the recreation ground. Didn't we cover that in the house-to-house yesterday?'

'Yes,' Anna confirmed, bringing up the records of the interviews on her computer screen. 'Sergeant King and Constable Appleton spoke with a Mrs Mason. She told them that she walked through the playground on the way to the shops, only a few minutes before Abigail was taken. She was the person who said she saw a white woman with fair hair approaching the buggy shortly before the abduction must have happened.'

'Yes – I remember. She gave a good enough description that we were able to match it up with one of the women who was still in the playground when the police arrived.' Jonah thought for a moment. 'Something about this doesn't feel right, but I can't quite see what this woman can have to do with Abigail's disappearance. And yet … I never trust co-incidences. Did Social Services say any more about this Felicity Mason?'

'They sent someone round to check out her story,' Monica told him. 'It looks as if she *did* have a baby. There were all the usual things – toys, pram, that sort of thing – and she showed the social worker a birth certificate. She told her that she couldn't stand the baby's screaming so she left her in the church, but now she's regretting it and wants the kid back. I've got the number of the social worker who called, if you want to talk to her.'

'Yes. Thanks. I think I might do that.'

'Yes?' Ruth said nervously. The secretary who had answered the phone had told her that a DCI Porter wanted to speak to her and she was wondering what it could be about. 'Ruth Hammond here. What can I do for you?'

'I'm DCI Jonah Porter. I'm investigating the disappearance of a baby from the Margaret Road

Recreation Ground yesterday. One of the witnesses was a Mrs Felicity Mason. I gather you've spoken to her today about her claim that she's the mother of the baby that was left in St Anselm's Church?'

'Yes. That's right.' Ruth was puzzled. What had Felicity's impulsive abandonment of her own baby got to do with the missing child? And was the inspector intending to imply that he thought she was lying when she said that the baby was hers?

'How did you find her?' Jonah asked. 'I mean – what sort of state of mind was she in?'

'Upset that we couldn't just give the baby back to her then and there.'

'So, you are convinced that she's the mother, are you?' Jonah asked sharply.

'Well, we'll have to go through some

checks, but it does seem likely. There's certainly been a baby in that house recently. They've got all the equipment – you know: pram, toys, dummies, feeding bottles and steriliser – and she showed me the birth certificate, with her name on it as the mother.'

'And the father?'

'He had the same surname, so is presumably her husband. They're both teachers apparently. It all looked very normal to me.'

'Except that she claims to have dumped her baby in a church porch and gone off and left her. That's not very normal behaviour.'

'I don't know,' Ruth said thoughtfully. 'I daresay a lot of mothers have thought of doing something like that – on those days when the baby just won't give you any peace and you're shut up alone with it for hours on end. She says it was a heat-of-the-moment thing. The baby wouldn't stop crying, so she took her out for a walk in the hope that the motion of the pram would send her off to sleep. As she was passing the church, she got to the stage when she couldn't bear it any longer; so she took the baby out of the pram and left her in the porch – knowing that the vicar would be along in a few minutes and would find her. Now she regrets her impulse and wants her baby back.'

Jonah thought for a moment. Somehow, this story didn't quite stack up, but he couldn't put his finger on what was wrong. Oh! Of course!

'Where did the box come from?' he asked incisively.

'What box?' Ruth was puzzled.

'The box that the baby was in when

the vicar found her. She was in a cardboard box lined with blankets. If it was all so sudden, where did she get it from?'

'Are you sure?' Ruth queried anxiously. It was beginning to look as if Felicity Mason had been less than straightforward with her.

'It's all here in black and white, in the report from the officers who attended,' Jonah told her. 'She was in a good strong cardboard box, with plenty of padding to make her comfortable. It must have taken a bit of pre-planning to rig it up – which doesn't square with your Mrs Mason's story that it was all done on impulse when she'd already got to the church.'

'You're right,' Ruth said slowly, thinking hard. 'Still – it doesn't mean she isn't the mother. Maybe she just thought it sounded better to say she only thought of it when the crying got unbearable and she left the baby in the nearest place she could – rather than admitting that it was pre-meditated. After all, it's definite that she *had* a baby, and I didn't see one in the house when I went round, so her baby must be somewhere and, if she says it's the one that was left in the churchyard, that seems the most likely place, doesn't it?'

'It would certainly be a nice neat ending,' Jonah agreed. 'But my problem is that she's also a witness to this other baby's disappearance. If she's been bending the truth when she was talking to you, how do I know I can rely on what she said about what she saw in the park yesterday? That's why I started off by asking you about her state of mind. Did she seem rational to you?'

'Oh yes!' Ruth said decidedly. 'But then, I didn't know that she wasn't being completely honest about leaving the baby in the churchyard. I don't know now quite what to think.' She paused for a few seconds. 'I've got the name of her GP,' she went on, brightening up. 'I'll see if they can tell me any more about how she was coping with the baby and if there were any signs of … mental instability, I suppose. If she isn't able to admit that she deliberately tried to abandon the child, it will be difficult to be confident that she won't do it again if we let her have her back.'

Jonah ended the call and turned to address Bernie.

'Right! We're going to interview Mrs Felicity Mason,' he said decisively. 'Andy – you come with us. Anna – can I leave you to follow up on the most likely leads out of your list of mothers who've lost babies? Take Philipson with you. She could do with the experience.'

***

Flick looked at her reflection in the bedroom mirror. She looked a mess! No wonder that social worker had been reluctant to believe that she was a fit person to care for a baby. What must she have thought, seeing her still in pyjamas in the middle of the afternoon? And look at the state of her hair! She must tidy herself up, clean the house, and get ready to show the world that she deserved to have her baby back.

She headed for the bathroom, feeling more purposeful and cheerful than at any time since Mia had been taken from her. She would show everyone what a good mother she was; and they would give Mia back to her; and everything would be alright again.

***

It was mid-afternoon before Debra made it back down to the kitchen. Now fully dressed, she sat idly flicking through Facebook pages on her phone while she waited for the kettle to boil. A photograph caught her eye. It was of a baby, wrapped in a pink blanket, lying asleep. The caption beneath it urged readers to share the picture with the hope of finding the mother of the child. Debra clicked the link and read on. How strange! A baby had been found in just the same area of Oxford as John's baby – she was sure that it was John's baby – had gone missing. Someone had left her baby in a churchyard for anyone to find. What sort of mother would do that? How could anyone do that, when there were others who so desperately wanted a baby?

***

'And now, on the line from her home in Headington,' the voice on the radio said, as Sam Mason switched it on to be sure of catching any traffic news during his drive home, 'is the woman who says she is the mother of the baby that was left in St Anselm's church this morning. She says that she is suffering from post-natal depression and left her baby, Mia, in the church because she felt that she couldn't cope. Now she's appealing for the baby to be returned to her.'

Mia! Why did the wretched woman have to choose that name? He hoped that Flick would not have heard the news bulletin. The mention of another baby with that name might reawaken all those feelings of loss and disorientation that he was hoping she might have been starting to put behind her. Not that there had been much sign of that when he left her that morning …

'Yes,' a woman's voice came over the radio. 'I'm appealing for help from the public, because Social Services are refusing even to let me *see* my baby.'

It was Flick's voice! What *had* she done now?

***

A call came through to Jonah's phone as they were turning into Quarry Rise from the ring road. It was Ruth Hammond.

'DCI Porter?' she asked anxiously.

'Speaking.'

'I've been on to Mrs Mason's GP.'

She sounded breathless and troubled. She paused.

'And?' Jonah prompted.

'Her baby died about a month ago. It was quite sudden and unexpected – a cot death.'

For a few moments, there was silence as everyone took in this unexpected news.

'I asked how she'd been since the death, but the GP said he hadn't seen her – too busy to start worrying about patients who don't come to see him, and assumed if she didn't bother him she must be OK.'

'You said there was lots of baby equipment lying around the house,' Jonah said, at last, having processed the information and now keen to follow a new, and more sinister, train of thought. 'Do you think it was just stuff that she'd not got round to putting away after the baby died? Or …?'

'I don't know,' Ruth said cautiously. 'When I was there, it somehow *felt* as if there'd been a baby in the house very recently. I really believed her when she said she'd fed her baby that morning and then taken her out in the pram. Things like having to clear toys off the sofa before anyone could sit down. But maybe … maybe she just hadn't felt able to move anything that belonged to her baby.'

'OK,' Jonah said, nodding thoughtfully. 'Thank you for letting us know. This certainly puts a different perspective on things.' He ended the call and looked towards Andy, who had turned round to speak to him from the front passenger seat.

'Well!' Jonah said emphatically.

440

'That's all very interesting, isn't it? It looks as if Mrs Mason fits the profile we've got in mind for the abductor of Abigail Johns rather well, doesn't she?'

'But, sir – if she *has* already taken Abigail, why would she want to claim this other baby? It doesn't make sense.'

'Andy's right,' Bernie agreed. 'She ought to be keeping her head down, not drawing attention to herself like this.'

'Logically, yes, but perhaps she just couldn't help herself,' Jonah argued. 'If we assume that her grief at losing her own baby is making her act irrationally, perhaps one baby wasn't enough – or perhaps this baby is a better match for hers and she wants this one instead.'

'If that's the case – and she really *has* got Abigail,' Bernie said grimly, 'let's hope she doesn't decide to give up on caring for baby number one, because she's hankering for baby number two!'

'On the other hand,' Andy pointed out, 'if she's decided that this second baby is hers, she may be more willing to give back Abigail without a fuss.'

'Always assuming she *has* got her,' Jonah agreed, as they pulled up outside the Masons' house. 'Well – the only way to find out is to see for ourselves.'

'Mrs Felicity Mason?' Andy said, a few minutes later, holding up his warrant card towards a woman of about his own age, who stood on the doorstep, looking out at him with deep brown eyes. Her long brown hair was tied back neatly and her face looked newly scrubbed – perhaps in an attempt to hide the redness around her eyes, which was still faintly visible. 'I'm Detective Sergeant

Lepage and this is DCI Porter. We need to talk to you–'

'Is it about Mia?' The woman interrupted eagerly. 'How is she? Are you going to let her come home?'

'No, Mrs Mason,' Jonah answered, taking control of the conversation. 'It's about the statement you made regarding the abduction of a baby from the Margaret Road recreation ground yesterday. We need to clarify some points. May we come in?'

'I suppose so,' she nodded, stepping back to make room for Jonah's wheelchair to enter. 'Although I don't see what else I can tell you. Haven't you found the baby yet? I would have thought –'

'No,' Jonah cut in sharply. 'We haven't found her – which is why we need to ask *you* some more questions.

As a mother yourself, I'm sure you understand how important and urgent this is.'

They all trooped into the living room – now much tidier, with the toys all neatly packed away in a basket in the corner of the room and a copy of *Mother & Baby* magazine lying open on the coffee table – and sat down. Bernie took out her small laptop and prepared to take notes.

'Mrs Mason,' Jonah began, 'you told us that you took your baby daughter with you in her pram when you walked through the recreation ground on the way to the London Road shops yesterday afternoon.'

'Yes. That's right,' Felicity agreed.

'But that's not quite true, is it?' Jonah said gently.

'What do you mean?' There was a slight note of alarm in her voice, and she looked round at Bernie and Andy before resting her gaze on Jonah's face again.

'Social Services have spoken to your doctor,' Jonah told her, still speaking calmly and watching her face intently. 'He told us about your baby.'

'What about her?' Felicity's voice became more high-pitched and her eyes darted around the room.

'She died, didn't she?'

'No! That's a lie! I mean, the doctor must have made a mistake – got hold of the wrong notes or something.'

'I don't think so.'

'But I *told* you – I took my baby with me to the shops yesterday.'

'No,' Jonah said, calmly but firmly. 'I think you took an empty pram with you, when you went out. We have witnesses who saw someone answering your description pushing a pram across the recreation ground, but none of them looked inside it; and they say that you had the hood up and a sunshade across it.'

'Of course, I did! It was a sunny day. I didn't want Mia to have the sun in her eyes, or to get burnt. You have to be careful with babies.'

'Of course,' Jonah went on, still speaking calmly but with a hint of menace in his voice, 'it's possible that the pram *wasn't* still empty by the time you were crossing the field.'

'What do you mean?' Flick's voice rose in pitch as she started to surmise the real purpose of the police visit.

'I mean that you had ample opportunity to pick up Abigail Johns out of her buggy and put her in your pram without anyone noticing you doing it.'

'But ... but ...,' Flick gasped, her mind

racing to take in this sudden accusation. 'That's ridiculous! *My* baby is the one that was left in the churchyard. I don't need to steal someone else's – I just want my Mia back!'

'But she isn't your Mia, is she?' Jonah persisted. 'You're just hoping that we'll let you have her, because you need a baby to replace yours – just as you hoped that you would get away with taking the baby that you found in the park.'

'No! That's not true!'

'In that case, you won't have any objection to us taking a look round your house – just to make sure that you *don't* have her hidden away here.' Jonah turned his chair as if to go out into the hall.

'Stop!' Flick called, getting up and walking over to the door herself. 'You can't just search my house. You need a warrant for that.'

'Not if you give us permission. If you don't then we'll go and get a warrant, but we're in a hurry, because there's a baby out there who may be in danger. We need to eliminate all the false trails as quickly as we can. So, if you really have nothing to hide, please let us have a look.'

'I don't know,' Flick bit her lip. 'I'm not sure Sam would like it. He likes to keep our stuff private. He wouldn't want … but he'll be back soon, and he'll be able to tell you that I haven't stolen any baby … look! There he is now!'

She pointed towards the window and they all turned to see a man's silhouette crossing it on the way to the front door. Then there were the sounds of a key turning in the lock and the door opening.

Flick went out into the hall, closing the door behind her. Jonah could hear a whispered conversation going on. Then the door opened again and in came Flick, followed by a man of similar age with brown hair, thinning on top, and hazel eyes behind black-framed glasses.

'My husband, Sam,' Flick introduced them. 'And these are the police officers.'

'DCI Jonah Porter,' Jonah told him, 'and my assistant, Dr Bernie Fazakerley, and Sergeant Andy Lepage. We're sorry to intrude, but we have a missing child to find, and your wife's behaviour has been …,' he paused, trying to find a non-confrontational way of putting what he wanted to say, 'somewhat unusual,' he concluded. 'May we have a look around your house – just to confirm that she's telling us the truth when she says that the missing baby is not here?'

Sam looked round at them with an expression of bewilderment on his face.

'I don't understand,' he said, shaking his head slowly. 'What makes you think my wife could have taken the baby?'

'She was there at the time – with a convenient pram for carrying a baby away without being seen – and today a social worker visited and saw all the signs that a baby had been living here very recently – far *more* recently than when your baby died a month ago.'

'Oh! I see.' Sam stood for a moment, thinking. Then he beckoned to them to follow him out into the hall. 'Come with me and I'll show you the baby.'

'Andy and Bernie followed Sam upstairs, while Jonah sat impatiently in the hall, staring up after them.

'This is what you're looking for,' Sam

said, flinging wide the bedroom door and striding over to the bedside.

Bernie and Andy followed him in and stood staring as he snatched up the baby doll from the pillow and held it out towards them.

'This is what my wife has been pushing around in the pram for the last couple of weeks,' he told them. 'And feeding, and changing, and talking to it all the time. Last night I told her it had to stop. That's probably why she rang to say that baby they found in the churchyard is hers. She can't accept that Mia is dead. But she didn't steal that baby – really she didn't!'

15 CHILDREN YET UNBORN

'Another day and we're no further forward!' Jonah muttered bitterly as they got back into the car after taking their leave of the Masons. 'I don't know what I'm going to say to old Peter and the others. It makes you start to wonder if …,' his voice trailed off. He did not want to voice the fear that was starting to grip him, that Abigail might never be found.

'It's still early days,' Bernie pointed out, trying to sound optimistic. 'And one thing that this business with the Masons has shown us is how easy it would be for someone like her to keep a baby hidden. Lots of people must have seen her pushing the pram around with that doll thing in it and just assumed that it was the baby that they'd seen her with before. If whoever's taken Abigail *is* a mother who's lost her baby, it may be quite some time before anyone realises it isn't the same one – if, say, she's a single mother with no close relatives.'

'Bernie's right,' agreed Andy. 'And there's a good chance that DI Davenport will track her down in her list of mothers. It'll just take time, that's all.'

'I hope so,' Jonah sighed. 'But we can't afford to ignore the other possibilities – even though they don't bear thinking about.'

'Well, sir, we've got all the ports and airports on high alert, so, if it's traffickers they won't get her out of the country.'

'Maybe not, but she could have been stolen to order for someone in this country.'

'In which case, it may just take a bit longer,' Bernie said firmly, trying to convince herself as much as the others. 'If someone claims to have adopted a baby, sooner or later questions will be asked. They'll have to register them with a GP, for example. Or else someone will recognise her from the photos we've put out. We just have to keep on with the publicity, so that people don't forget about her. And there's another thing that Felicity Mason has taught us. I bet whoever took Abigail had a pram or a buggy with them and carried her away in that. We *know* that nobody saw anyone *carrying* a baby out of the playground, but they wouldn't notice if someone had a pram, would they? So, can we identify all the pram-pushers who were in the playground that afternoon?'

'You're right!' Jonah agreed, sounding more cheerful, now that there was something positive to be done. 'Let's get back to the incident room and start going through all the statements again.'

'No,' Bernie protested. 'Let's get on the blower to someone who's still on duty this evening to do it, while *we* get off home. Quite apart from it being knocking-off time and you and Andy having been hard at it since the crack of dawn, you owe it to Eddie and Crystal to keep them up to date with the investigation – even if there's nothing much to say.'

They dropped Andy off at his home in

Headington Quarry and then Bernie started the car again and headed for the roundabout where the ring road joined the A40, with the intention of going home. However, Jonah had other ideas.

'Carry on down the by-pass,' he ordered. 'I want to pay Philip Davenport a visit, before Anna gets home. We've got time.'

'Are you sure that's wise?' Bernie queried, nevertheless following orders and continuing along the dual carriageway. 'Interfering between man and wife? It's none of our business, is it?'

'If his behaviour is interfering with one of my officers being in a fit state to do her job, then it *is* my business,' Jonah insisted. 'But more important, he needs to face up to what he's doing and see how selfish he's being.'

'Maybe, but are you the right person to do it?' Bernie remained unconvinced.

'Absolutely I am! He's making out that he wants Anna to have an abortion because it's better for the child never to be born than to have to live with a disability. Well, when it comes to living with disability, I'm an expert in the field!'

'I'm not sure that he'll see it that way,' Bernie said doubtfully. 'And, after all, it is a bit different when it comes to a baby – I mean an acquired disability, like yours, is different from a congenital one.'

'Yes – different, and arguably worse.'

'And you aren't the one who's going to have to look after the baby, are you?' Bernie persisted, manoeuvring into the right-hand lane in order to come off the ring road at the Littlemore roundabout. 'Philip can legitimately complain that you have no right to tell him that he *has* to take on a disabled child, just because you think it's wrong to abort it.'

'Yes – if *that*'s his reason,' Jonah agreed. 'But that's just the point. I want him to admit that it's all because he doesn't want the bother of bringing up a child with spina bifida, and *not* out of concern for the child herself. If he can square that with his conscience then that's his problem – but I *won't* have him going round congratulating himself on his humanity towards the unborn child and criticising Anna for not wanting to save her baby from a fate worse than death.'

'OK,' Bernie sighed. 'On your head be it! Now, what number is the house?'

They pulled up outside a modest three-bedroomed semi-detached in the Rosehill area. Bernie noted with satisfaction that the step up to the front door was shallow and they would not need the portable ramp to enable Jonah to enter – that was, of course, if Philip Davenport were to invite them in. She still thought that he would be well within his rights to send Jonah packing.

She rang the bell and, after a short pause, the door opened to reveal a tall man in his early forties with yellow-blond hair and pale blue eyes. He looked at them with an expression of surprise, which turned to alarm as he worked out who Jonah was.

'What is it?' he asked anxiously. 'Is it Anna? Has something happened to her? Is she alright?'

'Please don't be alarmed, Mr Davenport,' Jonah said, pleasantly surprised that Philip appeared to be so concerned for his wife's well-being.

'Your wife is quite safe – and I've left orders that she's to come home on time today, whatever may be kicking off in the case. If I'm going to be bullied into knocking off promptly at the end of the shift, I don't see why she shouldn't as well!'

'So … why are you here then?' Philip looked from Jonah to Bernie and back again, with a puzzled expression on his face.

'I wanted to have a word with you about your daughter,' Jonah answered. 'May we come in? It won't take long.'

'About Jessica?' Philip queried, looking even more puzzled, but stepping back to allow Jonah to enter, with a little help from Bernie to negotiate the step.

'No. Your other daughter – the one you seem so keen not to be burdened with.'

'Oh! I get it! I suppose Anna's put you up to this.' Philip's tone changed from puzzlement to hostility. 'She's got no business discussing our private affairs with you – and you've got no business–'

'No. Anna knows nothing about me being here. And I have no intention of interfering in your private affairs. I just think that, when you're making life and death decisions about another person, you ought to be properly appraised of all the facts.'

'Meaning?' Philip demanded, with increased animosity in his voice.

'Meaning that, if you think you can justify pressurising your wife to have an abortion for the sake of the baby, you need to know what life would be like for that baby.'

'And you know all about that, I suppose?' There could be no mistaking the anger in Philip's voice now.

'Yes. I do – or at least I've got a much better idea than you can have. You've been told that the baby most likely has spina bifida, right?'

'Yes.'

'And what have they told you that will mean for her – from a practical point of view?'

'They said it'd mean paralysis – isn't that enough?'

'Enough to mean she'd be better off dead? No – not enough at all! Do you think *I'd* be better off dead?'

'No, of course not,' Philip said hurriedly. 'But that's completely different. You had a whole life before ... before ...,' Philip searched for the right words, struggling with embarrassment, '... before it happened, he finished at last. 'That baby of Anna's would be handicapped from birth. That's why it would be a kindness to finish things now. It's unfair to compare it with your situation. You were an adult – you could decide for yourself.'

'Well no, I couldn't actually. Under British law, *I'm* not allowed to decide that my life isn't worth living – or at least, only if I can figure out some way of killing myself without any help from anyone else! But that's not the point. You want to deprive your daughter of the opportunity of life – and you're *claiming* that it's because you don't think her life will be worth living. I'm just telling you that you can't possibly know that – and that, in fact, there's an awful lot of life that we poor cripples can enjoy just as much as you do.'

'And a lot that you can't,' Philip argued. 'A lot that this baby of Anna's would never have a chance to experience. *You* may be happy enough, but you can't speak for everyone. There are plenty of stories of people with back injuries who just want to die – and if it was up to me, I'd change the law to allow them to choose that.'

'Plenty of stories? Do you know a single one where it was someone *born* with a spinal cord defect? *Of course*, when you have a life-changing injury, you get depressed about it! There were times when I felt it wasn't worth the effort of carrying on – but I was wrong. I've still got lots to live for. And if I'd been born like this – well, it'd just be part of what I was like – part of being me. You ought to go and meet some people with spina bifida before you start writing them all off as *better off dead*.'

'It's all very well for *you* to talk,' Philip

argued. 'It's *our* lives that are going to be turned upside down if Anna insists on going ahead with having this baby. What makes you think you can come here, taking the moral high ground and telling me we've got to burden ourselves with-'

'Now that's a different argument altogether,' Jonah interrupted. 'And, if that's your line, I agree – it's none of my business. All I came to say is that, if you're going to continue to press Anna to have an abortion, you've got to come clean and admit – to her and to yourself – that it's for your own benefit and not out of some high-minded desire to prevent your daughter from suffering.'

'And stop calling it *your daughter* like that,' Philip went on. 'It's just another ploy to try to make me feel guilty. It's just a foetus – not a living, breathing human being.'

'But it will be – unless you succeed in persuading Anna to prevent it having the chance,' Bernie pointed out, coming to Jonah's defence against her better judgement, but feeling compelled to do so by a combination of loyalty to him and an instinctive belief that human life began at conception rather than at birth.

'All I'm asking you to do is think about it,' Jonah said, trying to adopt a more conciliatory tone. 'And to remember that being in a wheelchair isn't the end of the world and walking isn't all it's cracked up to be!'

'And being a carer has its up-sides too,' Bernie added. 'It's all just a matter of thinking positive.'

'OK, you've made your point,' Philip growled, keeping his anger in check with some difficulty. 'Now, if you don't mind, I've got dinner to get for my wife and my *actual* kids, which is rather more important than standing here speculating about hypothetical ones.'

'Fair enough,' Jonah nodded and began the tricky manoeuvre of turning his chair round in the narrow hallway. 'Good bye.'

Philip closed the door behind them and turned to go back to the kitchen, but a voice calling out from upstairs stopped him in his tracks.

'Dad!' Jessica called over the bannisters in an accusatory tone. 'Is that true, what he said? Are you trying to get Mum to have an abortion?'

'Jess! I thought you were in your room. How long have you been listening?'

'Since forever. I heard him say something about wanting to talk to you about your daughter. I thought he meant me, so of course I listened. Now answer my question.'

'Your mother and I are thinking about what to do,' Philip hedged. Why had Anna refused to listen to him, three months earlier, when he told her that there was no need for the kids to know that she was expecting? Time enough when her condition became obvious even to them – assuming that they had decided to go through with it. Everything would have been so much easier if she had allowed them to think that her morning sickness was simply a rather persistent stomach bug, instead of showing off the 9-week scan picture, as if she were delighted with the whole business. Then they could have got rid of it quietly, with no fuss, and Jessica and Marcus would have been none the wiser. 'The second scan showed up some abnormalities, which means we have to decide–'

'Whether to kill it or not,' Jessica interrupted. 'That's what you were talking about just now, wasn't it?'

'No Jess, it's not like that at all,' Philip protested. 'It's not a case of *killing*. All we're talking about is terminating an unwanted pregnancy. Women do it all the time.'

'But Mum doesn't want to, does she? It's just you!' Jessica sounded accusing.

'Naturally it's difficult for her to make a rational judgement,' Philip began. 'Her hormones–'

'Bollocks!' Jessica interrupted rudely. 'That's what men always say when they disagree with a woman. It's just a way of not having to admit that we've got a right to a different opinion. He's right – you just don't want the bother of having a disabled kid in the family. What about us? Don't Marcus and I get a say?'

'You don't understand,' Philip said as calmly as he could, resisting the urge to shout at his daughter to leave him alone and get back to her schoolwork. 'It's you and Marcus that I'm thinking about. You don't realise what an impact it would have on you both – on all of us – if your mother goes ahead with this. Handicapped children take up a lot of time. There'd be all sorts of things that we couldn't do together anymore.'

'But we could help,' Jessica argued. 'I wouldn't mind. You're just being so blinkered!'

'No! It's you and your mother that are being blinkered. You're just refusing to think about how difficult it's going to be.'

'And then there's Nan,' Jessica continued. 'When we move down to

Devon, she'll be able to help, won't she? She loves kids.'

'If your mother doesn't see reason, she won't be coming with us to Devon,' Philip retorted angrily. 'I'm not having my mum running round after a handicapped baby at her time of life!'

For a moment, there was a stunned silence. Then Jessica rounded on her father, shouting wildly.

'You can't be serious! You're leaving Mum? And you never told us! And all because she won't agree to kill *your* baby? I can't believe I'm hearing this!'

'Jess, Jess!' Philip implored, putting out his arm towards his daughter in a fruitless attempt to calm her. 'It's not like that at all. Of course I *hope* your mum will come round to seeing it my way and then we'll all be able to go down to Devon together. We didn't tell you and

Marcus because ... well, we hoped you'd never need to know about our ... disagreement.'

'Disagreement! You want Mum to kill a baby and you call it a *disagreement*!'

'Will you stop using that word? We're not killing a baby – we're just preventing a handicapped child being born. Surely, you can see that it wouldn't have much of a life – confined to a wheelchair, not able to do the things that all the other kids are doing?'

'Oh, I see!' Jessica said, sarcastically. 'If you can't walk, you'd be better off dead! Well, I hope I never have a serious accident, like DCI Porter, because I can see you'd be wanting to have me put down!'

'Now you're being ridiculous!'

'Am I? I don't think so.' Jessica turned and ran back upstairs and into her bedroom, slamming the door behind her. Philip stood in the hall, unable to decide what to do. Then the bedroom door opened again and Jessica shouted down to him, 'and if Mum stays here, I'm staying too! You can bugger off down to Devon on your own!'

16 NIGHT OF DOUBT AND SORROW

'Is there any news?' Peter asked the moment they entered the house. He had heard the car pulling up outside and was waiting for them in the hall. Bernie and Jonah both shook their heads.

'We thought we had a lead,' Jonah told him, 'but it didn't go anywhere. We've got people going through a list of women who might have a reason to want to take a baby, but nothing doing with that so far. A couple of minutes ago, there was a call came through that a woman in Sunderland has reported that her neighbour has been buying a load of baby stuff – pram, high chair, car seat, that sort of thing – but doesn't have a baby. Northumbria Police are following up on that.'

'That's a bit tenuous, isn't it?' Eddie commented, coming out of the living room with Ricky in his arms. 'They could be presents for someone else or anything.'

'And isn't Sunderland an awfully long way away?' Crystal added, joining them from the kitchen, where she had been helping Peter to prepare their evening meal.

'Yes and yes,' Jonah replied. 'But apparently the woman has been acting a bit strangely ever since her marriage broke down a couple of years ago – in fact, according to the neighbour, she hadn't been right since quite some time before that – something to do with her not being able to have children and not being able to come to terms with it. In other words, just the sort of psychological profile that *might* make her take someone else's baby. Anyway, on the principle of leaving no stone unturned, I've told the local police to investigate. They're going to call on her this evening, so we should have a full report by the morning.'

'And there really is no other news?' Crystal asked, trying hard not to sound reproachful. She knew that Jonah was doing everything that he could to find her little daughter.

'No. I'm sorry.' Jonah shook his head again.

There seemed to be nothing more to be said. Peter and Crystal returned to the kitchen, while Bernie joined Eddie and Ricky in the living room and Lucy came down from her bedroom to take Jonah through his daily physiotherapy session. She transferred him from his chair into the *Functional Electrical Stimulation*[5] machine that enabled him to exercise muscles over which he no longer had conscious control.

As he watched his legs moving on the exercise bike, Jonah pondered on the events of the last few hours. It had

---

[5] See, for example, Home-Based Functional Electrical Stimulation Rescues Permanently Denervated Muscles in Paraplegic Patients With Complete Lower Motor Neuron Lesion, H Kern et al., Neurorehabilitation and Neural Repair, May 2010. http://journals.sagepub.com/doi/abs/10.1177/1545968310366129 (accessed 15/12/16).

definitely not been a good day. They had started out with one distressed family and now they had three! Eddie and Crystal were distraught that Abigail had not been found. The baby in the churchyard had lost her family – and goodness knew what sad story lay behind her mother having abandoned her. And now there was Felicity Mason – grieving for her lost child and vainly hoping to claim a replacement. There was something very wrong with a world where those things happened.

His thoughts were interrupted by the ringing of the phone on his wheelchair. Lucy answered it.

'Hi Nathan!' she said, seeing his name and profile picture on the screen. 'Your dad's doing his physio, so hang on a minute while I move things around so he can talk to you.'

'It's OK. Don't interrupt him,' Nathan's voice came over the loudspeaker. 'I'm just ringing with a quick update on Rachel.'

'Rachel!' Jonah exclaimed from the other side of the room. He had been so preoccupied with the investigation into Abigail's disappearance that he had forgotten about his granddaughter's illness. 'Is she OK? Was she discharged today?'

'She's had a bit of a setback,' Nathan continued. He had not been able to distinguish all of his father's words, but he had heard the tone of anxiety in his voice. 'But the doctors still say there's nothing to worry about. They're keeping her in for another night and they're running the tests again – just in case – but they say they're still ninety-nine percent confident that it's viral meningitis and she'll throw it off in a few days.'

'Are you sure?' Jonah asked anxiously, his voice sounding clearer now that Lucy had moved the microphone closer to him. 'You're not glossing over the bad news for fear of worrying Poor Old Dad, are you?'

'No, Dad. I'm telling you exactly what they told us.'

'OK. Well, thanks for ringing. You will keep me informed, won't you?'

'Yes Dad, of course.'

There was an awkward silence. Neither man knew how to end the conversation without appearing abrupt, but neither could think of anything more to say.

'Give our love to Georgia,' Lucy chipped in.

'Thanks. I will. Well … I'd better go. I'll

ring again in the morning to let you know how things are going.' Nathan ended the call.

'I should have rung Nathan as soon as I got in,' Jonah muttered, angry with himself for having forgotten.

'They must both be dreadfully worried,' Lucy agreed. 'I was going to light a candle for Rachel, but then I wasn't sure if maybe Nathan and Georgia might not like it. Do you think they'd mind?'

'I can't imagine they'd *mind*,' Jonah answered in a tone that betrayed his deep suspicion of the practice. 'It's not as if it'll make any difference to anything.'

'I just wondered,' Lucy tried to explain, 'with Georgia being Jewish ... I mean, she might not like ... praying for them in a church, I mean.'

'I don't see why – it's all the same God, isn't it? I just don't see why you think He'll be impressed with candles!'

'I don't,' Lucy protested. 'It's not that at all. It's …,' she hesitated, unsure how to explain her feelings. 'It just makes me feel that I'm *doing* something,' she finished at last.

'Hmmph!' Jonah snorted. 'It all seems a bit too much like superstition to my way of thinking. Or magic. You go through the right rituals and something miraculous happens.'

'But it's not like that at all,' Lucy argued. 'It's just another way of praying, really.'

'Father Damien has been praying to St Anthony for Abigail's safe return,' Peter joined in the conversation. He had come into the room to let Jonah and Lucy know that the meal was nearly ready. 'We'll be dishing up in ten minutes. Let me give you a hand with getting ready.'

Lucy switched off the exercise machine and started carefully removing electrodes from Jonah's body. Peter, meanwhile, brought over the hoist that they would use to transfer Jonah to the bed, where they could dress him most conveniently.

'St Anthony!' Jonah exclaimed in a disparaging tone. He had been brought up as a Baptist and found veneration of the saints incomprehensible, if not idolatrous.

'He's the patron saint of lost things,' Lucy told him. 'Lots of Catholics talk about praying to St Anthony when they want to find something they've lost.'

'It sounds like a lot of mumbo-jumbo to me.' Jonah was more worried by

Nathan's news than he cared to admit and it was making him argumentative. 'Setting up all these saints and worshipping them like little gods.'

'Like I was telling Peter yesterday,' Lucy said, 'it's not like that really. When they say they're praying to a saint, they really just mean they're asking the saints to pray for them.'

'I don't need to ask some plaster saint to pray on my behalf,' Jonah argued. 'What's the point? I'd rather go direct to the top.'

'It's only the same as when people ask for prayers from living people,' Lucy countered. 'You know – prayer request books in church and that sort of thing. You get lots of requests for prayers on social media too. What's the difference between that and asking the saints to pray for us?'

'Well, for a start, they're all dead.'

'I thought they were all supposed to be part of the Church Triumphant.' Peter interjected, surprising himself, as well as the others, by his intervention on the side of Catholic credulity. 'Didn't there used to be a bit in the old communion service about us all being part of the church, militant here on earth, triumphant in heaven?'

'In my opinion, once you're dead, you're dead – until the second coming. That's what St Paul said.'

'So, don't you ever talk to Margaret?' Peter asked, in a tone of surprise. 'I talk to Angie.'

'Maybe I do,' Jonah conceded reluctantly. 'But it's just habit. I know she can't hear me. And I don't understand why *you're* talking like this, Peter, when you don't even believe in God or an afterlife or anything.'

'I was only saying that talking to dead people is a natural thing to do, so I suppose, it's not that different talking to saints who've been dead a lot longer.'

'Well, however you dress it up, it still seems to me like trying to get round God by asking one of his special friends to try to influence Him. I mean – presumably, that's the idea? *I'm* not important enough to carry much weight with God, so I'll ask some saint to talk to Him on my behalf!'

'Or maybe,' Lucy suggested, remembering her conversation with Peter the day before, 'it's more that it's easier to believe that they'd understand where you're coming from. Like the way it's easier to talk to someone about a problem, if you know they've had a similar experience. Nathan rang,' she added, turning to Peter, as she remembered the incident that had sparked off this conversation. 'They're keeping Rachel in hospital for another night.'

'Why?' Peter's voice was immediately filled with concern. He looked towards Jonah with compassion in his eyes. 'Is she going to be alright?'

'So the doctors say, apparently,' he answered. 'According to Nathan it's just a precaution – but they're doing more tests, which doesn't sound that good. So we'll just have to hope that there's more in Lucy's candle-lighting and your chattering to the dead than meets the eye, won't we?' he added, trying to make light of the situation. 'Now, I'm dressed, so if you'll just get me into the chair again, perhaps we can eat.'

Victoria peered hopefully out of the window. Yes! This time it was no false alarm; the car that had drawn up outside was a taxi and the man who was climbing out on to the pavement was John. There was no mistaking that thick thatch of red hair. He had sent a text from the airport to say that he was on his way, and she had been on tenterhooks for the last hour awaiting his arrival. She hurried out into the hall and opened the front door, ready to welcome him.

It seemed to take an age for him to pay off the driver and collect his bags from the back, but at last he looked towards her, smiling and calling out, 'Vicky! I've missed you!'

Then he was with her in the hall,

holding her tight in his arms and kissing her. For a few minutes, they might have been the only two people alive in the world. Then, he released her and looked around.

'And now, I must see her,' he said excitedly. 'Where is she?'

'Upstairs. She's still supposed to sleep most of the time. I'll go and get her.'

'No. Don't disturb her. I'll come up. I'll take my case up to our room and then I'll just have a peep in at her.'

A few minutes later, they were both standing in silence, looking down into the cot. Esme shifted in her sleep and made a grunting noise, but she did not wake. John put his arm round Victoria's shoulder and drew her closer to him.

'She's beautiful,' he breathed.

'I think she takes after her dad,'

Victoria whispered back.

They went downstairs again and Victoria served the casserole that she had prepared earlier and left keeping warm in the oven in readiness for John's return. If only Esme would stay asleep for long enough for them to enjoy it together!

'That was wonderful!' John declared a few minutes later, pushing away his plate and leaning back in his chair. 'It's so good to be home again! And I really do mean it this time – I'm not going off abroad any more. Brian can look after the overseas business from now on. I'm determined to be here for you and Esme.'

After the meal, they slumped together on the sofa in front of the television set, half-watching the news channel. John was finding it difficult to keep himself awake. It had been a long day of travelling and, by now, it was the early morning in Beijing. Victoria rested her head against his chest, listening to the slow thump, thump of his heart with one ear while keeping the other alert for sounds from the bedroom above. Esme was being unusually well-behaved this evening. It was as if she understood that Mummy and Daddy needed some time together on this special day. Perhaps the worst was over now. Perhaps everything was going to work out alright after all.

'Concerns are growing for the welfare of six-week-old Abigail Johns, the baby who was snatched from her pram in the Headington district of Oxford yesterday afternoon.' John sat up straighter and listened intently to the news report, alerted by the familiar place names and the mention of a baby. 'There is still no news of her whereabouts and the police have renewed their appeal to members of the public to be vigilant and to report anything that could help them to track her down.'

'Isn't that the recreation ground at the bottom of the road?' John asked, watching the screen intently as the camera displayed the array of flowers and soft toys lying along the railings, and the uniformed police officer standing next to the plastic tape that still cordoned off the playground.

'Yes,' Victoria agreed. 'It's frightening to think that it was so close to here, isn't it? And I must have passed the baby only a few minutes before it happened. I took Esme out for a walk to get her off to sleep, and we went across the rec. In fact, I think I may even have seen the baby. She was asleep in a double-buggy, under the trees.'

The scene changed again, showing a tower block and a young woman standing outside it, with a toddler in a pushchair and an older child fidgeting beside her.

'Shona Knight lives in a neighbouring flat and knows the Johns family,' the reporter was saying. 'This must have come as a shock to families in the neighbourhood,' she went on, holding out a microphone for Shona's reply.

'Yes,' agreed Shona. 'We're all in shock at the moment, I think. Nothing like this has ever happened here before. And they're such a lovely family. It's heart-breaking to think that someone could do such a thing.'

'I'm glad you're home now,' Victoria said earnestly, pulling John back down beside her and settling her head under his chin. 'I'll feel safer with you here. I know it's stupid, but I was getting paranoid that someone might somehow get in and steal Esme from her cot. It's just so awful to think there's someone out there who would do something like that.'

The scene changed again, to show a re-run of Peter's appeal to the kidnapper for Abigail's safe return. Then the item closed with a close-up of the photograph of Abigail that the police had put out to the public. She lay there smiling up, her green eyes shining and her red hair sticking out around her head.

'I suppose all babies look quite similar,' John said, still staring at the screen, 'but that one does bear a remarkable resemblance to that photo you sent me of Esme – except for the hair, of course.'

'And the eyes,' Victoria added. 'Esme was asleep, so you couldn't see, but I'm sure her eyes are a different colour.'

***

'Bed time!' Bernie declared to Jonah, looking at her watch. 'It looks as if you'll have to put up with me getting you sorted this evening.'

Lucy had gone out on her errand to St Cyprian's and Peter was up in the attic rooms with his son and daughter-in-law, leaving Bernie and Jonah alone together making rather desultory conversation.

'OK,' Jonah agreed. While he would never have admitted it, he was feeling exhausted after a busy and frustrating day, and the worrying news of Rachel's relapse. 'I'll just call into the incident room one last time, in case there have been any developments.'

As he had expected, there was little to report. There had been a few more possible sightings of Abigail by members of the public in various parts of the country, none of them very convincing. The likely identities of three of the boys who had made racist remarks to Crystal in the street the week before had been established. A growing list of mothers of babies of roughly Abigail's age had been investigated and eliminated from the enquiry.

Northumbria Police had visited the home of the woman whose neighbour had reported that she was accumulating equipment for a non-existent baby, but she was not there. Another neighbour had come out and told them that the woman had left in her car three hours earlier. She was confident that the car had contained a child's safety seat, but she had not been able to see whether it was occupied. Police across the country had been alerted to watch out for the car and its occupant, who had been named as Mrs Debra Middleton.

'It feels very much like clutching at straws,' Jonah remarked to Bernie, as they made their way into his bedroom and began the daily routine of preparing him for the night. 'Why would you travel all the way from Sunderland to Oxford to steal a baby? And, as Eddie said, there are a million perfectly innocent explanations for her behaviour.'

'I suppose, if you *were* intent on stealing a baby, you might feel safer taking one from somewhere a long way from home,' Bernie suggested. 'It would reduce the chances of the baby being recognised, wouldn't it? I mean – if you'd stolen a baby, you wouldn't want any risk that you might bump into the real parents in the street, would you?'

'Well, my money's on us waking up to hear that she's just become an auntie or a godmother or taken up fostering or something. The nosey neighbour is probably exaggerating and everything is completely normal really.'

'It's not like you to be so pessimistic,' Bernie commented as she gently sponged his face. 'What's happened to the usual DCI Porter total confidence in your abilities to solve every crime in record time?'

'The stakes aren't usually so high. I'm afraid of letting you all down.'

Bernie pondered this remark.

'We won't hold it against you,' she said at last, 'even if ...'

'No. I know, but it'll still feel ...,' Jonah

groped for the right words. 'And right now … It doesn't seem as if we're getting anywhere … and then there's Anna's baby … and that poor woman, Felicity Mason …'

'And Rachel in hospital,' Bernie finished for him. That was it, wasn't it? Like Peter, Jonah was feeling impotent to protect his son from the heart breaking circumstances that they were in. 'Yes. It does feel as if everything's going wrong just now.'

'I suppose we'll just have to hope that all Lucy's candle-lighting does the trick,' Jonah said with a short laugh, trying to make light of the situation. However, Bernie detected the mockery and bitterness in his voice.

'Don't be like that,' she chided. 'I know you don't believe in that sort of thing, but there's no need to imply–'

'I just can't understand how someone as intelligent as Lucy can think it's going to make any difference.'

'That's because you're not looking at it the right way,' Bernie told him as she loaded Jonah's toothbrush with paste. 'You're thinking about it as if it's some sort of bargain with God: so many candles equals so many prayers granted. It's not like that at all.'

She brushed Jonah's teeth vigorously, taking advantage of his temporary inability to answer back, to expand on her theme.

'When I was a child, I used to go to church with my dad every Saturday to light candles for my mam. It was our regular routine: confession and then, while we were both in a state of grace, a candle each for her. I suppose you'd have said that it didn't do a blind bit of good, seeing as her MND still progressed just the same; but that wasn't what it was all about. It was … I don't know … It was a sort of public admission that here was something that we couldn't sort out ourselves, I suppose. And it was Dad's way of showing me that he cared about Mam. I mean, he wasn't that articulate; he'd never have stood up in one of your Baptist prayer meetings and prayed for her or anything like that – or even written her name in one of those prayer books they have in the back of churches these days.'

She held a bowl under Jonah's chin so that he could spit into it, and reached for the glass of water that she had got ready for him. He swilled it round in his mouth and then spat again, while Bernie continued with her defence of the candle-lighting ritual, speaking less seriously now.

'And you're behind the times, if you still think candles are half-way to Rome,' she teased. 'Lots of protestant churches are starting to realise that they've been throwing the baby out with the bathwater and they're starting to use them again. I bet there were candles lit at that all-night prayer vigil at Cowley Road. It's a way of people feeling they're *doing* something. Just like the way complete strangers keep leaving flowers and teddies and things by the playground where Abigail went missing – they don't know what they can do to help, but they want to make some sort of gesture.'

'Hmmph!' Jonah was still unconvinced. 'I suppose next you'll be telling me that I ought to be enlisting the help of St Anthony to find Abigail!'

'No,' Bernie sounded puzzled. 'Where's that coming from?'

'Peter told me that some *Father Damien* has been praying to St Anthony on her behalf.'

'And how has Peter come to be talking to Father Damien?' Bernie wondered. 'I suppose he must have called round while we were out. He's at St Cyprian's. He prepared Lucy for her first communion – I think she gave him rather a hard time! Praying to St Anthony is just his way of saying that he's concerned about Abigail having gone missing. I don't suppose he really means it literally.'

Jonah was prevented from answering by the cloth with which Bernie was now gently wiping his face, so she continued.

'If you asked him, I'm sure he'd tell you that, when Catholics say they're praying to the saints, they're really just talking to them – asking them to pray to God on our behalf. It's only the same as asking for prayers from a friend.'

'That's what Lucy said,' Jonah admitted, as soon as his mouth was free to speak again. 'But I still don't get it. For a start, I don't think I ever would ask anyone to pray for me. That's not how I see prayer at all. It's not about asking him to do things. It's about giving praise and thanks, saying sorry, and sharing the things that concern me, and then hoping that he'll show me how to fix some of the things that are wrong with the world. I don't see how you can do that through an intermediary.'

'But that's how Catholics see it too – at least, no, I'm sure there are plenty of people in every denomination who haven't got past the idea of prayer being a shopping list of things that they need God to deal with because nobody else can – but if you asked a Catholic theologian, I'm sure they'd agree with you. Take Mother Teresa of Calcutta, for example. She said something along the lines of "I used to believe that prayer changes things, but now I know that prayer changes us and we change things." Now, let's get you into bed.'

'So where does that leave praying to saints?' Jonah wanted to know.

'That's it!' Bernie said excitedly, as she carefully manoeuvred the hoist to transfer Jonah from the bathroom into his bed. 'I think I've just worked it out. You shouldn't say, "praying *to* saints". It's "praying *with* the saints"! It's like having a prayer meeting – which I'm sure you Baptists do a lot of – and all sharing together, the way you talked about just now.'

'I suppose so,' Jonah conceded, still sounding doubtful, 'if you imagine the saints as being up there in heaven looking down on us and listening in to our conversations.'

'And why wouldn't you? At least – I'd dispute *up there*. It's more like *out there*, all around us. You know – the great cloud of witnesses and all that.'

'So you don't agree with the idea that, after you die, the next thing you know is the last trump and Judgement Day? That's how I've always pictured it.'

'I don't know,' Bernie said slowly. 'I think it's all to do with how you reconcile time and eternity. I mean, God is assumed to be outside of time, isn't he? What if, after we die, we will be too?'

'How d'you mean?'

'Well,' Bernie paused for a moment to

marshal her thoughts. 'I suppose we all think of time as being like a straight line. And we can only move along it in one direction. It's one-dimensional, if you like. But suppose it's really a line in space? The way I see Eternity is as multi-dimensional Time. So now, suppose that when you die, you fall off the one-dimensional time line and into 3-D Eternity. From out there, you can see the whole of the time line, right the way from minus infinity to plus infinity! Does that make sense?'

'I suppose so,' Jonah said again, 'but I still don't see the point of praying to – or with – saints. Why make things any more complicated than they already are?'

'Look – I'm not asking you to understand. Just don't dismiss people who do it as ignorant or childish.'

'I never said anything of the sort!' Jonah protested indignantly.

'No. I know.' Bernie checked that Jonah was lying in a comfortable position and drew the covers over him. Then she leaned forward and kissed him softly on the cheek. 'But that's how it comes across sometimes.'

She straightened up and turned to go, but Jonah called her back.

'Bernie?' he asked earnestly. 'Do you think Margaret is out there – watching us?'

'Yes.' Bernie knelt down next to the bed and put her arms around Jonah's shoulders. 'Yes – I do.' She paused for a few moments before going on. 'But that's just my way of looking at it. You could be right. It could be that they're all in a big sleep until the last trump. I'm not trying to –'

'But *you* think she can hear me when I talk to her?'

'Yes.'

'And she knows about Rachel?'

'I think so.' Bernie hugged Jonah tighter. There seemed to be nothing more to be said.

***

Eddie and Crystal lay awake in their attic room. The house was silent. They could hear Ricky's soft breathing from his cot in the corner. Eddie stretched out his hand and grasped the small alarm clock on the shelf next to the bed. He held it in front of his face and peered at it. Only one o'clock! It was still hours to go before they could get up, and more hours still before they could expect news on how the search for Abigail was progressing.

'Eddie?' Crystal said, feeling the movement and realising that he too was awake. 'What happens ...,' she paused, fearful of voicing her thoughts, and yet knowing that it was something that she needed to share with her husband. 'What happens if they *never* find her?'

'I'd been thinking about that too.' Eddie put down the clock and took Crystal in his arms. 'I've told them at work that I'll be in on Monday, whether or not. They said I could have as long as it takes, but I can't expect them to wait forever and we can't afford to lose this job. In any case ...,' he trailed off, unwilling to admit that he would welcome a return to the routine of work and something to take his mind off constantly wondering what had happened to his daughter.

'I know.' Crystal hugged him. 'It's the

waiting that's the worst – and the not knowing – and especially the not knowing if we'll ever know. And that's why I asked. I mean – how long do we wait before we …?'

'I think we ought to go back to the flat,' Eddie said, glad of the opportunity to start making decisions for themselves again. 'We've got to try to get back to normal.'

'Yes,' Crystal agreed. 'I know your dad would like us to stay here, but it'll only be more difficult for Ricky to settle there again the longer we leave it.'

'And it's not fair on Jonah,' Eddie added, 'coming home after he's been working on looking for her all day and having to face us all evening.'

'I hadn't thought of that. Do you think he *ought* to have handed it over to someone else?'

'Yeah. Probably. I'm surprised Superintendent Brown didn't make him. I can only think they all expected it to be over so quickly that it wouldn't matter.'

'You mean, they thought they'd have found Abby by now?'

'Yeah – maybe.'

'So – do you think …? I mean, would they have found her now, if they were going to?'

'No! Well, maybe. I don't know, do I?' Eddie's frustration got the better of him and he was unable to restrain the irritation that he felt at these questions.

'Sorry,' Crystal said humbly, conscious that she had annoyed her husband. 'I didn't mean to–'

'No,' Eddie broke in, '*I'm* sorry. I shouldn't have snapped at you. It just …,' he sighed.

They lay together in silence.

'I should never have brought you here,' Eddie said suddenly.

'What do you mean? It was your dad's idea – and we agreed we're going to move back tomorrow.'

'No. I didn't mean this house. I meant over here – to England. If we'd stayed in Jamaica, this would never have happened. I should never have dragged you and Ricky over here – away from your family and all your friends.'

'I'm making new friends over here,' Crystal objected, trying to stem the flow of Eddie's self-denigration.

'It's not the same,' Eddie answered dismissively, determined to vent his feelings of guilt and frustration. 'I shouldn't have rushed to take the first job that came along. I should have waited. Something would have turned up. We'd have managed somehow. You had your job. And your parents said they'd help out. It was all my fault for not wanting–'

'No, Eddie. We both decided to come,' Crystal insisted. 'I didn't want to move in with Mum and Dad any more than you did. It was fine having them just round the corner, but I'd have gone crazy living in the same house with them. And your dad's been lovely. I really like him. And Ricky's taken to him really well too.'

'You don't have to pretend–,' Eddie began, strangely reluctant to give up his role as the cause of all their misery.

'I'm *not* pretending,' Crystal answered sharply. It was her turn to feel irritated with her spouse. 'I really do think we did the right thing, coming over here. It wasn't doing us any good having my mum dropping in every five minutes with food – as if she thought I'd let you all starve if she didn't bring us supplies all the time.'

'If we'd stayed, Abby wouldn't have been taken,' Eddie insisted. 'You can't get away from that.'

'Or if I'd kept a proper watch on the buggy, while I was playing with Ricky,' Crystal said in an undertone. 'Everyone's been very careful not to say it, but it *is* all my fault really, isn't it? I shouldn't have just left her like that.'

'No!' Eddie's exclamation disturbed Ricky and he whimpered in his sleep. 'No,' Eddie resumed more quietly. 'It's not your fault. You weren't to know. You just did the same as anyone would have done back home.'

'What do you mean?' Crystal was puzzled.

'I mean, it's different here. People

keep themselves to themselves. They don't look out for each other the same. You can't trust –'

'So you *do* think it's my fault!' Crystal interrupted in an angry whisper. 'You think that I ought to have *known* that someone might want to take Abigail. That's what you're saying, isn't it? You're saying I'm just an ignorant Jamaican who doesn't know how to keep her kids safe over here, because I'm too trusting.'

'I wasn't saying that at all,' Eddie whispered back indignantly. 'I was only saying that, over here, there are a lot more people who –'

'I can't believe I'm hearing this!' Crystal cut him off again. 'I never thought you were a racist.'

'Where's that coming from?' Eddie was stunned. 'I never said anything!'

'You *did* though.' Crystal insisted. 'You're saying that you can't trust white people.'

'I never said anything of the sort. I was just pointing out that society is different over here – not so close-knit – more disjointed – everyone out for what they can get. It's nothing to do with race.'

'OK then,' Crystal conceded. 'Maybe race isn't the right word – though I still think, when you say *society* you mean *white society* – but you *are* saying that British people are less trustworthy than Jamaicans.'

'Don't be silly. *I'm* British, remember?'

'Yes – and so are all those people who've been leaving flowers and things outside the park where Abby was taken.'

'Yes. I suppose so.' Eddie thought for a few seconds. 'But I still think it wouldn't have happened if we'd stayed in Jamaica.'

'Why? Because nobody in Jamaica ever wanted a baby so badly that they were tempted to … that, when they saw one that they thought had been abandoned, they couldn't stop themselves from taking her? Don't you remember what your dad said – and the police too? Whoever took Abby, it's probably because they desperately want a baby. And don't you remember how *we* were feeling only a couple of years ago, when *we* thought we might never have any children? Don't you see …?'

'I just meant that if we hadn't moved here then it wouldn't have been Abby who was the baby that whoever it was decided to take, that's all.'

'Maybe. But we couldn't possibly have known that, so there's no point blaming yourself for bringing us here.'

They lay in silence for a few more minutes. Then Crystal sat up and switched on the bedside light.

'What're you up to?' Eddie asked.

Crystal got out of bed and padded across to the dressing table where she had left her handbag. She got out a small notebook and a pen. Then she came back and got in beside Eddie again.

'I'm writing out what I'm going to say,' she told him. 'I've decided that I want to make an appeal to the kidnapper to give Abby back. Your dad was great, but I think I might get through to her – whoever she is – better than he could. I can talk to her as one mother to another, and show her I understand how she feels.'

17 A TABLE SPREAD

'I've made up my mind,' Jonah said to Bernie as she carefully rolled him off the bed and into his chair the following morning. 'I'm going to ask the Chief Super to find someone else to lead the investigation.'

'Not Khan!' Bernie said sharply, positioning Jonah's left hand on the control panel and fastening the Velcro band that held it in place. Finding himself once more in control, Jonah brought the chair up from its recumbent position so that he was moved from lying flat on his back into a sitting posture.

'No. I think she'll have to bring someone in from outside Oxford – someone who never worked with old Peter. The disadvantage is that they won't know the area at all, but ...'

'I know. It's all a bit too personal, isn't it?'

'I thought it'd all be over in the time it'd take to find someone,' Jonah tried to explain. 'I thought it'd be a day at most. But now ...,' his voice trailed off again. He hated to admit to doubting his own ability to solve a case, and this case was one that he particularly wanted to come to a speedy conclusion.

'It's still less than two days since Abigail went missing,' Bernie pointed out. 'Although it feels more like half a lifetime,' she added with a grim smile.

'Don't say anything to Eddie and Crystal,' Jonah instructed her. 'Not until we've got my replacement lined up and briefed and ready to go. I don't want them to think we're letting up on looking for Abigail while we rearrange the deck chairs on the Titanic. I'm going to be giving this my very best shot right up to the moment DCI Superman takes over. I just hope Alison Brown has someone good she can get over here.'

Nobody had much to say at breakfast that morning. As he sat waiting for his tea to cool down, Jonah rang through to the incident room for any overnight news that might have come in. Alice Ray told him that Debra Middleton's car had been picked up on cameras at a service station on the M1, and that PC Gavin Hughes had called in with a rambling story about how he thought he might have recognised the baby in the churchyard. Apart from that, there was nothing new to report.

'I'm sorry,' Jonah said to Eddie and Crystal, who were listening eagerly to his end of the conversation. 'I'm afraid we still don't have any idea where Abigail's being held. We'll carry on following up on the leads that we have and-'

'I want to make an appeal,' Crystal broke in. 'Like Peter did, only woman-to-woman. I've got it all worked out. I wrote down what I want to say here.'

She put down her notebook on the table in front of Jonah. He looked down and read the opening lines: I think I can understand why you took Abigail. I know how it feels to want a baby so much that it hurts. I don't want you to be punished …

'OK,' he said looking up again. 'We can organise that. And there's something else that you can do to help. I'm thinking that a reconstruction might be a good idea. It might help to jog a few memories. So, we'll need you to walk us through exactly what you did on Tuesday, to make sure we get it right. Then we'll stage the reconstruction this afternoon, at the same time as it actually happened. Is that alright with you?'

'Yes. Yes, of course!' Crystal said eagerly. It was a great relief to feel that she was doing something at last to help get Abigail back.

'Good. I think the best thing will be if you come with me and Bernie, and I'll hand you over to Anna – you remember

DI Davenport, don't you? – and she'll take you back to your flat and do the walk-through with you. Leave Ricky here with Peter and Eddie. It could take some time and he'll get bored if he comes with you.'

***

'I got up early so that we could have breakfast together,' Sam told Flick, coming into the bedroom carrying a tray.

He put it down on a chest of drawers that stood next to the bed and then got in beside his wife. She lay there motionless with her eyes closed, as if she had not heard him. He looked down at her pale face, wondering what to say next. There was so much he wanted to talk to her about, and so little time before he would have to set off for work.

'I rang your mother,' he ventured,

tentatively at first and then with more decisiveness. 'She's on her way. She said she'll be here before ten and she can stay for as long as we need her.'

Flick opened her eyes and stared up at him.

'You didn't need to bother Mum. I'm OK. I don't need a minder. I'm not going to do anything stupid.'

'You're going to need someone to fend off all the reporters and busybodies who're queuing up to talk to you after your little performance yesterday,' Sam told her, trying to make light of the situation while in reality feeling considerably worried. 'I've turned off your phone and taken the landline off the hook, but I'm afraid it won't be long before they find out where we live and start calling at the house.'

'Oh Sam!' Flick pulled herself up to a

sitting position and grasped her husband's hand. 'I'm sorry! It was a stupid thing I did! I just thought ... I thought, *there* was a baby that nobody wanted and *here* was I, wanting Mia back so badly ... and it all seemed so obvious that she belonged to me. I really believed it when I told everyone that it was my baby. I know that sounds ridiculous now.'

'No, no. Not at all,' Sam assured her, thankful to have managed to elicit a response of any kind. At least now, they were talking – and Flick appeared more rational than she had seemed for some time. He reached over to the breakfast tray and picked up a mug of coffee, which he handed to Flick, feeling disproportionately pleased when she murmured her thanks and took it from him. It almost felt as if they were starting to get back to normal life again.

'I wish I could stay with you,' he said, picking up his own mug and resting it on his knees. 'But there are already a couple of staff off sick and I can't –'

'No. Of course not.' Flick sounded more decisive than he had heard her for months – not since Mia died. 'I'll be OK – and you said Mum was going to be here soon. Don't worry. I'll manage.'

'Yes. I'm sure you will.' Sam hoped that his words sounded sincere. He had been saying this sort of thing to Flick for so long, without believing it, that it felt very false and he was afraid that she would think that he was just humouring her. Perhaps he was – but he felt more hopeful this time. There was something about her tone of voice and demeanour that felt more like the old Flick, whom he had started to fear had gone forever.

They ate their breakfast and Sam got out of bed to take the tray back down to the kitchen.

'I'll take these down and then I'll have to go.'

'Don't bother with the washing up. I'll do it later. You get off. Don't worry!' Flick added, seeing the doubt in his eyes. 'I won't just go back to bed and try to pretend it isn't happening. Look!' She threw back the duvet and swung her legs over the side of the bed. I'm going to have a shower and get dressed and then I'll go and sort the spare room out for when Mum gets here.'

'Good.' Sam's face lit up in a smile. 'And don't answer the door to anyone except your Mum, will you?'

'No. I'll be careful. And …,' Flick hesitated. She was not sure how to put what she wanted to say next.

'Yes?'

'You said you knew someone who'd had counselling after a miscarriage?'

'Yes.'

'Would you ...? I mean, could you find out ...? I think maybe that's what *I* need.'

***

'I can't stay.'

Georgia looked up at the sound of her husband's voice. She had spent another night at the hospital. As a nursing mother, a room had been found for her to sleep in near to the paediatric ward, where Rachel was still causing concerns by her continuing high temperature and rapid breathing. However, there was no space for Nathan, so he had tossed and turned in their bed back in the house in St Albans before rising early in order to pay a flying visit on the way to his daily commute.

'I just wanted to see how she is,' Nathan continued, crossing the room and gazing down into the cot.

Rachel lay there, twitching sporadically in her sleep, the intravenous drip still attached to her tiny arm.

'She's been feeding better,' Georgia told him, putting down the slice of toast that the nurses had brought her and getting to her feet. She stood next to Nathan, slipping her arm through his. 'And she hasn't been sicking it all back up the way she was.'

At the sound of her mother's voice, the baby's eyes opened and she looked up. For the first time in more than two days, she gave a smile of recognition and gurgled baby noises. Georgia smiled back and leaned over the cot to gather her daughter up in her arms.

'Are you feeling better, darling?' she murmured.

***

'Is something wrong?' Anita Khan asked her husband, watching him staring glumly down at his breakfast cereal. 'Is the milk off or something?'

'No. Nothing like that.' Arshad sighed. 'I'm just not looking forward to facing Porter and the rest today. I really blew it with the Johns family yesterday and I won't be surprised if they put in a complaint. Even if they don't do anything official, they're bound to tell DCI Porter and he'll probably feel obliged to report it to the Chief Super.'

'So, what did you do that was so terrible?'

'Oh, nothing much!' Arshad sighed again. 'I just added to the troubles of a couple whose baby has been abducted by suggesting that they might not have been able to bond with her because she's a different colour to them, and made them think that I was accusing them of being involved in the abduction themselves.'

'And do you think that could have been what happened?' Anita asked. 'It did strike me as odd that it was the grandfather who made the appeal for her return and not the parents.'

'No, not really. It's just one of the things that we have to consider, alongside all the other possibilities. The trouble is, then the baby's father – Edward Johns – remembered that I'd been involved in investigating his mother's death, which was another occasion when I messed up big-time.'

'I'm sorry – you've lost me.'

'Well, you remember I said that DI Johns's first wife was killed and I was part of the team that investigated it?'

'Yes. And you said you didn't manage to find out who did it.'

'That's right. I interviewed Johns shortly after it happened. I can't remember what I said exactly, but he took offence and Bernie – that's the woman who became his second wife and who is now PA to DCI Porter – asked me to leave. It turns out that I managed to create the impression that I thought that Johns was responsible for his wife's death in some way.'

'It seems to me that was understandable under the circumstances – if he was already hanging around with this Bernie woman.'

'No – I didn't mean like that. There was never any question of either of them doing away with the first Mrs Johns. No. Like I said before, I just thought that Peter Johns didn't understand what it was like for his wife and kids being black in a white world and that, as a consequence, he made them more vulnerable to racial abuse.'

'Do you still think that?' Anita asked. 'You said the killers *were* brought to justice in the end. *Was* it a racial attack?'

'Not of the sort I was expecting. Poor Johns! It was all to do with him, in a way. The killers objected to the idea of a black woman marrying a white police officer. Oh! And I don't think I told you – it was DCI Porter who finally got to the bottom of it all.'

'I still don't see that you have anything to reproach yourself about,' Anita insisted. 'You only did what you had to.'

'Yes, but I ought to have managed to do it without upsetting the victims the way I did. I really admire the way Johns manages to see the good in everyone. And the last thing I want is to make it any more difficult for the missing baby's parents. I ought to have been able to ask them about people's reactions to a black couple with a white baby without making them think I'm accusing them of something.'

'Maybe you're just the wrong person for this case,' Anita suggested. 'Why don't you ask your boss to find someone else – someone who doesn't have your past history with the family?

***

'Mum?' Marcus Davenport said through a mouthful of cereal. 'Jess says you aren't coming to Devon with us. Is that right?'

'I haven't decided yet,' Anna answered, wondering how much her daughter had told Marcus of the conversation that they had had the previous night, after Jessica had demanded to hear her side of the story. 'It's a big step. There are a lot of things to consider.'

'She said you and Dad are splitting up because there's something wrong with the baby and he doesn't want to have anything to do with it.' His mother did not respond, so Marcus continued, 'I told her Dad wasn't like that. It isn't that – is it?' his voice became more uncertain as he realised that his mother was not rushing to deny the accusation.

'It's more complicated than that,' Anna said at last, trying to find a way of explaining Philip's attitude that would neither compromise her own principles nor destroy her son's faith in his father. 'Dad has a lot on his mind at the moment, with this partnership idea coming up and everything.'

'But the baby,' Marcus persisted. 'Jess said he was leaving because you wouldn't have an abortion. *She* said the partnership in Devon was just a smokescreen.'

'No – that's not fair. Dad must have been discussing that with his friend Brian for months. The contract is all ready for him to sign. And Gran told me, when I rang her yesterday, that he'd told *her* about it when we were down there at Easter.'

'So why did he only tell *us* on

Tuesday?'

'I expect he didn't want you and Jess to be disappointed if the move to Devon didn't come off. He knows how much you like it down there.'

'For a holiday!' Marcus protested. 'When we're visiting Gran. That's not the same as moving down there to live. What about my GCSEs? And all my mates?'

'You can have your mates down to stay with us, once we're settled in,' Philip said, coming into the room and catching the tail end of his son's complaint. 'And until then, you can keep up with them all on Facebook and Instagram and all those other things that kids these days use all the time. And you'll find a whole load more mates, once you're in a school down there.'

Marcus pulled a face, but did not

reply. Instead, he turned back to his mother.

'You never answered my question – about the baby. *Is* there something wrong with it?'

'The second scan showed up a malformation of the spinal cord,' Anna told him. 'The doctors think she's got a condition called *spina bifida*, which means –'

'Which means,' Philip cut in, 'that the kid will probably never walk and may have all sorts of other problems, like incontinence and –'

'Which means,' Anna continued, ignoring the interruption, 'that she'll need a lot of extra caring and Dad doesn't think it would be fair on your gran to expect her to cope with that at her age. So I'm going to stay here, while you and Dad go down to live with her.'

'What if I don't want to go?' Marcus demanded angrily. 'Jess said she was staying with you. I want to stay here too. You can't make me go.'

'Technically, we can,' Philip said. 'You're only fifteen. It's up to us to decide.'

'That's not fair! Jess said you told her she could stay. And it's much more important for me – I'm right in the middle of my GCSE course.'

'Jess thinks she's going to help with the baby,' Philip told him, trying but failing, to keep the distaste out of his voice at the mention of his unborn child.

'*I* could help. It can't be that hard. And if you cared about any of us,' he added, rounding on his father, 'you'd stay here and help too.'

There was a long silence after this outburst. Anna wiped her mouth and carried her bowl and mug over to the sink.

'I'm sorry,' she said, looking from her husband to her son and back again. 'I'm going to have to go. DI Porter rang to say he wants me to organise a reconstruction of that child abduction that we're investigating and he's bringing the mother in to see me first thing.'

***

'How are you this morning?' Victoria asked John as he wandered into the kitchen in his dressing gown. 'I hope Esme didn't keep you awake. I tried to get to her as soon as she started.'

'I still feel as if I don't know if I'm coming or going,' John answered. 'But don't worry – it'll wear off. And no, Esme didn't wake me. I was so done in last night, you could have played the 1812 overture in the nursery and I wouldn't have noticed!'

'I've made coffee and there's bread in the toaster. I was going to bring you breakfast in bed. You ought to take it easy, after all that travelling. Sit down and –,' she broke off and stood for a moment with her head on one side, listening. 'There's Esme. She's ready for *her* breakfast too. I'll go and change her and then I'll bring her down and you can feed her if you like.'

'Yes. I'd like that.' John sat down and poured himself some coffee. This was just how he had imagined it would be. This was the family life, for which he had been waiting for so long.

The doorbell rang.

'I'll get it,' Victoria said, jumping to her feet. 'You're doing a great job there,' she added, as she passed John on her way out into the hall. 'Esme's really taken to you. She must know that you're her dad.'

She opened the door and looked out. There were two uniformed police officers on the step. The man looked vaguely familiar – could he be one of the officers who had called on Tuesday evening to ask her about the baby that had been taken from the park? The woman stepped forward and greeted her.

'Good morning, Mrs Norris. 'I'm sorry to disturb you. We're visiting mothers in the area to remind them to remain vigilant and to report anything suspicious – until we find out who took the baby from the playground on

Tuesday.'

'How is your little one?' the man asked. Yes. Victoria was sure that he was the older of the two policemen who had come round on Tuesday – the one who had shown so much interest in Esme and had asked to see her. 'Esme, isn't it? Such a pretty name.'

'She's fine. And don't worry – I'm not letting her out of my sight for a moment – except indoors, of course.'

'That's good,' the policewoman told her. 'We don't want to make you overly anxious, but it's as well to be on your guard.'

'What's all this?' John Middleton came up behind Victoria and stood staring at the two police officers. He was holding Esme in an upright position on his shoulder while he gently patted her back to bring up the air that she had swallowed during her feed.

'It's nothing, John,' Victoria told him quickly. 'Just the police warning us to take special care of Esme while this baby-stealer is on the loose.'

'You've still not caught them, then?' John asked, looking at PC Hughes, whom he subconsciously assumed to be the more senior (being both older and a man).

'I'm afraid not, sir. That's why Sergeant Burton and I are doing the rounds of families in Headington to check that their babies are being kept safe.'

'Do you mind giving us your name, sir?' Tracy added. 'For the record.'

'Middleton – John Middleton. I'm Esme's dad. I've been away on business since before she was born. I only got back yesterday, so I'm only just getting to know her. Isn't she beautiful?' He shifted Esme off his shoulder and cradled her in his arms. Gavin stepped forward and gazed down admiringly at the small, pink face and short fuzz of hair.

'You certainly are!' he said, in the voice that adults use when talking to babies. 'I'm so glad I came back to see you again. You were asleep last time, so I couldn't see those lovely eyes of yours. Are you glad your daddy's back?' He put out his hand towards her and she took hold of his index finger in her small fist. Gavin smiled with pleasure. Then he looked up and saw Victoria looking at him and he gently withdrew his hand and took a step backwards.

'We'll let you get on,' he said, looking towards Victoria and John, who were now standing very close together, barring the way into the house. 'You must have a lot to talk about, after being away for so long. Thank you for letting us see Esme again – she's lovely.'

18 YOU SEARCH ME AND YOU KNOW ME

Jonah watched as Anna and Crystal made their way out, past the cluster of officers, who were waiting for his orders regarding their duties for the day. As soon as the door closed behind them, he turned to speak to Alice.

'Has anything else come in since we spoke on the phone?'

'Yes, sir – just now, while you were briefing DI Davenport about the reconstruction. A patrol car has spotted that silver Nissan that we're tracking. It's parked at the Travelodge by the Pear Tree Park-and-Ride.'

'Really?' Jonah was suddenly alert and thinking fast. That could not be just a coincidence, surely? 'And what about the woman? Has anyone seen her?'

'They checked with Reception and the car belongs to a Mrs Middleton – which fits with the name that Northumbria gave us.'

'Right! It looks as if we may be getting somewhere at last. Andrews!'

'Yes, sir.' DI Rupert Andrews stepped forward, ready for action.

'Take Andy and get over to Pear Tree Travelodge right away. Make sure that the staff there know not to say anything to Mrs Middleton about the police having enquired after her. Then keep a watch on her and keep me informed of her movements. I reckon Abigail was probably stolen for her, and she's down here to collect her. So, if we can avoid spooking her, she'll most likely lead us to her.'

Jonah watched the two men out of the room and then turned back to address his remaining officers, but he was interrupted by a phone call. It was Tracy Burton.

'I thought I ought to ring you right away, sir. We went round to the home of a Ms Victoria Norris, in Headington, this morning. Gavin thought that her baby might have been the baby in the churchyard, because he'd been round there on Tuesday and he thought they looked the same. Anyway, now we've seen the baby again, and he says it looks like the missing one – Abigail Johns – just with her hair cut off short.

Gav says it isn't the same baby as he saw before, but I don't see how he can tell,' she added, somewhat apologetically, 'they all look alike to me.'

'Right! We'll take it from here.' Jonah ended the call and turned to Bernie. You and I had better get round there right away and check this baby out. We need to find out if there's any chance it really *is* Abigail before letting Crystal or Eddie know that there's a possibility that she's been found. Arshad – can you take charge here, while I'm gone?' he added, rotating his chair to face DCI Khan. 'You'll need to be ready to respond if Andrews has news on Mrs Middleton's movements.' Then, without waiting for an answer, he headed for the door. It was not long before they were in the car and on their way.

'What chance do you think there is

that Hughes has got this right and it really *is* Abigail that he saw?' Jonah asked, as they made their slow way through the rush hour traffic. 'He's not exactly the brightest button in the box, is he?'

'Maybe not, but he *does* have identical twins, which I imagine may well make him better than average at telling babies apart,' Bernie answered. 'And you may be underestimating him. Peter used to reckon he was very good in his own way – a bit slow, but solid and reliable. He always used to say that Gavin was like a St Bernard – large and dependable. You, on the other hand,' she added with a grin, 'are more like a terrier.'

'Tenacious, you mean?'

'Always racing around getting under everyone's feet and making a nuisance of yourself!'

'Hmmph! I had been about to say that it was just like old Peter to stick up for Hughes because he always tried to see the best in people.'

'He doesn't have a lot to say in DCI Khan's favour,' Bernie pointed out.

'No,' Jonah agreed. He was silent for a few moments. 'Khan seemed a bit strange this morning, didn't you think? Sticking with the canine theme, I'd say he was like a dog that knows it's done something wrong and has got its tail between its legs waiting for its master to find out and give it a whipping. Did you see how relieved he seemed when I sent Crystal off with Anna? It was as if he were uncomfortable being in the same room with her. Do you think he could have had words with Peter when he called round yesterday to talk to them?'

'Peter never said anything about it,' Bernie shook her head.

'Mr Norris?' Jonah enquired, looking up at the man who had answered the door.

'No. I'm John Middleton.' The man looked down at Jonah with an expression of puzzlement mingled with suspicion.

Bernie held up Jonah's warrant card and her own ID for him to see.

'I'm DCI Jonah Porter and this is my personal assistant, Bernie Fazakerley,' Jonah went on. 'I need to speak to a Victoria Norris, in connection with a case of child abduction. I believe she lives here. Is that right?'

'Yes,' Middleton admitted. 'She's my

… partner,' he finished, after some hesitation. It felt absurd to call a woman in her mid-thirties his girlfriend, and inaccurate to claim her as his wife.

'May we come in?' Jonah asked.

'Is that really necessary? I mean, it's not a good time. We've just got our baby daughter off to sleep.'

'We'll try not to disturb her,' Jonah assured him. 'Now please – I really do need to speak to Ms Norris.'

'Very well.' Middleton opened the door wider and stepped back as Bernie set down the portable ramp, which she had brought from the car, and Jonah drove his wheelchair up it into the hall.

A woman emerged from a room at the back of the house and came towards them. Jonah studied her face. She looked anxious – and not at all welcoming of his presence.

'This is another policeman,' Middleton told her. 'He says he needs to talk to you about that baby being stolen.'

'Victoria Norris?' Jonah asked. The woman nodded. 'I'm very sorry to bother you, but it's been reported to me that you have a baby here that bears a remarkable resemblance to the one that was abducted from the Margaret Road recreation ground on Tuesday afternoon.'

'But that's ridiculous!' Middleton intervened. 'The only baby we have here is our own daughter.'

'Nevertheless,' Jonah answered calmly, 'I'm afraid that we have to follow up on any such reports. It should be straightforward enough. If you could just let us see your daughter, so that we can check?'

'No. Why should we?' Victoria said

sulkily. 'You tell them, John. They can't just come round here like this demanding to see Esme.'

'She's right,' Middleton said combatively. 'Surely you need a warrant for that sort of thing.'

'Where the safety of a child is concerned, the police have considerable discretionary powers to act,' Jonah told him smoothly. 'But let's not get into all that. It's a simple enough request. We just need to have a look at your daughter. After that, assuming that we can see that she's *not* the missing baby, I'll be able to confirm that this was a false alarm and you won't be getting any more hassle from us.'

'No,' Victoria repeated. 'You lot have already seen her. That nosey policeman has been round and looked at her twice. Isn't that enough?'

'Constable Hughes reported that the baby that he saw this morning looked different from the one you showed him on Tuesday,' Jonah explained. 'That is why we need to check. So please – tell us where your daughter is so that we can have a quick peek at her to set our minds at rest, and then we'll get out of your hair.'

'She's upstairs,' Victoria told him, still sounding sulky. 'And I'm not disturbing her bringing her down here for you to look at. It's all a load of nonsense. This is police harassment!'

'Nip up and take a look, will you Bernie?' Jonah said at once. 'Don't worry,' he added to Victoria, as she slipped quietly upstairs.

Victoria gave him an angry look and then hurried after Bernie, leaving Jonah and John looking at one another in the hall.

'Middleton,' Jonah mused. 'You wouldn't, by any chance, be related to a Mrs Debra Middleton?'

'My ex-wife's name is Debra, why?'

'Does she live in Sunderland?'

'Yes, she does. Look – what is this? What has any of this got to do with Debra?'

'Are you expecting a visit from her?' Jonah asked, ignoring his question.

'No. She never comes here. And I don't suppose she even knows I'm back in the country. I've been in China the last three and a half months. I only got back yesterday. I was looking forward,' he added pointedly, 'to a nice peaceful time getting to know my new daughter.'

'Yes, I'm sorry we've had to disturb you like this – but, getting back to your wife: do you have any idea why she drove down to Oxford last night with a carful of baby equipment? Could she have been bringing it to give to you? To show there are no hard feelings over the divorce, for example?'

'No,' John shook his head in bewilderment. 'She never even knew about the baby. I was keeping it from her, in case it upset her.'

'So you hadn't promised her that *she* could have your baby – Esme, I mean – or that you and she would bring her up together?' Jonah suddenly put together two ideas that had been going through his mind. 'Victoria wasn't acting as a surrogate for you?'

'No!' John said indignantly. Then, in a more measured tone, 'I don't know what may have been going through Debra's mind. You've got to understand – she's not always rational; not where babies are concerned. She's not well. That's why we split up. I just couldn't cope anymore.' He lowered his voice at the sound of footsteps above 'Please don't say anything to Vicky about Debs coming to Oxford.'

Bernie came downstairs, followed closely by Victoria. Jonah looked up at her enquiringly and she nodded.

'I reckon it's Abigail' she said in a low tone when she reached the hall. 'Have a look for yourself.'

She held her phone in front of Jonah displaying a photograph of a sleeping infant. 'That's the baby that's upstairs here,' she told him. 'And this is the picture that we distributed of Abigail.'

Jonah watched as Bernie switched between two photographs. 'Do you have one of Abigail asleep?' he asked 'So that we can compare.'

Bernie obligingly flicked through photographs until she found one. Jonah studied them carefully. Then he looked at John and Victoria.

'Have a look at this,' he invited them.

Victoria held back, but John came round behind Jonah's back and peered at the phone over his shoulder.

'The baby's hair has definitely been cut off,' Bernie went on. 'It looks quite different from when it hasn't started to grow yet. And it feels like soft stubble. I'm as sure as I can be that that's Abigail up there.'

That's a load of nonsense!' Victoria protested. 'Just 'cos our baby looks a bit like the one that got taken!'

'Well, there's a very simple way to settle this,' Jonah said quietly. 'We just need to take an easy non-invasive sample from your daughter and compare her DNA profile with yours and with the parents of the missing baby.'

'No!' Victoria was indignant. 'Why should Esme have to go through all that, just because you're all so desperate to avoid admitting that you can't find the baby?'

'It won't hurt her,' Jonah assured her. 'It's just a matter of collecting a few cells from inside her mouth.'

'Well, I'm not going to give permission. You can't make me.'

'No,' Jonah agreed, 'but if you really are the mother of that baby up there, surely you can't have any objection to proving it and clearing up this business once and for all?'

'He's got a point, Vicky,' John added. 'I say, let's have the test, prove that Esme's ours, and then perhaps we can be left in peace to get on with our lives.'

'I'll get on to it right away,' Jonah told them. 'We can have someone out here within half an hour and then it'll all be sorted, and no need to disturb your daughter at all.'

'No! I won't let you,' Victoria insisted. 'Tell them, John, tell them we won't. Why should Esme have to be tested?'

'I'm sorry, Vicky. I don't understand. They said that the test won't hurt Esme.' John turned to address Jonah. 'Go ahead. I'm happy for you to take a sample from Esme – and from me too, if that will help.'

'It's the principle. We're innocent. It shouldn't be up to us to prove that Esme's ours.'

'I'm sorry, Vicky, I still don't see your problem,' John said in a puzzled tone. 'What are you afraid of?' he added, a note of suspicion creeping into his voice.

'Is there something you haven't told me?'

'No, of course not!' Victoria's voice rose and there was a hint of panic in it.

'You would tell me, wouldn't you, if this DNA test is likely to turn up something I'm not expecting?'

'I told you – I'm not letting Esme have a test.'

'But why? You have to tell me?' John took hold of Victoria's arm and pulled her round so that he could look her directly in the eyes. 'There's something wrong, isn't there? Am I not Esme's father? Is that it?'

'No!' Victoria pulled her arm away and stood with her head bowed as if staring at the floor. Then she raised it again and looked up at John. Jonah saw that it was wet with tears.

'Why don't we all go and sit down?'

he suggested. 'And then perhaps you could explain what's been going on.'

They trooped silently into the front room. John and Victoria sat down on the sofa while Jonah positioned his chair where he could watch them both. Bernie took a small packet of tissues out of her pocket and pressed them into Victoria's hand. Then she moved an easy chair next to Jonah and sat down in it. Jonah looked expectantly towards Victoria.

'I'm sorry John,' she said, dropping the tissues into her lap and using both hands to grasp one of his. 'I'm so sorry! I've messed everything up.'

'But Vicky,' he said, slipping his hand out of hers and putting his arm around her shoulders, drawing her closer to him so that her head was resting against his chest. 'I still don't understand. What is it you've done?'

'That's what we'd all like to know,' Jonah added quietly. 'Although I think I've got an idea.'

'I so wanted you to love Esme,' Victoria began.

'But I do,' John objected. 'What makes you think I don't?'

'I wanted you to love her,' Victoria repeated, 'and for us to be the family that you'd been waiting for – hoping for – all these years. But she was always crying and she wouldn't stop – hours and hours just screaming and crying – and I never got any sleep. And I thought it would be no good for you when you came back and you'd never be able to stand living in the same house with her. And they said the brain damage might be permanent and she might never be able to do the things that other children do. And I just kept thinking that it wasn't fair on you and it was all my fault.'

'What brain damage? How your fault?' John asked in a bewildered voice. 'I don't understand.'

'It took too long. Her heart stopped. I was so tired. I couldn't push anymore. I'd already failed as a mother before she was even born. And then I couldn't feed her properly and she just kept on crying and crying and ...,' Victoria's voice trailed off and she wiped her eyes on a tissue.

'But none of that was your fault.' John still sounded confused. 'If anyone was to blame it was me for going off to China and not being there to help.'

'She isn't crying all the time now,' Jonah said gently. 'You solved that problem in time, so that John wouldn't see his daughter like that. Tell me how you did that.'

'I took Esme out in the pram, like I said. And she dropped off to sleep just as we got to the playground; so I sat down there and had my lunch. And I saw this baby lying asleep in a buggy. I looked down on her and she had all this long ginger hair – just like yours, John. And I thought *this is what Esme ought to be like*. And I looked around and I couldn't see anyone about – except for a black woman playing with her little kid on the slide. I thought that nobody wanted that baby. She had been left there all on her own. I felt that she must have been left there for me to find. That's how it felt – as if she was *meant* for me. I – I – I just couldn't stop myself. I picked her up and put her in the pram next to Esme. She didn't even wake up. She just stirred a bit and then settled down to sleep again. Only it woke Esme up and she started crying again, so I went off and walked round a bit – just like I told you – and then I went home.'

Victoria collapsed into sobbing, burying her head in John's shoulder. He held her in both arms and gazed round at Jonah and Bernie, a look of bewilderment on his face. Nobody spoke. Eventually the sobs died away and Victoria sat up and blew her nose.

'So the baby upstairs isn't our daughter after all?' John asked, still not quite able to take it all in.

'No,' Victoria said with a little gulp, dabbing her eyes as the tears threatened to take over again. John looked at her, his eyes wide open in disbelief.

'So where is the real Esme?' he asked sharply. 'What have you done with her?'

'Don't worry,' Jonah intervened. 'She's quite safe. Social Services have found a temporary foster home for her. She's being well looked after.'

'Vicky?' John pressed her. 'Tell me what you did.'

'You left her wrapped up safe in a cardboard box in the porch at St Anselm's church, didn't you?' Jonah prompted gently. Victoria nodded. 'Tell us about it.'

'I thought … I suppose I hoped that people would think that she was the baby that had been taken from the park. My first idea was to leave her there on one of the benches, but then I thought kids might find her and hurt her, or a dog might get in or something. I thought she'd be safe in the church, but the door was locked, so I could only get as far as the porch.'

She stopped and blew her nose again.

'I'd often been out round there in the morning before – trying to get Esme off to sleep after her feed – so I knew the vicar always came just before nine. I put the box down in the corner, out of the draft, and I put Esme in it. Then I went outside and waited in the lane until I saw him come across through the graves and go into the porch. Then I knew she'd be safe, so I came home again. What will happen to me?' she asked, looking towards Jonah. 'Will I go to prison?'

'It's not for me to decide,' he answered kindly. 'But I doubt it. I don't see how that would help anyone. The main thing now is to get Abigail back to her real parents as soon as we can. Then, after that, you two will both have to give formal written statements. After that ... well it'll be largely out of my hands. Right!' he went on, speaking more briskly now. 'I think the best thing is for Bernie to drive us all back to the police station. Do you have a baby safety seat we can use?'

'Yes,' Victoria nodded. 'It's upstairs. I'll get it.'

She got up and made for the door, Bernie followed her closely, anxious in case, despite her apparent contrition, she tried to make off with Abigail or to harm her in any way. John and Jonah remained downstairs, eyeing one another, trying to size one another up. After a few moments, John broke the silence.

'This really isn't like Vicky, you know. She's never done anything like this before. She must have just been at the end of her tether. It's not really her fault. I should have been here for her.'

'No point beating yourself up about that now,' Jonah advised. 'You're here now, that's the main thing. Now, I need to make a few phone calls.'

By the time that Bernie and Victoria reappeared, with Bernie carrying Abigail – now awake and staring round with wide, green eyes – strapped into a car safety seat, Jonah had completed his calls to Anna and Peter, telling them to bring Crystal and Eddie to the police station to meet them. Bernie kept hold of Abigail while instructing John on the correct way to fold up the ramp and return it to the car after Jonah had made his exit from the house. A few minutes later, they were on their way.

19 HOME, WEARY WANDERER HOME!

'Inspector Porter, sir!' The desk sergeant greeted them as they entered. 'I was told to tell you, there's a Mrs Middleton here. She came in a few minutes ago, claiming to be the mother of the baby that was left in the churchyard. Obviously a total loony – she looks older than my mum. DCI Khan's with her in Interview Room 3.'

'Thank you, sergeant. I'll look in on them later. First – are the Johns family here?'

'DI Davenport's with them in your office. Shall I ring through to let them know you're here?'

'No. Bernie – you take Abigail straight up to them. I'll be there as soon as I've found people to take Mr Middleton's and Ms Norris's statements.'

'Look who I've got!' Bernie called out as she entered the office, throwing the door open dramatically and striding across the room to deposit Abigail in her mother's arms.

Crystal's face registered surprise and then broke into a wide smile as she hugged her baby to her and rocked her back and forth on her lap. She was too happy to speak. Abigail made soft cooing noises and reached out a small hand to touch her mother's face. Eddie, who had been standing by the window, came round behind her chair and bent over his wife's shoulder to look at Abigail, as if he were checking that this really was the right baby. Then, apparently satisfied, he looked towards Bernie.

'Where was she?' he demanded. 'Is she OK? I mean ... did they do anything to her?'

'She's absolutely fine,' Bernie assured him. 'The woman who took him has been looking after her just as if she was her own. Jonah will tell you all about it later – just don't worry.'

'Can we go home now?' Crystal asked timidly, looking from Bernie to Peter, who was sitting inconspicuously in the corner of the room with Ricky on his lap.

'Yes. Jonah said he'll need to talk to you both, but you can go home and we'll come to you when he's ready.

***

'Let me get this straight, Mrs Middleton, you say that you drove down all the way from Sunderland on Monday evening and stayed overnight in a hotel in order to leave your baby in a church in Oxford?' DCI Khan sounded incredulous. 'Why, might I ask, did you go to all that trouble, instead of leaving her somewhere closer to home?'

'My husband lives in Headington,' Debra explained. 'He left me to go off with a younger woman. I was planning to leave her with him – get him to take a turn looking after her. But there was nobody in when I called round, so then I got to thinking and I decided that he probably wasn't a very suitable person to look after her anyway.'

'But what made you leave her in the church?'

'I don't know,' Debra shrugged her shoulders and looked down at the table that separated them. 'I suppose I wasn't thinking straight. I walked round and round the roads, trying to decide whether to go back and try John again and then I saw the church and I thought that she'd be safe there and someone was bound to find her and look after her. At the time, it was just such a relief not to have to worry about her all the time. It's so difficult being all on your own!' She looked up with a pleading expression. 'Now, can I see her, please? I want to take her home.'

'I'm sorry, Mrs Middleton,' Jonah said quietly. He had entered the room silently and had been waiting patiently for her to finish speaking. 'The person who really left the baby in St Anselm's church porch has come forward. I'm satisfied that she is the real mother.'

'No! That's not true!' Debra protested. 'She must be lying. The baby's mine – she belongs to me!'

'You might as well know,' Jonah went on, speaking quietly but firmly, 'seeing as it is bound to be on the news, that it was your husband's new partner, Victoria Norris.'

'There you are! She's stolen John from me and now she's trying to steal my baby!' Debra's voice rose and she sounded increasingly hysterical. 'Give her to me! You can't let her take her away from me!'

'I'm sorry,' Jonah repeated. 'I'm afraid it's quite impossible that you could have left the child in the church as you say you did. Your neighbour saw you arriving home in Sunderland on Tuesday night. And your car was still on your drive on Wednesday morning.'

'I told you – I left her in the church before I went home on Tuesday.'

'Impossible. The church choir practises on Tuesday evenings. They would have seen her there. Besides, when she was found it was clear that she had recently been washed and changed. So, Mrs Middleton, I would urge you to abandon this pretence and go home.'

'OK,' Debra said, looking first at Jonah and then at Arshad. 'OK,' she repeated as if thinking fast, trying to work out a new strategy. 'I admit it – I lied about it being my baby – but it *is* John's baby. I'm his wife, so I *should* have her! *She* doesn't want her – she tried to get rid of her. Why can't you give her to me?'

'I'm sorry, Mrs Middleton,' Arshad said, getting up and taking her by the hand. 'That's not how it works. Come with me and I'll find someone who'll get you a coffee and arrange for you to go home.'

***

'She's gone down straight away,' Georgia reported, coming into the kitchen. 'Quicker than usual.'

'She's probably glad to be home,' Michelle answered, pouring coffee into two mugs. 'I know *I* am.'

She picked up the mugs and carried them into the living room. Georgia followed her.

'Yes,' she agreed. 'I was beginning to

think I was going to be camping out in
the hospital forever. It's good to be
back.'

20 NEVER FORGET TO SAY, 'THANK YOU'.

'Mrs Johns? It *is* Mrs Johns, isn't it?'

Crystal turned to see a woman of about her own age. Next to her was a red-haired man, some years older, pushing a baby buggy containing a child that looked to be about six months old.

'Yes – that's right,' Crystal answered with a puzzled smile, bending down to tuck in the rug that Abigail had been repeatedly kicking off, exposing her feet to the coldness of the November day. 'Do I know you? I'm sorry – I'm not always very good with faces.'

'I was hoping we'd meet sometime,' the woman continued. 'I'm so grateful to you.' Crystal continued to look puzzled. 'I'm Victoria Middleton and this is my husband John.'

'We wanted to thank you for getting the police to drop the charges,' he told Crystal. 'It was very generous of you. It gave us the chance to make a new start.'

'Oh! I see now! You're the woman who took Abigail.'

'Yes. I'm so sorry. I don't know what came over me. Looking back, I just can't believe that I did such a dreadful thing.'

'We'd have quite understood if you'd wanted to push for a prison sentence,' John added. 'Which is why we're so grateful to you.'

'It was nothing – really,' Crystal

assured them, feeling embarrassed at their effusive thanks. 'It's not as if you hurt her at all. And when I heard about *your* baby – I mean, I know what it's like being left alone with a baby. When my husband went abroad to find work, I don't know how I'd have coped with Ricky if I hadn't had my mum just round the corner.'

She looked down at the child asleep in the buggy. Only her face was visible, framed by the hood of a pink fur-fabric suit topped with rabbit's ears.

'How *is* your baby? She looks like a little angel at the moment.'

'Much better since we switched to a new feed,' Victoria told her. 'It turned out that she's very intolerant of cow's milk, and all that crying she used to do was because she had tummy-pains.'

'Nobody thought to investigate,

because they all just assumed it was to do with the brain damage,' John added. 'It was only after …'

'After my stupid escapade,' Victoria finished for him. 'All of a sudden the Health Visitor got much more interested in her, and she arranged for her to be tested. I feel so stupid now, not taking her to the doctor, but they said at the hospital that she might cry a lot more than normal babies, so I thought it was something I just had to put up with.'

'I'm so pleased for you,' Crystal said sincerely. 'I felt so sorry when the police explained about why you … about what happened.'

'She's still quite a long way behind in her development,' John continued, but her hearing and sight are both OK – which was one of the things they were afraid might have been affected when she was born.'

'And she's got some floppy muscles that they say will probably delay her becoming mobile,' Victoria added. 'But the main thing is – now she's stopped crying all the time, we can relax enough to think about doing things to help her.'

'Yes,' Crystal nodded in understanding. 'It's so difficult to think straight when you've got a baby that won't stop crying.'

'And what about *your* little girl? How is she doing?' Victoria crouched down to look at Abigail, reclining in the double buggy next to her brother. Seeing a new face approaching, the baby looked up with wide green eyes, unsure at first and then breaking into a smile. She waved her arms around to show appreciation for the attention and caught Victoria a glancing blow with the plastic rattle that she was holding in her tiny fist. Victoria laughed.

'I'm sorry I cut off all your pretty hair,' she said, returning the smile. 'I'm glad it's grown back now. You're going to be a real stunner when you grow up, I can see!'

'Wing!' Ricky announced loudly, banging a toy digger, which he had insisted on bringing with them, against the side of the buggy in which he was sitting. 'Wing! Wing! Wing!' He thought it was high time his mother stopped chattering to these boring grown-ups and took him to the playground, as she had promised.

'Alright, Ricky darling, I'll take you on the swing in a moment.' Crystal turned back to Victoria and John. 'I'm sorry. He tends to get a bit impatient, and I promised him that we'd call in at the playground on the way back from the shops. I'd better go, before he starts shouting out and disturbing the neighbourhood.'

Victoria and John watched as Crystal pushed the double buggy down the road towards the recreation ground. Victoria slipped her hand through her husband's arm and they turned the other way along the road, heading homewards.

'I'm glad we bumped into them,' Victoria murmured. 'I'd been wanting to say thank you for ages, but I didn't like to go round in case it upset them.'

***

Flick let go of Sam's hand and knelt down to remove the dead flowers from the tiny grave in the area of the cemetery reserved for children. Then she looked up at him and he handed her the new bunch of purple and white chrysanthemums that they had brought with them. She arranged them in the vase, while he stuffed the old flowers into a carrier bag. She scrambled to her feet and they stood holding hands together for a few minutes, looking down at the black marble stone and its gold inscription:

Mia Sophie Mason

April – May 2017

Always in our hearts

'We must never forget her,' Sam said quietly.

'No,' Flick agreed. 'But we must be careful. We mustn't let the new baby grow up thinking they've got to *be* Mia. We must let them know we love them for themselves.'

***

'Aunty Debbie! Aunty Debbie's here!' Hearing the key in the lock, three-year-old Luke Bolton raced down the hall and flung himself at Debra as she entered. She bent down and swept him up in her arms, kissing him on both cheeks before carrying him down the hall and into the kitchen.

'Deb-Deb!' his brother Ian shouted excitedly, banging his spoon on the tray of his high chair.

'Sit down and pour yourself a cup of tea,' their grandfather called out, turning round from the sink where he was washing up after breakfast, and smiling at her. 'You'll need it if you're going to be helping me with these two all day!'

Debra sat down at the table and took Luke on her lap. He looked up at her eagerly. Granddad's new friend – Mummy called her his *girlfriend* but she seemed quite old to Luke – was currently his favourite person in all the world.

They had met her one day in the supermarket when he had accidentally tipped a shelf-full of toilet rolls on the floor by putting his hand out as Granddad pushed him past in the trolley. She had helped to pick them up and then rummaged in her handbag and given him a strange object to play with while they finished the shopping. It was a plastic disc, which opened up to reveal a mirror in one half while, in the other there was a cluster of little white dots. Debbie had shown him how you could push up from behind and these magically turned into a tiny round hairbrush – like a hedgehog putting up its spines.

She had her handbag open now.

Luke peered into it as it lay on the table in front of them.

'Now let's see what I've got for you today,' Debra said, putting in her hand and drawing out a small rectangular box. She opened it and Luke looked in eagerly.

'It's paints,' he said, sounding a little disappointed. 'But I've already got some.'

'Not like these,' Debra said mysteriously. 'These are special ones that you can use on your face. Would you like me to turn you into a tiger?'

'I'd rather be an elephant.'

'I'm not sure I'm clever enough to make you into an elephant. How about a zebra? Or a stripey cat – like Tabitha Twitchet?'

'She's a *girl* cat!'

'Tom Kitten then?'

'Yes! Will you do it now? Right away?'

'If that's OK with Granddad.'

Soon Luke was sitting on a chair while Debra carefully applied pale brown face paint to his cheeks and smoothed it out gently.

'No talking now,' she said. 'You don't want to get face paint in your mouth, I'm sure it tastes horrid.'

Paul Bolton came across and stood behind her, watching the transformation of his grandson.

'I wish I'd met you when Cathy was small,' he said. 'If you'd been there to help, maybe I wouldn't have made such a hash of bringing her up after Penny died.'

'Don't be so hard on yourself. She hasn't turned out so badly, has she? She's holding down a good job – which is saying something with two young children.'

'Her mum would have been horrified at the idea that she's still only twenty two and she's got two kids – by two different fathers, neither of which stayed around long enough even to see them born.'

'Better than leaving it too late and then regretting it,' Debra said with feeling. 'You should be pleased that you've got grandchildren when you're still young enough to enjoy them. Don't knock it.'

***

'Ups-a-daisy! Come and have a sit on Grandpa Jonah's lap.'

Michelle bent down and picked up Rachel from where she was sitting on the floor, surrounded by the débris of several towers of wooden bricks, each built painstakingly by her grandmother and knocked down in a moment by a single swipe of a small hand. She placed the child carefully on Jonah's knee, with her back supported by his chest. Then she picked up his right hand and placed it across Rachel's body so that its weight held her safely in place.

It still felt strange to be manipulating the limbs of an adult who was, in many ways, more helpless than her baby grandchild, but Michelle was starting to become more confident in her dealings with her daughter's father-in-law and no longer shrunk from touching him for fear of doing something inappropriate. He smiled his thanks.

'Well now, Miss Rachel,' he said solemnly. 'Shall I take you for a ride?'

He took the chair on a turn around the room, pointing out landmarks – the

window, a bookcase, her toy cupboard –
in the tones of a tour guide escorting a
group around an historic town. Then he
brought the chair to a halt next to the
sofa where Michelle was sitting. A
movement of his left index finger on the
controls made it rise up so that Rachel
could look down on her grandmother's
head. She cooed with delight and
clapped her hands.

Jonah brought the chair back down to
its normal height and bent his head
forward to whisper in Rachel's ear.
'Shall we show Grandma how we play
see-saw Margery-daw?'

He made the chair recline so that
Rachel was lying on his chest; then he
brought it back into an upright position
before reclining it again. As he did so,
he began singing the well-known
nursery rhyme. Abigail smiled broadly

and clapped her hands again. Michelle looked on, smiling. Whoever would have thought that Jonah would have been capable of playing with his grandchildren? What a lot she had learned, in the eight months since Rachel's birth, about what a paralysed man could do – with a little help from his friends and some advanced technology!

Jonah finished the song and brought the chair to rest in its upright position. Then he proceeded to keep Rachel entertained with a sequence of short videos on his computer screen. She leaned forward eagerly to point at a cat performing various amusing antics and laughed out loud when it disappeared through a gap under a gate that appeared far too small to accommodate it.

'Have you got a date fixed for your

retirement?' Jonah asked Michelle.

'Yes. I've told them I'm going at Christmas. That will give me a couple of months to establish some sort of routine with Rachel before Georgia's maternity leave ends.'

Much to everyone's surprise – including her own – Michelle had decided to take early retirement in order to devote herself full-time to the care of her granddaughter.

'Will you miss your work?'

'No.' Michelle's answer was confident. 'The more I see of Rachel, the more I realise how much I missed out by going back right away after Georgia was born. I was so determined not to be like *my* mum – with nothing in her life except cooking and cleaning and looking after the kids – that I threw the baby out with the bathwater rather. I'm glad Georgia's only going back part-time. That'll be much better for both of them. I just hope I can make a better job of things this time round.'

'Don't beat yourself up about it. I don't think there *is* a right way to be a parent. Margaret and I both kept working full-time, and sometimes I worry that I wasn't there on occasions when the boys needed me; but then I think about how embarrassed I used to be when my dad came to my primary school sports day. All the other dads were at work – or so it seemed to me – and he *would* insist on sitting on the front row. And one time he told me off in front of everyone for cheating in the sack race.'

'How *can* you cheat in the sack race?' Michelle asked, amused at Jonah's description, which reminded her very much of the way her own mother used sometimes to behave.

'I didn't jump with both feet together the way you're supposed to,' Jonah explained. 'I just pushed my two feet into the bottom corners of the sack and ran. The teacher said it was a good example of lateral thinking, but my dad said I should be disqualified. He was a bit like that – everything was very black-and-white with him and there tended to be only two ways of doing anything – *his way* and *the wrong way*!'

'My mum was just the same,' Michelle agreed with a smile. 'I think that was one reason I went back to work so soon. Ever since we got married, she would come round almost every day, telling me how to wash the clothes, how to clean the floor, what furniture to buy, what clothes to wear. After we'd been married about six months, she started wanting to know when she was going to become a grandmother and asking us if there was anything wrong and had I seen a doctor. And then, when Georgia was on the way, she went on and on about what I should and shouldn't be doing and what a big responsibility it was having children. I decided that it would be easier to go back to work and let *her* look after Georgia than to have her coming round all the time criticising the way I was doing it.'

'My dad was on the PTA committee at my secondary school,' Jonah went on, declining to give an opinion on the behaviour of Michelle's late mother. 'I was mortified! All my friends thought it was hilarious. None of their parents could be bothered. And I was always afraid that my dad would be talking about me to the teachers behind my back.'

'My mum was *chair* of our PTA committee,' Michelle said, smiling but with a hint of resentment in her voice. 'She used to organise fund-raising events and expected me and my sister to help at them. I was *so* embarrassed one year when the headmistress presented her with a bouquet at speech day and she insisted on calling us both up on to the stage with her. I thought I'd never live it down.'

'And it all bears out my contention that, whatever you do, you'll never get it right,' Jonah insisted. 'I bet if you were to ask him, Nathan would have a long litany of things that I got wrong when he was growing up. I know, for example, that he and Reuben resented being expected to do their share of the housework. But, if Margaret or I had given up work to be at home with them, I'm sure the boys would have had another list, just as long. All we can do is to follow our instincts and try to do what feels right at the time.'

'Are you having fun with Grandpa Jonah?' Georgia came in and swept Rachel up in her arms. Then she turned to speak to Jonah and Michelle. 'Lunch is just about ready. I'll take Rachel and put her in her high chair.'

'Before you go,' Jonah said, winking at Michelle. 'Tell me – when you were a kid, were you ever disappointed that your mum didn't come to see you in school plays and concerts and things?'

'God no!' Georgia exclaimed, smiling round at them both. 'It was bad enough having Gran there, talking in a loud voice about how well I was doing and clapping in all the wrong places. I used to tell my friends that she was going senile and couldn't help it! And the worst of it was the way that afterwards – after she'd been telling everyone else how perfect I'd been – she'd tell *me* all the things she thought I'd got wrong. There was no pleasing her. I don't know how you and Aunty Carole put up with her when you were kids,' she added, to Michelle.

***

'You looked just like your father when you asked that – don't you think so, Peter? – sort of anxious and eager-to-please.' Bernie looked from her daughter to her husband. Peter shrugged.

'Don't ask me. Richard was never eager-to-please where I was concerned – he was my boss don't forget.'

'Do I really look like him?' Lucy asked, forgetting for the moment the subject upon which she had been seeking Bernie's opinion, and sitting down next to her. 'Of course!' she added, seeing the photograph album open in her mother's lap. 'It's his birthday, isn't it? Is that what made you think of it?'

'I don't know,' Bernie answered. 'It's difficult to say – after all, for a start, you aren't six foot two and about to turn sixty – but I suppose he must be responsible for the way you've shot up like a beanstalk these last couple of years. I'm getting quite an inferiority complex being the shortest in the family!'

'When he was younger,' Peter ventured, 'your dad had curly yellow hair like yours.'

'The thing I notice most is your hands,' Bernie told her. 'Sometimes

608

when you're playing the piano I look down and it's as if he was back here. You've both got musician's fingers – not like my short stubby ones.'

Lucy held out her hands in front of her comparing them with her mother's. Then she leaned over to look at the photographs.

'It's strange to think about how it would've been if he hadn't died. I'd like to have known him, but I can't really imagine what it would be like not to have Peter as my dad.'

'He'd still have been your godfather,' Bernie pointed out.

'It's not the same though. And then there's Jonah – would my dad have wanted him to come and live with us?'

'If your dad hadn't died, I don't suppose we'd ever have got to know Jonah. I only met him because he came to the funeral, after all.'

Lucy sat in silence, digesting this information. 'Is it awful of me to say I'm glad things are the way they are?' she asked at last.

'Of course not!' Peter said decisively. 'You never knew him. How could you miss him? And I'm very flattered that you seem to think I've done a reasonable job of filling the gap.'

'Peter's right,' Bernie agreed. 'And – although I *do* miss him – I can't help feeling that he's a lot more use as a father to you up there,' (she pointed heavenwards), 'than down here with us! I'm quite sure he'd have driven me crazy, wanting to protect you from all the unpleasantnesses and dangers of life. We're both much better off this way.'

'And you really think he *is* "up there" looking down on us?' Lucy asked.

'Well, it's not exactly scientifically demonstrable, but yes. Of course, a lot of people would say it's only wishful thinking to imagine that we survive at all after death; and a lot of other people – Jonah, for example – would say that the dead are asleep, waiting for the last trump to take us all up into heaven together. Both camps would probably say that it's all just psychological that I feel that Richard is out there and that he can see what we're up to. I suppose *you pays your money and you takes your choice*. Now, what was it you were asking me about?'

'It's this,' Lucy said, holding up a cot-size patchwork quilt. 'I made it for Anna's baby. Do you think it's OK?'

'Well, *I* think it' a masterpiece,' Peter declared. 'I'm sure she'll love it.'

'And she won't mind?' Lucy asked

anxiously. 'I mean – I don't really know her. I just wanted to do something to show her I thought she'd made the right decision about ... you know.'

***

'You should have been there,' Jessica told her brother, Marcus, as he stood staring down into the plastic cot next to his mother's bed in the maternity unit. 'It was awesome! And the midwife let me cut the cord and help with cleaning her up – and then I was the first to hold her.'

After Philip moved down to his mother's house in Devon, at the beginning of the school summer holiday, Jessica had taken over. She had managed the house with a quiet efficiency that had surprised Anna greatly, and she had been so solicitous of her mother's welfare, and that of her unborn child, that she had easily persuaded her to allow her to be present at the birth.

'No way!' Marcus was quite certain that the delivery room was no place for a teenage boy. He continued to look down, struggling to find something to say about this strange new creature, sleeping peacefully beneath the cream-coloured hospital blanket. 'She's very small,' he ventured at last. 'And her face is all wrinkled – like an old woman.'

'She's big, actually,' Jessica informed him. 'Eight pounds three. And *your* face would be wrinkled if it'd been underwater for nine months!'

'It's alright, Marcus,' Anna intervened with a smile. 'You don't have to pretend to admire her. All babies look ugly when they're born. She'll start looking a bit more human in a month or two.'

For several minutes they were all silent, looking down, watching the slight rise and fall of the blanket as the baby breathed gently.

'I came as soon as I heard.' Anna looked up at the sound of a new voice and was surprised to see Philip standing behind Marcus. He was clutching a bunch of carnations in one hand and an attaché case in the other. 'Are you OK? And the baby?'

'We're both fine,' Anna told him.

'I brought you these,' Philip held out the flowers.

'Thanks. Jess – perhaps you could go and ask one of the nurses if they've got a vase for them.'

Jessica took the flowers and went off, treating her father to a scowl as she passed him. She had not forgiven him for his attitude towards the new baby or for going through with his plan to move away. As a protest, she had refused even to spend the usual two weeks at her grandmother's house in Devon that summer, preferring to remain with her mother in Oxford.

'And mum knitted this for the baby,' Philip added, taking a small paper parcel out of his case and laying on the bed in front of his wife. Anna opened it and took out a green and white matinée jacket and a matching bonnet.

'That's very kind of her.'

'And she says she hopes you'll all come down to stay with us for Christmas this year, seeing as you'll be on maternity leave and so can't be on duty for once.'

Anna nodded and smiled, but did not reply, wary of committing herself to anything until she was more certain of how Philip and his mother really felt about the recent addition to their family. She looked towards the cot, and Philip, following her gaze, suddenly seemed to recollect himself and went over to inspect the infant.

'She looks normal enough,' he found himself saying before he could stop himself. 'I mean – she looks just like I remember Jess being when she was born.'

'Of course she does!' Jessica said scornfully, arriving back with the vase of flowers just in time to hear her father's ill-judged comment. 'What were you expecting – some sort of monster?'

'No, of course not. I just thought … I don't know,' Philip sighed, 'I suppose … I suppose I was expecting somehow that it would be more obvious that there was something wrong with her, that's all.

I'm sorry.' He turned to his wife. 'Presumably the ante-natal tests were right? She does have …?'

'Yes.'

'And have the doctors said anything about …?'

'She's down for an operation to repair the hole in her spine tomorrow. After that, there'll be all sorts of tests to assess the extent of the damage and then they'll sort out a plan for physiotherapy and things. She doesn't have hydrocephalus, which is good, but they seem to think it's almost certain her legs will be affected. That could mean a wheelchair or maybe just leg braces to help her walk.'

'I see. Well, if there's anything you need – anything I can do – you *will* tell me, won't you?'

'As if *you* care!' Jessica growled.

'Of course I–,' Philip began. Then he bit back the angry response that had leapt to his lips and started again. 'I'm sorry about the way things are,' he said, addressing his wife and avoiding Jessica's eye. 'I still don't think you made the right decision, but she *is* my daughter too and, now she's here, I want to do the best I can for her. Does she have a name, by the way?'

'Donna,' Jessica told him, before Anna could answer. 'We've called her Donna.'

'Donna Charlotte,' Marcus added. His new sister's middle name had been his contribution and he did not want it forgotten.

'Donna Charlotte,' Philip repeated. 'I like that.' He looked at his watch. 'I suppose I'd better be going. I told Mum I'd be on the quarter to six train. Unless

…,' he paused. 'I've got an overnight bag with me. If you wouldn't mind me staying at the house, I could come and see you and Donna again tomorrow.'

'That's up to Jess,' Anna told him. 'She's in charge until we get out.'

Philip looked at his daughter. She looked back, eyeing him up and down as if she could not decide whether she could bear to have him in the same house with her.

'OK,' she said grudgingly. 'So long as you don't make a mess. I'm trying to keep the house nice for Mum and Donna when they come home.'

'Thank you,' Philip answered seriously, restraining the urge to smile at the thought that his daughter had suddenly been transformed into a paragon of domestic virtue. 'I'll do my best.'

***

'Careful now, Ricky!' Peter knelt at the rail in the side chapel at St Cyprian's and held his grandson's hand firmly, guiding him as he lit the candle and set it in its place. 'That's right. Now let's go and have a word with Mary and ask her to keep an eye on baby Donna, shall we?'

Ricky nodded and set off across the church, while Peter followed with the buggy. Soon they were standing looking up at the statue of the Virgin and Child.

'Up! Up!' Ricky said impatiently, patting the folds of the figure's long robe and looking up expectantly at Peter, who obligingly lifted him up so that he could embrace Mary around her neck and whisper in her ear. Then he turned to the Christ child, kissing him on the cheek and stroking his curly black hair.

'Well, well! If it isn't Abigail Johns! Haven't you grown since I saw you last?'

Peter turned at the sound of Father Damien's voice behind him.

'You're on grandparent duty again today, I see,' he greeted him with a smile. 'I'm pleased to see you're giving them a good Catholic start in life.'

'One of my colleagues gave birth to a baby girl today,' Peter explained. 'We came to light a candle for them.'

'I'll hold them in my prayers,' Father Damien promised. 'Can you give me their names? It doesn't matter, but it helps me to focus better.'

'Anna – and the baby's called Donna.'

'Thank you. I won't forget. Was there any special reason?'

'Yes, but, well it isn't really my

business to spread it round. They've just got a tough time ahead, that's all.'

'I see. It doesn't matter – like the names don't really matter. God knows. That's all that matters.'

'Yes. God and ...,' Peter looked up at the Virgin's anxious face, which had seemed to mirror his own anxiety six months earlier when Abigail was missing.

'And Our Lady,' Father Damien agreed.

They stood in silence for a few minutes, before Ricky became impatient and demanded to be put down and allowed to run about the church. His footsteps on the tiled floor echoed around the walls.

'We'd better go,' Peter said, turning the buggy towards the door. 'Come here, Ricky! Time to go home now.

Lucy'll be back from school soon.'

'Are you still OK for tomorrow?' Father Damien asked, as they walked down the aisle together. 'You're welcome to bring the kids if you need to.'

'Thanks, but it's Crystal's off-duty day to tomorrow, so I've got a day off too. Don't worry. I'll be there.'

'I'm looking forward to it. I always come away from our classes feeling that I've learnt more than you can possibly have done.'

'I don't know about that,' Peter shrugged. 'I never feel I know much about anything.'

'And you're sure you want to go through with this?' Father Damien sounded anxious. 'I mean, formally being received into the Catholic Church? I'm quite happy for us to continue our little chats, without you committing yourself.'

'I promised,' Peter said firmly, turning to look back at the statue of the Madonna. 'I promised her, if Abigail came home safe and sound, I'd give it a go.'

'And what about your family? How do they feel about it? Wouldn't you be more comfortable in their church?'

'I didn't think it was supposed to be anything to do with being comfortable, is it? But, to answer your question, Jonah thinks I'm mad – principally because he was brought up to think of all this,' here he gestured with his arm to indicate the whole interior of the church, taking in its statues, stained glass windows and the painting that adorned the ceiling, 'as graven images. That and thinking that praying to Mary is idolatry, not to mention it being a waste of time.'

'I was thinking more of your wife and stepdaughter – and your own kids.'

'I haven't told Hannah yet, but I don't think she'll be bothered. I don't think she's that interested in religion. Eddie *says* it's up to me what I decide, but I think secretly he's inclined to agree with Jonah that it's all a bit weird and probably idolatrous. He's putting down my *obsession with Mary*, as he calls it, to me still not having properly got over losing my first wife. Bernie prides herself on being broadminded, so she's backing me up against Jonah. Her take on the Mary question is that Mary is a representation of the feminine side of God. I don't know how that fits in with orthodox Catholic doctrine. Anyway, whatever she thinks about me converting, she can hardly complain, can she? Seeing as she still classes herself as a Catholic whenever it suits her. Lucy thinks it's cool that we'll all be able to go to mass together after I've been done – that is assuming you don't feel obliged to excommunicate Bernie for her unorthodox views on Marian devotion. Oh! And Bernie says to tell you that you'll need to set aside a good long time for hearing my first confession!'

Father Damien laughed. 'I'll make a note of that.'

'Seriously though,' Peter concluded. 'I think that Bernie and Lucy – and even Jonah – are pleased that at last I've got off my agnostic fence and admitted that God is probably real.'

'I should think they are! I'm quite relieved myself,' Father Damien joked. 'I was beginning to think *I* might be joining

Lucy's sit-down strike on the steps outside the pearly gates, saying to St Peter, "I'm not coming in until you let in Peter Johns!"'

Peter laughed. 'You needn't have worried. He'd never have been able to hold out once Our Bernie started working on him!'

He lifted Ricky into the buggy and strapped him in next to his sister. Father Damien knelt down and made the sign of the cross over each child in turn, murmuring a blessing. Then he stood up and put his hand on Peter's shoulder.

'Don't worry,' he said quietly. 'Remember the words of Lady Julian: "All shall be well, and all shall be well and all manner of things shall be well." I won't forget your friend or her baby – and neither will God.'

THANK YOU

Thank you for taking the time to read Sorrowful Mysteries. If you enjoyed it, please consider telling your friends or posting a short review. Word of mouth is an author's best friend and much appreciated. Thank you,

Judy.

A NOTE ON THE CHAPTER TITLES

The titles of chapters within this book are taken from hymns. The references below are included so that the interested reader may explore them. I have tried to include at least one source for the lyrics and, where possible, links to where a recording and additional background information may be found. For those that are included in *Singing the Faith*, published on behalf of the Trustees for Methodist Church Purposes by Hymns Ancient & Modern Ltd, 2011, the

629

relevant hymn number is given. Please do not read anything into the choices of hymns, which in many cases are quite contrived. Inclusion of any hymn in this list, should not be taken as endorsement of the sentiments contained therein, either by the author or by Bernie and her friends. I hope you enjoy exploring them.

1. *Mother dear, remember me* is the first line of the chorus of the Catholic hymn to Mary, *Mother dear, O pray for me!* The words may be found here: http://www.catholicfirst.com/thefaith/pray ers/marianhymns.html.

2. *For the joy of human love, brother, sister, parent, child* are lines from the hymn *For the beauty of the earth* by Folliott Sandford Pierpoint. The words and a tune may be found here:

http://www.hymnary.org/text/for_the_be auty_of_the_earth. It is 102 in Singing the faith.

3. *We hold our breath in horror* is the start of a line from the hymn entitled *The boy in the ambulance*, by Andrew Pratt. It was written in response to the photo of five-year-old Omran Daqneesh, rescued from a bombed building in Allepo, Syria, in August 2016.The lyrics, and some more information about the hymn may be found here: http://www.singingthefaithplus.org.uk/?p =14713.

4. *Where there's despair in life, let me bring hope* is a line from *Make me a Channel of Your Peace*, by Sebastian Temple, which is a metrical version of the prayer of St Francis of Assisi. It is 707 in *Singing the Faith*.

5. *I will weep when you are weeping* is a line from *Brother, Sister, let me serve you* by Richard A M Gillard. It is 611 in Singing the Faith.

6. *Come, let us sing of a wonderful love* is the first line of a hymn by Robert Walmsley. It is 443 in *Singing the Faith*.

7. *With hopes and fears we come* is a line from William Cowper's hymn *Heal us Immanuel! Hear our prayer*. It is 650 in Singing the Faith.

8. *The pain that will not go away* is the first line of the second verse of the hymn *We cannot measure how you heal,* by John Bell and Graham Maule of the Iona Community. It is 655 in *Singing the Faith*.

9. *We often dread tomorrow* is a line from *Lord we come to ask your healing,*

by Jean Holloway. It is 652 in Singing the Faith.

10. *Morning has broken* is the first line of a hymn by Eleanor Farjeon. It is 136 in *Singing the Faith*. There is more information about the hymn and its author here: http://www.singingthefaithplus.org.uk/?p=1660. There are several recordings available online, including this one: https://www.youtube.com/watch?v=h5D3LEjGF8A.

11. *What child is this* is the opening of a Christmas hymn by W Chatterton Dix. The lyrics and tune may be found here: http://www.hymnary.org/text/what_child_is_this_who_laid_to_rest.

12. Seeking the lost is a line from Come, let us sing of a wonderful love by Robert Walmsley. (See 6 above.)It is 443 in

Singing the Faith.

13. *Sweet Spirit comfort me* is the refrain of a litany to the Holy Spirit by Robert Herrick. The words may be found here: http://www.bartleby.com/101/275.html, and there is a recording by *Schola Caeciliana* here: https://www.youtube.com/watch?v=VW4 8eJ3MI0U

14. *Behold the amazing gift of love* is the opening line of a hymn by Charles Wesley. The words and a tune may be found here: http://www.hymnary.org/text/behold_the _amazing_gift_of_love.

15. The phrase, *cradle children yet unborn,* comes from the hymn *We cannot measure how you heal,* by John Bell and Graham Maule of the Iona

Community. (See 8 above.) It is 655 in *Singing the Faith*.

16. *Through the night of doubt and sorrow* is the opening line of a hymn by Bernhard Severin Ingleman, translated by Sabine Baring-Gould. The lyrics may be found here: http://www.hymnary.org/text/through_the_night_of_doubt_and_sorrow.

17. *Author of life divine, who has a table spread*, are the opening words of a communion hymn by Charles Wesley. It is 572 in *Singing the Faith*.

18. *O God, you search me and you know me*, is the opening line of a hymn by Bernadette Farrell, based on Psalm 139. It is 728 in *Singing the Faith*.

19. Home, weary wanderer, home! is a line from Come, let us sing of a

wonderful love, by Robert Walmsley. (See 6, above) It is 443 in Singing the Faith.

20. Never forget to say, 'Thank you'. is the second line of the hymn, Always Remember, never forget, by Lynda Masson. It is 70 in Singing the Faith.

A NOTE ON THE LOCATIONS

Most of the locations and institutions that feature in this book are real. Their inhabitants and employees, however, are purely fictional. In particular:

- There is no St Cyprian's Roman Catholic Church in Headington and the church of this name described here is not based on any church in Oxford or elsewhere;

- Father Damien is a fictional character, and is not based on any Catholic priest in Headington, the Oxford area or anywhere else;

- There is no St Anselm's Church in Headington and the church of this name described here is not based on any church in Oxford or elsewhere;

- Rev. Alan Chambers and his wife Marion are fictional characters and are not based on the incumbent and spouse of any church in Headington, the Oxford area or anywhere else;

- The behaviour of the police officers in this book should not be construed as in anyway representative of Thames Valley Police or any other police service.

WHAT ARE THE SORROWFUL MYSTERIES?

The rosary[6] is a traditional form of prayer used in the Catholic Church. Prayers are counted using a necklace of bead, arranged in five *decades* or groups of ten. The rosary is a

---

[6] See, for example, http://www.usccb.org/prayer-and-worship/prayers-and-devotions/rosaries/how-to-pray-the-rosary or http://www.catholicity.com/prayer/rosary.html.

contemplative prayer system and while praying each decade, thought is given to one of the *Mysteries* of the rosary. Each mystery represents an episode in the life of Christ. Traditionally, there are fifteen mysteries, grouped as the *Joyful Mysteries*, the *Sorrowful Mysteries* and the *Glorious Mysteries*. Pope John Paul II introduced a fourth set, called the *Luminous Mysteries*.

The Five Sorrowful Mysteries are traditionally prayed on Tuesdays and Fridays, and on the Sundays of Lent. They are:

- The Agony in the Garden;
- The Scourging at the Pillar;
- The Crowning with Thorns;
- The Carrying of the Cross;
- The Crucifixion and Death.

The rosary begins with the Apostles'

Creed, the Lord's Prayer (or 'Our Father') and three Hail Marys (one each for Faith, Hope and Charity). Each decade comprises ten Hail Marys followed by the *Gloria*, the Fatima prayer and the Lord's Prayer. After the five decades have been completed, there is a final prayer to Mary.

Bernie was taught to pray the rosary by her father, who was a cradle catholic. Her mother, a salvationist, did not hold with such things and Bernie, therefore, grew up with a healthy dose of scepticism about this form of devotion. She did, however, introduce Lucy to it, as part of ensuring that she was aware of her Catholic heritage. To Peter, brought up in the National Children's Home (a Methodist Foundation), the whole idea of prayer beads and Marian devotion is strange and foreign. To

Jonah, the son of a Baptist pastor, it is anathema.

LIST OF POLICE PERSONNEL

The following police officers recur in many of the Bernie Fazakerley Mysteries. This list is provided to give some background to them and for reference.

- **Rupert Andrews:** Detective Sergeant 2000, Detective Inspector 2012.

- **Malcolm Appleton:** Police Constable 2007, Sergeant 2018.

- **Alison Brown:** Detective Inspector 1989, DCI 2004, Chief Superintendent 2015.

- **Tracy Burton:** Police Constable 1999, Sergeant 2005.

- **Anna Davenport:** Detective Sergeant

2007, Inspector 2015. Married in 2001 to Philip Davenport. Separated in 2017. 3 children: Jessica (2001), Marcus (2002), Donna (2017). Archaeology and Anthropology graduate from Cambridge.

- **Jordan Fox:** Police Constable 2001, Sergeant 2006, Inspector 2018
- **John Gamble:** Police Constable 2017
- **Pamela Gregson:** Custody Sergeant.
- **Gavin Hughes:** Police Constable 1988. Specialises in community policing and building bridges with rough-sleepers.
- **Peter Johns:** Police Constable 1969, Detective Constable 1973, DS 1978, DI 1993, retired 2011. Married to Angie in 1978 and to Bernie in 2006. Father of Hannah (1980) and Eddie (1982). Stepfather to Lucy (2000).
- **Arshad Khan:** Detective Sergeant

2002, Detective Inspector 2006, DCI 2014. Specialises in cases involving ethnic minority victims. Married to Anita.

- **Aaron King:** Police Constable 2001, Sergeant 2009.

- **Andrew Lepage:** Detective Constable 2007, Detective Sergeant 2015. Graduate in criminology (1st class) from Leicester University in 2005. Lives with his mother in Headington Quarry.

- **Monica Philipson:** Detective Constable 2002, Detective Sergeant 2008. An ambitious police officer, who studied at Keble College, Oxford.

- **Richard Paige:** Detective Constable 1960, Detective Sergeant 1967, DI 1973, DCI 1981, Detective Superintendent 1995, died 1999. Married to Bernie in 1997. Father of Lucy (2000).

- **Joshua Pitchfork:** Detective Constable 2015

- **Jonah Porter:** Police Constable 1977, Detective Constable 1979, Detective Sergeant 1983, DI 1987, DCI 1996. Married to Margaret in 1982. Widowed in 2014.

- **Louise Otterbourne:** Police Constable 2017

- **PD Q:** Police Dog 2014. General Purpose dog. German Shepherd Dog.

- **Alice Ray:** Police Constable 2015, Detective Constable 2016

- **Melanie Stanton:** Police Constable 2009 and Dog Handler 2014

- **Ben Timpson:** Police constable 2018

- **PD Wesley:** Police Dog 2015. Drug and firearms search dog. Spaniel.

MORE ABOUT BERNIE AND HER FRIENDS

There are now nine Bernie Fazakerley Mysteries. These are (in chronological order of the action):

1. Two Little Dickie Birds: a murder mystery for DI Peter Johns and his Sergeant, Paul Godwin.

2. Murder of a Martian: a double murder for Peter and Jonah to solve.

3. Grave Offence: an assault and a suspicious death that Peter investigates, while Jonah is in rehab in the spinal injuries centre.

4. Awayday: a traditional detective story set among the dons of an Oxford college.

5. Death on the Algarve: a mystery for Bernie and her friends to tackle while on holiday in Portugal.

6. Mystery over the Mersey: a murder mystery set in Liverpool.

7. Sorrowful Mystery: Jonah investigates a child abduction and Peter embarks on a new journey of faith.

8. In my Liverpool Home: Bernie and her friends return to Liverpool to investigate a suspicious death in Aunty Dot's Care Home.

9. Organ Failure: a body is discovered under the organ in St Cyprian's Church and Jonah is called in to investigate.

Bernie also appears in two other novels:

• Changing Scenes of Life: Jonah Porter's life story, told through the medium of his favourite hymns.

• Despise not your Mother: the story of Bernie's quest to learn about her dead husband's past.

There is also a book of short stories, in which Peter narrates his side of the story:

• My Life of Crime: the collected memoirs of DI Peter Johns. This includes some episodes that appear in other books, but told from a new perspective, as well as some completely new stories.

Read more about Bernie Fazakerley and her friends and family at https://sites.google.com/site/llanwrdafamily/

Visit the Bernie Fazakerley Publications Facebook page here: https://www.facebook.com/Bernie.Fazakerley.Publications

Follow Bernie on Twitter: https://twitter.com/BernieFaz.

ABOUT THE AUTHOR

Like her main character, Bernie Fazakerley, Judy Ford is an Oxford graduate and a mathematician. Unlike Bernie, Judy grew up in a middle-class family in the South London stockbroker belt. After moving to the North West and working in Liverpool, Judy fell in love with the Scouse people and created Bernie to reflect their unique qualities.

As a Methodist Local Preacher, Judy often tells her congregation, "I see my role as asking the questions and leaving you to think out your own answers." She carries this philosophy forward into her writing and she hopes that readers will find themselves challenged to think as well as being entertained.

www.ingramcontent.com/pod-product-compliance
Lightning Source LLC
Chambersburg PA
CBHW070535030726
47505CB00001B/49